The Angels are Talking to You

The Angels are Talking to You

DEATH OF THE SUICIDAL LOVE?

SAMANTHA SCANTLEBURY

authorHOUSE®

AuthorHouse™ *UK Ltd.*
1663 Liberty Drive
Bloomington, IN 47403 USA
www.authorhouse.co.uk
Phone: 0800.197.4150

Published by AuthorHouse   02/22/2014

ISBN: 978-1-4918-9081-3 (sc)
ISBN: 978-1-4918-9082-0 (e)

Contents

Preface

SINGLE, PENNILESS, DEPRESSED and suicidal. You could expect somebody to have one or two of these problems, at some time during their lifetime. But could you imagine Claudia, an attractive, successful solicitor, suffering all of these things simultaneously? With the force being so powerful, that it becomes unbearable.

Claudia is single, even though she's beautiful. She's poor, even though she has a successful career and she's depressed and suicidal, even though she has a lot to be grateful for.

Her pride doesn't allow her to fall apart in public, as she smiles and remains competent at work. Her emotions won't allow her to break down in front of her friends, as she portrays herself as a confident altogether woman.

Claudia suddenly falls madly in love with Ricardo, her former partner and father of her child, even though she despised him for so many years.

Throughout her trials and tribulations, she turns towards two people for support.

But can she really trust these people, or do they have an ulterior motive?

Has Claudia allowed herself to become a nervous wreck or is this how somebody wants her to be?

If the suicidal love is destroyed, then Claudia will live, but if it the suicidal love survives, then Claudia will die.

Acknowledgements

FIRSTLY, I THANK God. I am here because of you.

To my parents, you are my never-ending support network. I thank you for your unconditional love and for giving me, an upbringing instilled with good, strong values.

To Peter, the help, support and advice you have given me over the years has been priceless and Devon, you unintentionally became my career's advisor, when you suggested that I write the book.

Thank you to my book publishers. Kathy, Eugene, April and Lily, you made the book publishing process a very pleasant one.

To all my special friends who supported me through my challenges. You are all amazing.

As a first time writer, I enjoyed the experience. Taking on board the comments and feedback from my best critic, my beautiful daughter Leanne.

Thank you Leanne, for changing my life. You're funny and you're smart and I'm very impressed with your desire to be successful at your young age.

'The Angels are Talking to You' took me just under two years to write, I am pleased with my debut novel and I hope you are too.

This book is dedicated to those who survived their struggles.

Chapter 1

NEW TERM

CLAUDIA RACED TO the bus stop after school, to avoid sharing her journey with those unmanly kids from the neighbouring school, who always misbehaved and spoke about their personal business in front of all the passengers.

It was a bright afternoon and the last of the English summer was quickly coming to an end. Claudia had just celebrated her 13th birthday and although a new school term had begun, she was still in holiday mode.

Claudia made her way upstairs and sat at the back of the double decker bus. While she rummaged through her school bag to find her chewing gum, a strange thing happened to her. Claudia heard a softly spoken voice, which said, "You are going to find it hard to meet a boyfriend in the future." But actually, it was more like a premonition that she got.

Claudia quickly jumped out of her thoughts and for a moment, she wondered why she would get this message at all. A relationship was the last thing on her mind, not to mention the fact that her parents would hit the roof if they knew she had a boyfriend at her young age.

The bus soon arrived at Claudia's stop, she jumped off and walked the short distance home. After letting herself in, she made her way to the dining area, where she saw her mother and Miss Gloria watching a black and white movie.

Her mother was peeling the vegetables for dinner and Miss Gloria was helping her. "You're home already?" Claudia's mother, Maureen asked. "Yes mum, I got the early bus. Hello Miss Gloria." Miss Gloria didn't reply, she just smiled at Claudia.

"Miss Gloria, as I was saying, when I was in labour with Claudia, the doctors realised that she was a breech baby, so her feet were down instead of her head." Maureen explained. "The doctors turned her 3 times and each time she turned herself back the other way." Claudia's mother said proudly.

Claudia sighed, she had heard this same story time and time again and it definitely wasn't the first time Miss Gloria was hearing it either. "She was so determined to be born feet first," Claudia's mother continued, "So eventually the doctors gave up and let her have her way."

"Seems like you gave your mother a lot of trouble." Miss Gloria said to Claudia, as she patted her on the head. Claudia responded with a fake smile. Miss Gloria was not Claudia's favourite person. There was something about her mothers' friend that Claudia didn't like, but she couldn't quite put her finger on it. Anyway, Claudia tried to be polite and pretend to smile whenever Miss Gloria graced them with her presence.

"You know, Claudia's Godmother, who herself was born feet first, told me that it's supposed to be harder for curses to harm you if you are born in this way." Claudia's mother revealed. "Really?" Miss Gloria's eyebrows rose.

Claudia left the pair laughing and joking, she couldn't

bear to hear anymore. She didn't believe in curses and much of the things her mother had told her, she put it down to old wives tales. In Claudia's opinion, such stories should be prohibited in these modern days.

The weekend quickly arrived and Claudia was home alone on a rainy Saturday afternoon. She decided to switch on the video recorder to watch a movie. But, before that, she went to arm herself with enough snacks to serve her throughout the film.

As she headed towards the kitchen, she noticed a small shadow on the wall in the hallway. Claudia immediately stopped, then the shadow began to move slowly along the wall. Claudia continued to watch this shadow travel down the hallway and enter her parent's bedroom. However Claudia didn't runaway, she was more puzzled and bemused, than scared, as she tried to comprehend what she had just seen.

Claudia's eyes followed the shadow into the bedroom until the image stopped beside the radio. Claudia's father always had the radio switched on low, but all of a sudden, this thing appeared to have turned up the volume of the radio until it was blaring loud and then it disappeared.

Still at this point, Claudia did not run away, but instead she calmly walked up to the radio and reduced the volume. Although it seemed like something had turned up the radio, as far as Claudia was concerned, this could not possibly happen in real life. She thought that her eyes were just playing tricks on her. Claudia shrugged and she casually returned to the front room to watch her movie.

By the time the film had ended, Claudia's brother, Clint had arrived home. "Hi sis." Clint said as he poked his head into the front room. "Alright bruv?" Claudia responded. She dare not tell Clint about the shadow she saw, because he would definitely ridicule her and accuse her of being crazy. Claudia decided to wait until her parents came home.

A short while later her mother arrived. "Hi Claudia, is Clint home?" Claudia's mother asked. "Yes," Claudia replied. "Good, that boy is always hanging about on the street with his friends. He's treating this place like a hotel." her mother mumbled to herself, as she put her apron on to prepare the dinner.

Claudia followed her mother into the kitchen. "Can I tell you something?" Claudia asked, feeling a bit awkward. "What is it?" her mother said curiously. "Well this afternoon, I saw a shadow on the wall and it moved towards your bedroom and then the radio went loud." explained Claudia all flustered. "What?" her mother said in horror.

Maureen had a worried look on her face. "You saw something move across the wall and then it turned up the radio in our bedroom?" her mother repeated, clarifying the statement that Claudia had just made. "Yes mum, why do you sound so shocked?" asked Claudia, oblivious to the meaning of what she had just witnessed.

"Because sweetheart, that shadow you saw was an evil spirit." her mother revealed. "Ahhh" Claudia shrieked. "Mum please do not tell me that I saw a ghost. I'm really scared now." Claudia said as she began to cry. "Come here Claudia," her mother said as she hugged her "Don't worry, I'm going to get Mr Nelson to come and pray the spirit out of the house." her mother said reassuringly.

Mr Nelson was a long time friend of the family. He was a pastor and a faith healer and had helped Claudia's mother in the past "Will he be able to deal with it?" asked Claudia, very worried and concerned for her well-being. Claudia obviously had seen those scary movies where the evil spirit inflicts fear and misery into the lives of the good people but she didn't expect this could happen in real life. "Don't worry Claudia, everything will be okay." her mother said convincingly. Claudia smiled bravely, but she was still scared.

When Claudia's father, Leonard came home, he noticed that Claudia's eyes were red. "Claudia, have you been crying?" asked Leonard. Claudia had a sad look on her face. Maureen decided to tell Leonard about Claudia's earlier experience. "Don't worry, you don't have to be scared. I am here now and nothings going to happen to you." her father said as he hugged her in an attempt to protect and reassure Claudia, but her fear grew as night fell.

Claudia couldn't sleep, so she got up in the middle of the night and sheepishly asked her parents if she could stay with them. She was 13 years old and theoretically too old to sleep in her parent's room, but under the circumstances, she didn't care. Although, she wouldn't want her parents to advertise this to Clint.

The next day, over breakfast, unfortunately her secret became public. "Did you have a better sleep in our room?" her mother said. "What? Claudia slept in your room last night?" Clint asked and then he began to giggle. "It's not funny. Claudia saw a spirit and she got scared." explained her mother. Damm, now the second secret had been disclosed to Clint as well, thought Claudia.

"Claudia do you really believe that you saw a ghost? Don't make me laugh, they're not real, silly." Clint said as he pinched Claudia's cheeks. "Go away. Mum, tell him to leave me alone?" Claudia said angrily as she attempted to slap Clint, but he had ducked just in time. "Clint she's upset. Just leave her." Maureen said firmly.

It was unfortunate for Claudia, that Clint got to hear about the two things she didn't want him to know about and now she would have to endure him ridiculing her over the next few days, until he loses interest. "Crazy Claudia." Clint shouted as he got up and ran out of the room.

As Claudia prepared to leave for school, her mother came into her bedroom to reassure her that everything will be ok. She reminded Claudia that, Mr Nelson will be coming around in the evening, to carry out an exorcism in order to get the spirit out of the house.

At school, Claudia was very quiet as she reflected on the events that occurred at the weekend. As Claudia and her friends walked down the playing field, they began joking with each other. "Hey did you see the music awards last night?" asked Deena "Yeah, that new group were rubbish, I can sing better than them." laughed Shari.

"Claudia, Claudia, hello. Are you with us?" Shari asked, as she waved her hands in front of Claudia's eyes, to get her attention. "Yes" a pre-occupied Claudia replied. "What's up girl. I'm worried about you. You've been too quiet today and that's definitely not like you." Deena said in a concerned way. "Yeah, I'm cool." pretended Claudia.

She knew that she could never tell her friends that she saw a ghost in her house. They will definitely think she was crazy, the way Clint had. The girls hurried back to class for their Maths lesson. "Girls, you are late. Quickly take a seat." Mrs Gold said impatiently. "Sorry Miss." They replied.

The girls settled down and Mrs Gold proceeded with the lesson. Claudia was in her own world, gazing through the window. Her experience worried her and she still felt fearful. "Claudia, are you able to answer the question?" Mrs Gold asked. Claudia suddenly sat up in her chair. "What question Miss?" she replied nervously. "Well if you were paying attention, you would have heard what I had asked." said Mrs Gold sarcastically.

Mrs Gold turned to Deena "Deena, can you help Claudia

out?" A flustered Deena replied, "Sorry Miss, I didn't hear the question." Mrs Gold became cross. "I suppose you didn't hear the question either, did you Shari?" assumed Mrs Gold.

"Well Miss, I did hear the question." Shari said boldly, as she came to the front and wrote the answer on the board. "Okay," Mrs Gold said embarrassingly and then she snapped. "Well, you three Musketeers are not allowed to sit together anymore. Deena and Claudia, you will be staying behind after class."

As the students left at the end of the lesson, Deena and Claudia remained in their seats. "Right, you have been asked to stay behind, because I do not feel that you are taking your education seriously. Classroom daydreaming is not going to help you pass your exams, therefore I have given you a 30-minute detention. Complete sections 25 to 30 in your workbook and I'll be back shortly." Mrs Gold explained and then she left the room.

Normally the girls would have been messing around during their detention, but with the mood that Claudia was in, they decided to behave and quietly work on their questions. When the time was up, they left the school grounds and said goodbye to each other.

As Claudia arrived home, she walked into the front room to find Mr Nelson praying. "In the name of Jesus, I command you evil spirit to leave this house, right now." shouted Mr Nelson. Claudia looked bewildered, as she felt the power in Mr Nelson's voice. All of this stuff was weird and creepy for Claudia, but she didn't care as long as it solves the problem once and for all. Maureen on the other hand was very keen for this to be finished, before disbelieving Clint came home.

Mr Nelson slowly walked around the room with a lit candle as he commanded the spirit to leave. "I can sense that the spirit is in your bedroom, at the moment." explained Mr

Nelson as he turned to Maureen. He went around the house and repeated his prayers, blessing every room and forcing the spirit out. "Maureen, the spirit has left the house now." said Mr Nelson reassuringly. Over the next few days, Claudia's fear gradually faded away and she began to live a normal life again.

It was the weekend and Maureen was in the kitchen preparing the dinner. Clint was being annoying as usual and Claudia was very bored. She decided to go and see her mother in the kitchen. Claudia propped herself up against the worktop, with her chin in her hand.

"What's wrong with you? You look fed up," asked her mother. "Aren't you seeing your friends today?" Claudia replied. "Nope, Shari's gone to visit her granny and Deena can't come out because her parents are celebrating their wedding anniversary." Claudia. sighed. "Well you can help me peel these vegetables." Claudia's mother suggested. "Yeah alright" Claudia said unenthusiastically.

Claudia grabbed a knife from the draw and began to peel the vegetables. She then unexpectedly asked about her mother's friend. "Why isn't Miss Gloria married?" "Mind your own business." replied Maureen sharply. "Well she's quite old. I mean, you got married when you were in your twenties, you'd think she would be married by now." explained Claudia. "Why are you so interested in Miss Gloria all of a sudden?" asked her mother.

"Well it's not all of a sudden, I've been wondering for a while. All parents get married. Shari's parents are married, Deena's parents are married, everyone at school has married parents so I find it quite weird that she's not."

Claudia continued, "And then she keeps introducing us to different men all the time. Why don't her relationships last?" Claudia asked with a puzzled expression. "Well, Miss Gloria believes that her Auntie blighted her life by putting a curse on her, to prevent her from meeting a partner and settling down. I don't know if that's true." Claudia's mother explained.

Although at one point, Miss Gloria almost broke the curse, when she received her one and only marriage proposal. But, then she blew it, when her husband to be, came home early from work and found her in bed with one of her former boyfriends.

"Anyway, I don't want to talk about Miss Gloria anymore and you need to have respect for your elders." explained her mother.

Claudia stayed silent while she continued to peel the vegetables. She washed them before putting them into a pan of boiling water and then she turned towards her mother and said, "Curses are not real, those things only happen in story books like beauty and the beast." Then she left the kitchen and went upstairs to her room.

As the months passed, Claudia noticed that Miss Gloria had stopped coming to the house. Apparently, Mr Nelson warned Claudia's mother that Miss Gloria was no good. So one day, When Miss Gloria came to visit, for the first time Claudia's mother stood upright at the doorway and did not invite her in. Miss Gloria got the message and never came back to the house again.

Chapter 2

GRADUATION

It was 8am on a wet Saturday morning. The post arrived and two letters dropped on the mat. Claudia ran to the door in anticipation. She noticed that one of the letters was from the examination board. Her results had finally arrived.

Claudia nervously opened the envelope. She gently pulled out the paper and carefully unfolded it. She eagerly looked across the paper to find her results. "Yes," Claudia shouted excitedly. She shouted so loudly that she woke her parents up.

Claudia ran into her parent's room to give them the good news. "Mum, Dad, I've got 6 A's and 2 B's, that's more than enough to get into college." Claudia said happily. "That's wonderful Claudia." her mother beamed with joy. "Well Claudia, you definitely get your brains from me." Claudia's father said jokingly.

Claudia phoned Shari and Deena to give them the good news. Although they also achieved good grades, they were not interested in furthering their studies. Claudia was the only one who wanted to go to college, where as Deena went to work in her fathers company and Shari decided to travel around Europe.

Claudia looked through the prospectus of her local college and selected the course she wanted to study. She applied and prepared to enrol in the autumn.

On the day of enrolment, Claudia was nervous. She felt that she was now entering the big wide world. Her National Insurance Number came through permitting her to work however, she did not feel ready to be an adult and take on all those responsibilities that go with it.

"Let's look forward to new beginnings." Claudia mumbled nervously, as she entered through the double doors of the old-fashioned college. There seemed to be a lot of interest in the course that Claudia had chosen because the queue spilled out into the hallway.

Claudia patiently waited her turn. While she waited for the queue to go down, Claudia's shyness did not allow her to talk to anyone in her line. She just smiled back at those that smiled at her.

"Hello," Claudia heard a voice coming from the back of her and she turned around. "I'm Marcia, pleased to meet you." Marcia said as she reached out her hand to Claudia. "I'm Claudia, pleased to meet you too." Claudia said as she shook Marcia's hand. Marcia was a docile, pleasant girl. She was tall, slim and very fashionable.

The pair talked and got to know each other as the line slowly went down. Because Claudia was so used to wearing a school uniform, she was concerned about how to dress for college. So, before the term started, Claudia got her hair done at the salon and went shopping to update her wardrobe.

On the first day of college, Claudia wore her hair in a neat ponytail tied up in a circle comb with a long wavy fringe combed down on one side of her face. She wore a nice pair of denim jeans, a black and white striped sweater and a new beige Mac. Claudia felt good.

Claudia met her lecturers and members of her class. She could see how college was so different to senior school, with the new found freedom, the respect given to her by the lecturers and the exciting activities, including the monthly parties organised by members of the Student Union Association.

Claudia and Marcia would often attend these parties, exhausting themselves by dancing all night and when the slow tunes played, Marcia would always find a boy to dance with whereas Claudia would end up talking to her fellow classmates. Nevertheless, Claudia enjoyed college life, working diligently on her assignments and revising for her exams to achieve good grades.

Claudia quickly made many friends but she realised that the young men at college were not interested in her in a romantic way. Claudia found this strange but she put it to the back of her mind. "Maybe I haven't met my soul mate yet. Anyway I have plenty of time, I'm only 16." Claudia thought.

During her 3 years at college, Claudia did exceptionally well in her examinations and passed all three levels of her course with distinctions. Claudia was now ready to find employment and earn some money, however, her friends and her tutor encouraged her not to stop there. Because of her intelligence and evident capabilities, they advised Claudia to go to university. Claudia listened to there advice and decided to study law.

The summer break was coming up. Claudia's cousins, Felecia and Janet were planning a family holiday and they decided to invite Claudia along. The vacation was going to be at the end of Claudia's final term, which fitted nicely into Claudia's timetable. She was very much looking forward to getting away because the last time she had a holiday abroad, she was a young child with faded memories.

The holiday approached and Claudia was all packed and ready to go. "The cab is here." Claudia said. "Come on, let me help you with your luggage." her father said as he carried her case to the car. Her parents waved goodbye to Claudia, as she set off towards her cousin's house. When she got there she helped Uncle Max and her cousin's with there luggage and then they headed to the airport. When they arrived, they off loaded their suitcases and quickly checked in.

A few hours later an announcement was made, "Passengers for flight number 252, please board at gate number 4." Claudia and her family proceeded to queue up, to board their flight.

"First thing we are going to do when we arrive, is check out the club scene. I'm thinking of hiring a vehicle, because I'm sure the taxi fare over there is expensive." Felecia explained. "Ok, I applied for a student loan and I managed to get a few hundred pounds so I definitely can contribute towards the cost." said Claudia. "That's good, but it's a shame that you're too young to contribute to the driving. You need to hurry up and get your licence." Janet laughed.

The flying time of 7 hours and 35 minutes had passed quickly and the crew prepared for landing. The "Fasten your seat belt." sign flashed. "Good afternoon passengers," said the co-pilot. "Please could you return to your seats and fasten your seat belts, as we are about to descend. The estimated time of arrival is 2:30pm and the weather is currently warm and hazy with light rain. I would like to wish all passengers a lovely holiday and thank you for flying with us."

As the plane glided towards the Island, Felecia's ears became blocked and after a few seconds they popped. "Ow, my ears." howled Felecia. "Here chew on this gum. It will help." said Claudia. Felecia popped the gum in her mouth and chewed rapidly to get quick relief from the pain.

The plane slowly approached the runway and landed smoothly. As the plane stopped, everyone proceeded to exit. Claudia and her family quickly passed through immigration and subsequently boarded a waiting taxi.

When they got to the guesthouse, Oliver, the owner of the house, greeted them when they arrived. "Good afternoon, welcome to Sunny Beach Apartments." Oliver said warmly. "Thank you Sir." Uncle Max said as they shook hands.

As they stood under a mango tree, Claudia noticed that the tree was shaking. When she looked up, she could see something moving in the trees. As she looked harder she realised it was a monkey eating a mango.

Claudia tapped Felecia. "Look up there." Felecia looked up and smiled "You better save some of those mangoes for us." Felecia shouted to the monkey. Then suddenly, the monkey threw the mango skin down and it landed on Felecia's face. Everyone laughed as Felecia wiped off the remnants of the fruit with the back of her hand.

Uncle Max then introduced the girls to Oliver who showed them around. "We have a two bedroom apartment on the ground level, with two shower rooms, air conditioning and all other amenities. We also have a one bedroom apartment upstairs, so take your pick." explained Oliver. "Dad," Felecia said with a smile, "You can have the upstairs apartment and we girls will stay down here." Felecia suggested. "Okay." Uncle Max agreed.

The girls left Uncle Max to settle the bill while they settled into their apartment. "Right, this is my bedroom, with the ensuite." Felecia said excitedly. "Hey, have you forgotten? There's only two bedrooms?" Janet pointed out. "Oh no, does that mean I have to share with you?" Felecia said cheekily.

"You two sisters can share this room and I'll have the smaller room next door." Claudia suggested. The girls agreed and prepared to unpack and shower. They ordered a takeaway and brought some food upstairs for Uncle Max. Then they settled down for the night.

The early morning sun shone brightly, forcing its way through the curtains, which prevented the girls from sleeping any longer. Janet and Claudia took turns to shower, while Felecia put the kettle on. Then she telephoned Uncle Max.

He explained to Felecia that he had a busy schedule this week and told them not to worry about his meals. "So you'll be doing your own thing this week Dad? Okay take care of yourself." Janet got dressed and went into the dining room. "Oh my god, it's 6:30am, I never get up this early back home." Janet said astonishingly.

Felecia showered and the girls put on their denim shorts and their pastel coloured tops and now they were ready to let the locals know they were in town. As the girls got off the bus and walked into the town centre, a group of guys watched the girls as they walked up the narrow street towards them.

One of the guys made a hissing noise like a snake, another one from the group repeatedly chanted the words, "English, English." The girls smiled but continued walking. "How do they know we are English? We could be American." Claudia said bemused.

"Well, mum used to say that they can tell where we are from by the way we dress, because English girls dress differently to American girls and the hissing noise means that they like us. That one in the red vest top was nice, I can't wait to hit the club tonight." said Janet excitedly.

The girls went to the cafeteria to have some lunch and then they stopped off at the local supermarket to stock up on food before heading back to the apartment. The girls were glad to get out of the heat. "I am so hot, someone please put the air conditioning on." Claudia instructed, as she flopped down in the chair.

The beach was a stones throw away and the girls were eager to bathe their bodies in the blue clean seawater. "Right girls, shall we go for a swim? Let's shower and change into our bikini's." ordered Felecia.

The girls wrapped their sarongs around their waists and strolled towards the beach in their flip-flops. "Aaahh, look at that sheep over there. How cute." said Claudia, as she ran up to feed it some grass. "Yeah and those chicks look so sweet, waddling together." said Janet.

By now it was 3:30pm. The girls chose the right time to swim, as the strength of the heat is not as strong as it would be between the morning and early afternoon. They found their spot, laid out their towels and sat down to enjoy the sun on their backs.

"So Claudia, I don't hear you talking about a boyfriend, are you hiding him away?" Janet asked curiously. "No," Claudia said uncomfortably, "I'm just," she mumbled quietly, "Well, I don't have a boyfriend, at the moment, because I want to focus on my education first and now that I'm studying, I don't really have a social life. So there's not much chance of meeting a man anyway." Claudia said shyly.

"Girl, you're young, free and single. You need to get out there and stop acting like you're old before your time." Felecia advised, "You're ten years younger than I am. I'd love to be your age."

Felecia is a kind-hearted bubbly girl who married young. She had two children but unfortunately her marriage ended after 5 years. Felecia is now very ready to move on. Since her divorce, she kissed a few frogs but she is confident that she will meet the right man in time, as she has not been short of dates recently.

By the time the girls returned to the apartment, they hadn't had a moment's rest, before they were on the move again. They got themselves dressed up and they were ready to check out the club scene.

They realised that they were not going to do much driving as most of the amenities were near by, so they decided not to hire a vehicle after all and they travelled to the club in a taxi, instead.

As the girls walked up to the club entrance the local guys hollered over to them shouting out, "How are you beautiful English girls?" "We're fine" the girls replied.

They paid at the entrance and walked onto the large dance floor with florescent ceiling lights, flashing in sequence. The girls quickly ordered their drinks and boogied the night away.

"Girl, that guy over there has been watching you all night." Felecia said to Janet. Janet turned around and discreetly checked the guy out. "Ummm, he's nice looking. I wouldn't mind getting to know him a little better." smiled Janet.

"Hello, you lovely English lady," a tall, well-groomed man said to Felecia, "Would you like to dance?" he asked, as he offered his hand to her. Felecia became bashful, "Probably later, come and see me when they play the slow music." advised Felecia. The man nodded and disappeared into the crowd.

"Oooh, you have an admirer now." teased Claudia. The girls partied the night away and every so often, the men would pull at the girls to express their interest in them and they enjoyed the attention.

Felecia's admirer stood propped at the bar, watching her all evening, visually protecting her from other prey. As the end of the evening approached, the DJ switched the music and played the slow tracks.

"Please may I have this dance? You did tell me to come back later." Felecia's persistent admirer asked. "Okay." Felecia smiled as he pulled her close to him. After a few seconds, a man asked Janet to dance and she obliged.

Claudia on the other hand did not have a dance partner and she felt uncomfortable, standing on her own in the middle of the dance floor. She looked around the room and realised that nearly everyone had a partner to dance with except the weird people in the corner and she definitely was not weird.

She just couldn't understand why she never got any attention from the guys. She was always the one left on the shelf. This was not the first time she was without a dance partner. Being ignored by the guys had affected her enjoyment on this holiday and it slowly ate away at her confidence.

Now that she often attended parties, Claudia realised that these situations was a regular occurrence and when it happened, she would reflect on that premonition she got on the bus, when she was a young schoolgirl. "It's going to be hard for you to meet a boyfriend."

Claudia was now 19 years old and that message had haunted her since she was old enough to date. Again, she wondered why she would get a message like that and more importantly, she wondered if that message would prove to be true in her life.

Claudia avoided the embarrassment. She quickly got herself another drink and then made her way to the seating area at the back of the hall to hide herself away. As she sat sipping on her drink, she patiently waited for her cousins to come and find her. Eventually Claudia became so bored that she ended up falling asleep in the chair.

"Wake up, Claudia." Felecia said as she gently tapped

Claudia on her shoulder. "Hey sleeping beauty. You are getting old before your time. Why did you leave the dance area? I thought you had disappeared with a new man. How you gonna meet someone if you hide yourself away?" asked Janet.

"I'm just tired, anyway I hope you girls had a good time." said Claudia sleepily. "Yes we did." the girls replied simultaneously. "Well I got Darren's number, he wants to take me on a tour of the Island." Janet said happily. "Yeah and I've got Ray's number. Darren and Ray are good friends, you know." Felecia explained to Claudia.

The girls left the club and jumped into the cab that was parked outside. When they arrived home and walked towards the front door, Felecia screamed, "What the hell was that?" Claudia shrieked. They all ducked down and ran as they saw something fly past them. "That's a bat, look there's another one and another one." Janet shouted as Claudia put the key in the door, rushing to get inside the apartment as quickly as possible.

After fumbling with the key, they finally got inside the house and quickly shut the door. "Those bats look like rats with wings." Felecia said as she tried to get her breath back. "I didn't know that they fly so low?" Claudia said. "Well I'm going to make sure that I am inside this house before dark. That was scary." said Felecia. "Yeah right, if you won't be going out after dark anymore, then you're going to have to give up the night life." Janet pointed out. "Gosh, we have seen monkeys, sheep, chickens and now bats right outside our apartment. I feel like there's a zoo in our back yard." said Claudia. They all laughed.

The next day, there was an early morning phone call, which woke everyone up. Claudia got up to answer it, "Hello." said Claudia. "Good morning, is it possible to speak to Janet please? It's Darren." this man with a nice voice said. "Yes ok, hold the line. I'll just call her for you." replied Claudia.

Claudia ran into the girl's bedroom. "Janet, lover boy is on the phone." Claudia said cheekily. Janet quickly sat up in bed, "Oh my God. Did you say that Darren's on the phone?" Janet asked nervously. "Yes, girl." Claudia confirmed. "But why is he calling so early? I hate my voice in the morning, it sounds so croaky." said Janet. "Oh don't be so silly. Hurry up and go to the phone. You shouldn't keep the man waiting." teased Claudia.

Janet cleared her throat and then picked up the receiver, "Hi Darren." Janet said, as she made a feeble attempt to speak softly on the phone. "Hello, my beautiful lady. How are you today?" Darren replied with his deep sexy tone.

Before Janet could answer, Darren continued, "Would you and Felecia be available tonight? Because Ray and I would like to take you ladies on a boat trip around the Island. There will be great food, nice music and good entertainment. We could pick you up around 7pm, if you don't have any other plans of course." persuaded Darren. "Oh okay. I'll ask Felecia, then I'll call you straight back." Janet said excitedly.

Janet ran back into the bedroom "Hey, Felecia. I was just speaking to Darren." Janet said. "Really?" Felecia responded and then she began to wonder why her guy, Ray hadn't called her yet. "Darren and Ray want to take us on a boat trip tonight." explained Janet. Felecia's eyes lit up. "That's great, you told him yes didn't you?" asked Felecia. "Well I told him that I'll ask you first. I said I'll call him back with an answer." said Janet. "Call him back, right now and tell him yes." Felecia demanded.

Janet quickly ran to the phone and then she stopped and slowly turned around and walked back to the bedroom. "What about Claudia?" Janet said to Felecia, "It wouldn't be fair to leave Claudia out." Janet said sympathetically. "Yeah and it might make her feel bad, because she hasn't met anyone, yet." a caring Felecia replied. "We need to get Claudia hooked up with someone. This girl is so nice and she has a figure to die for. It won't take her too long to meet a man. In fact I'm surprised it hasn't happened already." said Janet.

Felecia and Janet were unaware that Claudia was standing by the bedroom doorway. "Ladies, I heard you," said Claudia, in an unimpressed way. "Thank you for the compliment, but I don't want anyone feeling sorry for me. Now you get on that phone and let your guys know that you will be meeting up with them tonight." Claudia insisted.

Janet did as she was told and she phoned Darren back with the good news. "That's great, I'll go and collect 4 tickets for tonight." Darren confirmed. Janet then lowered her voice and whispered, "Do you mind getting an extra ticket, because I would like to bring my little cousin Claudia. We'll give you the money for it." explained Janet. "I'll sort it, but I don't want the money. In this town, women do not pay for nothing. I'll see you later." Darren said charmingly.

The girls spent the rest of the day eating, listening to music and having fun. Claudia on the other hand was not her usual bubbly self and appeared to be quite sad.

As the evening approached, Felecia and Janet began to prepare for an exciting night ahead. They thought it was time to tell Claudia about her invitation to join them on their date tonight, to give her plenty of time to get ready.

"Claudia, Darren bought a ticket for you. We'd like you to come out with us tonight." Janet said excitedly, waiting for Claudia to reciprocate her happiness.

However, she didn't. Claudia tried to contain her feelings but her irritation showed. "Oh, thanks." replied Claudia. "You don't seem too overjoyed about it." Felecia said. "Well thank you for thinking about me but you two have already got partners." Claudia pointed out. "And you will meet someone too." reassured Janet, putting her arm around Claudia. "Okay, I'll get ready." Claudia said reluctantly.

She began to anticipate how the evening would be. Her cousins will be enjoying the night away, smooching with their partners. Which is typical for them as the pair are never short of male company, wherever they go. Where as Claudia will be sitting on her own as usual. She'd be lucky if even the less desirable of men notice her. Despite this, Claudia decided to make sure that she has a good time.

The sound of a car approached the girl's apartment. Claudia pulled back the curtains. "Ladies, there's a posh black Mercedes outside." shouted Claudia. "That can't be them, the driver is probably lost and has mistakenly parked up outside our house." explained Janet. "Wrong, this is definitely our ride because Darren's just stepped out of the car." Claudia said, smiling. "Have they really come to pick us up in such a posh car? Seems like they have money." Felecia said excitedly.

The doorbell rang and all three ladies went to open it. Darren and Ray greeted them. "Goodnight, ladies. Are you ready for an enjoyable evening?" Ray asked in his beautiful local accent. "Yes we are." Janet responded as she grabbed Darren's arm. Ray then opened out his two arms as an indication for Felecia and Claudia to hold on to him on either side. They then walked down the pathway and like true gentlemen, they held the car door open for the ladies before they drove off.

As they approached the pier, all that they could see in the midnight blue sky, was the beautiful white lights that decorated the entourage of boats, that docked at the harbour. They parked up and waited to board. "Oh what a beautiful ship." Felecia said admiringly. "Yes, this ship has been sailing the seas and serving the tourists for over 20 years." explained Ray.

They boarded and found a table which over looked the dark waters. "Can I get you all a drink?" Ray asked. "Yes please, rum punch for all of us." Felecia said boldly. As Ray and Darren left to get the drinks, Claudia nudged Felecia. "Oi, I can buy my own drinks thank you. I don't want your boyfriends to feel obligated that whatever they give to you, they have got to give the same to me." explained Claudia. She was embarrassed and still felt uncomfortable and out of place to be accompanying the double daters.

"What are you talking about? Don't worry, I won't allow him to give you everything that he is going to give to me, because his body is something he definitely won't be sharing." Felecia said as she teased Claudia. "Ha, ha you're very funny." smiled Claudia. "Anyway, I'm sure some good looking guy is going to whisk you away from us. We probably won't see you for the rest of the evening." Janet chuckled.

Darren and Ray returned with the drinks and they all sat down to enjoy the music as the boat gently sailed. "Oh I love this song," Felecia said as she got up. "Come on ladies lets dance." she said. Felecia grabbed Janet and Claudia's arm and they all hurried over to the dance floor.

After a while, the guys joined them. The evening was nice, the air was fresh and cool and the atmosphere was great. The DJ was playing the right tunes at the right time and the tiny lights in the distance pinpointed the location of the Island.

Later on in the evening, everyone queued to help themselves to a buffet dinner. "This cuisine is gorgeous." Janet said appreciatively, as they all returned to the table. "I agree." Claudia replied. They all remained silent, enjoying the food so much that they could not afford to speak.

There were a couple of hours left of the evening and the

entertainment started, which included a comedy act followed by fire-eaters, people on stilts and limbo dancing.

"Now everybody, we do expect the audience to participate in the limbo dancing." The host said. "Oh no I don't like stuff like that." Felecia revealed. "Shall we disappear? He's going to pick on us, because we're sitting near the front." explained Janet. "Yeah and this dress is really not the most appropriate item of clothing to be wearing when you're limbo dancing. Let's just quietly get up and make our way to the toilet." said Claudia.

As they walked between the rows of seats, they unintentionally brought unwanted attention to themselves. "Oh look at these lovely ladies. Where are you going?" The host asked. The girls looked up in horror and they dreaded what was about to happen next. "Can I invite you up to the front? Please clap for these ladies." announced the host.

As the audience applauded, the girls reluctantly and very slowly walked up to the front. "This is completely your fault, we should have just stayed in our seats. He probably wouldn't have seen us then." Felecia snapped at Claudia. "Don't blame me, you didn't have to follow me." whispered Claudia.

The girls arrived at the front to join the host. "So ladies, are you all enjoying your stay on the Island?" The host asked. "Yes, we're having a great time." Felecia replied on behalf of Claudia and Janet.

"Right, what's going to happen is this man over here, will show you how to limbo dance, properly." explained the host. A guy came forward, showing off a nicely oiled six-packed stomach, wearing nothing but a G-string and a grass skirt on top. "Umm he looks good." muttered Felecia. "Well honey you have your man already so he's all mine." Claudia joked.

The fire burning limbo bar was positioned very close to the floor. The crowd cheered as the dancer gyrated his waist and moved his body under the bar. He bowed as the audience clapped. "They don't expect us to limbo dance with the bar this low, do they?" Janet asked nervously. "And they better put that fire out as well." Felecia said unimpressed.

"Right ladies, obviously your limbo bar will be unlit and as you are wearing dresses we will not place the bar too low." But as the host raised the bar, the girls shouted, "Higher, raise the bar higher." So the male audience members reacted and began to shout out, "Lower, bring the bar down lower." Eventually the girls and the host agreed on a suitable bar level.

"Okay ladies, get into position." Instructed the host. The ladies lined up one behind the other. They took turns to lean backwards and move their hips from side to side to some calypso music until they completed the limbo bar. "Please give these ladies a round of applause for being a great sport." The audience clapped as they each received a souvenir. They thanked the host and went back to their seats.

"Well done." Ray said as they returned. "Thank you. We tried our best to avoid being chosen and look what happened." giggled Janet. "Never mind girls, we had a good time didn't we?" Claudia said.

A few hours before the night ended, the DJ slowed the music down. Ray and Darren invited Felecia and Janet to dance, whereas Claudia continued to sip her drink and dance to the music on her own as she watched them enjoy themselves.

After a while Claudia ordered another drink for herself and spent some time in the bar area before returning to her seat. She refused to let anything ruin her holiday even though the fact that she did not have a dance partner played on her mind. Sadly, not one guy on that ship had noticed her. It was strange but true. Claudia slowly sipped her cocktails until the night ended.

Soon the double daters came back to the table. "Well that was a great night." Felecia said as she waved her fan to cool herself down. "Claudia, where did you disappear to?" asked Janet. "Well I just spent some time on the top deck and enjoyed the vibe." Claudia replied.

The ship had returned to the harbour and everyone queued to depart. "I hope you all had a good evening. Please be patient while we lower the slope safely. We hope to see you again soon. Thank you and goodnight." said the manager as everyone headed for the exit.

"Ladies did you have a good time?" Ray asked. "Sure. Thank you for inviting us." smiled Janet.

They drove the short journey to the apartment and as the girls got out of the car, Janet and Felecia kissed their guys goodbye while Claudia went on ahead.

"I'm sorry that you're leaving the Island so soon. I wish I met you when you arrived, so that I could have spent more time with you." Darren said expressing his emotions. Janet smiled. "Never mind, we can keep in touch. I'll take your overseas number before your flight." Darren said as he hugged Janet. They waved goodbye to the guys as they drove off.

The girls congregated in Claudia's room to reflect on the great night that they had. "We can't say that we didn't have a good holiday." Felecia said feeling satisfied. "Yeah and sadly we're going back home soon. The holiday went by so quickly, we should have stayed for longer." Janet stated. The girls were very sleepy and quite drunk. They got themselves ready for bed and were asleep within minutes.

It was 6am. A knock at the door woke Claudia out of her sleep. She got up, put her dressing gown on and opened the door. "Hi Uncle Max," said Claudia. "Did you spend a nice time with your sister and her family?" Claudia asked. "Yes, I had a very good time Claudia." Uncle Max said as he followed her into the house. "Would you like some tea Uncle Max?" Claudia offered. "Yes, please, no sugar." he replied.

Felecia and Janet got up and came into the dining room. "Hi Dad, how have you been?" asked Felecia. "Well, I've been having a lovely time with the rest of the family. They really looked after me and fed me well." laughed Uncle Max, as he grabbed his tummy.

Claudia made a pot of tea and sliced some cake, which she brought into the dining room. "Anyway girls, I won't be leaving with you tomorrow." revealed Uncle Max. "Why, Dad?" Janet asked in a concerned way. "Don't look so worried. I have been having such a good time. Which is why I am not ready to leave yet. You all have jobs to go back to, but me I can stay as long as I like now that I'm retired." explained Uncle Max.

Uncle Max's wife died a few years ago and he was becoming lonely and depressed. It seemed like this holiday was just what he needed to put a spark back into his life. "So have you extended your ticket?" asked Janet. "Yes, I'm staying for another 6 weeks." Uncle Max revealed.

"So where are you going to stay, with Auntie?" asked Felecia. "Or will Uncle Max be staying with a lady friend?" Claudia said, teasing Uncle Max. "Oh don't be so silly, Claudia." Felecia snapped, unimpressed by her comment. "Well, you shouldn't think she's silly. I am not too old for romance, you know. Claudia is right. I have met a nice young lady." confirmed Uncle Max. "Young lady, how old is she?" Janet asked disapprovingly. "Well when I say young. She's just 10 years younger than me." explained Uncle Max "Oh, that's why we haven't seen much of you on this holiday. You go Uncle Max." Claudia said cheekily.

As the girls were leaving the next morning, they decided to have a restful day having dinner with Uncle Max and packing their cases. However, they didn't want to miss a final swim in the sea. The girls put on their bikinis and walked down to the beach and as usual, they attracted a lot of attention from the guys. Giving them a short-lived experience of what it would feel like if they were celebrities on the red carpet. They tired themselves out, splashing around in the cool sea and playing volleyball on the sand before returning to the beach apartment during the early sunset.

"We are back." Felecia shouted to her father. "Did you have a nice time at the beach?" Uncle Max asked. "It was lovely." Janet replied, "Well I had a lovely talk with Ray." revealed Uncle Max. "What?" Felecia jumped up in surprise. "Yes, well it seems like I'm not the only one who's enjoying a holiday romance." Uncle Max said, teasing Felecia.

"Well, I'm not the only one," Felecia said stammering her words and behaving like a naughty schoolgirl. "Janet has as well, she's going out with Darren." revealed Felecia. "Oi, Felecia," Janet reacted. "Dad's talking about you, there was no need to bring up my business in this conversation." defended Janet.

"Well I won't ask about Claudia, because you're too young. You just concentrate on your studies and forget the boys for now, they can be too much trouble." Uncle Max advised.

The last morning of the holiday had arrived and the girls rose early to get ready for their afternoon flight. However, because the place was untidy, they ran around in a haphazard state, desperately trying to put the apartment back to the condition that they found it.

The taxi arrived and Uncle Max helped them put their suitcases in the car. "Hey, I thought Darren and Ray were going to take us to the airport?" Claudia remembered. "Well we told them that we don't like goodbyes and I didn't really want to give him my home number, even though he was keen to stay in contact. There is plenty more fish in England. Anyway what happened on this Island stays on this Island." joked Janet, lowering her voice so that her father wouldn't hear her.

"Dad you look after yourself." Felecia said as they hugged. "If you need anything let us, know and don't take too long to come back home." Janet said as a tear dropped from her eye. "Girls, you get back safely and don't worry too much about me, I'll be fine." Uncle Max replied.

The girls waved goodbye and headed for the airport. They swiftly checked in their luggage and patiently waited to board the plane. They reflected on their holiday on the Island, knowing that they will leave with happy memories.

After having lunch, it was time for the girls to board their flight. As they climbed the steps towards the plane, they inhaled the last of the Island's smells and lapped up the final heat on their faces. There was little conversation as the tired girls took their seats.

When the plane ascended into the dark skies, Claudia looked back and silently said goodbye to her holiday, as the Island faded into the distance.

Chapter 3

WHO'S THAT GIRL?

THE SUMMER BREAK was almost over, Clint had married his childhood sweetheart and Claudia, after successfully passing her exams, was now preparing to go to university to commence her 3 year law degree. She enrolled and quickly settled into university life.

Claudia was a sociable girl but still a private person, so making many friends was not really important to her. "Friends cause you pain." her late grandmother would say, so she chose never to forget that.

Having one or two close reliable friends was better than having many unimportant friends who would probably let you down in the end anyway. Her main friend at university was her college friend Marcia. Claudia and Marcia would go around to each other's houses and continue to support each other in their studies as they had done when they were at college.

A couple of weeks into university life, Claudia began to suffer frequent headaches. She became concerned that these headaches could be a brain tumour so she decided to seek medical advice.

"Doctor, I've been getting really bad headaches. The pain starts at the back of my eyes and then I get a throbbing pain in the centre of my head. I then become sensitive to light. So I have to have all the lights switched off until it improves." explained Claudia.

The doctor listened attentively and came up with a diagnosis. "Well it seems like your symptoms suggest you're suffering with migraines. Studying can strain your eyes. It would be advisable to go to the opticians and get an eye test. But in the meantime when your migraines get bad, just take some tablets." suggested the doctor.

Claudia went home and told her mother what the doctor had said. "He also said that I should get my eyes tested, because recently I've noticed that I can't see the board clearly, so now I sit at the front." explained Claudia.

"Really, but you've always had excellent eyesight. It's strange that your vision has suddenly gone bad. You never had any problems at college." her mother said worryingly.

Claudia arranged for an eye test and had her eyes examined. The results were clear, she was short sighted and had to wear spectacles.

It was a sunny Monday morning, Claudia woke up in a panic, because her alarm didn't go off and she was running late for her exam. She remembered her mother saying to her that she must always have a hot drink in the morning but Claudia didn't have time today.

Claudia ran to the bus stop, jumped on the bus and made her way to the examination centre. She arrived 12 minutes late. Claudia was very lucky to make it just in time, because they would have shut the doors if she was more than fifteen minutes late.

The exam lasted 3 hours. Claudia quickly answered all the questions and sat patiently until the time was up. Claudia didn't want to hang out with her friends today as she felt a migraine coming on. So she avoided some familiar faces and quickly left through the back door.

As Claudia ran down the steps, a heavy hand touched her shoulder. Claudia quickly turned around "Hello, I'm Cheryl." said the girl. Claudia paused. She responded with an expression on her face that showed her irritation. Claudia was not in the mood for a conversation, all she wanted was to catch her train and take care of her pounding headache. But at the same time, Claudia didn't want to be rude, so she decided to give her a chance to speak.

"You go to the same university as me." Cheryl revealed. "Do I?" Claudia said surprisingly. "Yeah, we're studying the same law degree, but you're in your final year and I'm in my second year. I've seen you around the campus." Cheryl explained. "Right, I've not seen you before, my name is Claudia, by the way." Claudia said trying to be polite. She had reluctantly missed her train to talk to Cheryl.

"There's a student union party tomorrow night, are you going?" Cheryl asked. "Yes, but I'm going with my friends." Claudia replied.

Cheryl smiled, "Well if your friends can't make it, we could meet up and go together." Cheryl suggested. Claudia was wondering why Cheryl was so interested in her. Cheryl didn't know Claudia but she was friendly, a bit too friendly and for a brief moment Claudia wondered whether Cheryl liked girls.

Claudia quickly replied, "No, no, that's okay, my friends are driving so they'll give me a lift." After she said that, Claudia thought that it was not such a good idea to tell Cheryl, that she had transportation for tomorrow night, because she may then ask if Claudia's friends could pick her up on the way. "Okay, I'll see you tomorrow night." replied Cheryl. Claudia sighed with relief.

As they parted, Claudia wondered why Cheryl was trying to force her into a friendship. Claudia had never met anyone like Cheryl before. She seemed kind but a bit too pushy and loud for Claudia's liking.

Claudia was glad to get home as her migraine had become unbearable after the conversation she had with Cheryl who didn't stop talking.

"Hi mum, hi dad." Claudia said closing the front door behind her. "How was your exam?" her mother asked. "It was easy, I should definitely get a good grade." Claudia replied confidently. "Well you better pass because I only have intelligent people in my family." her father said in a comical fashion. "Ha, ha Dad." Claudia smiled as she left and went into her bedroom.

After taking two tablets, Claudia laid down and slept for a while. A couple of hours later, her migraine had disappeared. Claudia decided to ring Marcia to remind her about the dance at the university tomorrow night.

Unfortunately, Marcia gave up her studies during the first year of the course, to care for her sick mother. However, they remained close friends and Claudia would still invite Marcia to the parties because she always used to enjoy them when she was a student.

"Hi Marcia." Claudia said. "What's up, Claudia? How was the exam?" Marcia asked. "It seemed quite easy actually. I'll let you know how well I've done, when I get the results. Anyway the Student Union Party is tomorrow night, remember? Are you still coming?" Claudia said excitedly.

Marcia paused, then she proceeded to say, "Oh Claudia, you know tomorrow is Valentines Day, so I may have other plans, depends on what Carlton has arranged. I just didn't realise that your party is on the same day." Marcia explained.

Claudia felt disappointed. When Marcia mentioned about her boyfriend, it reminded Claudia that she was still a single girl and she had been throughout her teenage years.

"You know what Claudia?" Marcia said reassuringly, "I'll ask Carlton if he wants to come to the party, I'll call you back and let you know."

Claudia lay down on her bed. She looked up at the ceiling and began to reflect on her life. People of all shapes and sizes have someone in their life because there is supposed to be somebody for everybody, isn't there? Claudia thought.

Claudia couldn't remember the last time a guy came up to her and asked for her number, let alone invite her out on a date and a Valentines card, well she'd never been given one, except when she was six years old in infant school and sweet little Max asked her to be his Valentine.

The phone rang, which suddenly brought Claudia out of her thoughts. "Hi Claudia, good news, Carlton wants to come. He's never been to a student party before. We'll pick you up around seven thirty." Marcia said happily, as she did not want to let Claudia down.

As Claudia prepared to sleep, she couldn't help thinking about her singleness again and questioned why it was taking so long to meet someone.

Whenever her friends would split up with their boyfriends, within two or three months they would meet someone new. However, for Claudia, it had taken many years and she was still single. Her situation played on her mind and she spent the whole night worrying, unable to sleep.

The next morning, Claudia's mother called her from the

kitchen. "Claudia if you don't get up and have your breakfast you will end up being late for your lectures." Claudia was exhausted from the lack of sleep the night before. She looked at her clock and wondered why her mother would wake her up at 7:30am when she set her alarm for 8:25am. "Mum, lectures start late on a Wednesday. Why are you waking me up at this time?" Claudia hollered, annoyed that her sleep was broken.

"Oh sorry, I forgot, go back to sleep." said her mother. "Go back to sleep? It's not that easy to go back to sleep now that you have woken me up. I might as well get up now." Claudia mumbled to herself.

Claudia showered, had a cup of strong coffee and made her way to university early. As she got to the front entrance she saw Cheryl standing in the corridor. Claudia definitely was not in the mood for Cheryl today, so she quickly turned around and ran to the other side of the building to enter through the back doors.

Because Claudia had another hour to go before her classes, she decided to pass the time by having breakfast in the canteen. She saw her friends in there and she sat with them.

"Hey Claudia, where were you yesterday?" Candice asked. "We didn't see you in the examination room, were you there?" asked Trevor. "Of course I was there. Do you really think I would miss my exam? I sat at the back because I got there a bit late and then I was in a hurry to get home because I wasn't feeling well." Claudia explained.

"Anyway does anybody know a girl called Cheryl?" Claudia wondered. "Yes, I think I know her," Trevor stated, "Is she that weird looking girl, who has a disproportionate shape. Big on top and small on the bottom. Her sparrow legs almost seem too skinny to hold her up." laughed Trevor. "Yes, that's her. I tell you, I cannot believe this girl stopped me yesterday. She was talking to me as if we were best friends and now she wants to hang out with me. Cheryl even wants us to meet up at the party tonight." Claudia said.

"She's probably lonely, I feel a bit sorry for her, do you?" Candice responded sympathetically. "No, I don't know her, so why would I feel sorry for her?" replied Claudia.

The day passed quickly and everyone went home to prepare for the dance. "Have you got your garments sorted for tonight?" asked Claudia on the phone to Marcia. "Of course, what about you?" replied Marcia "Are you kidding me, I bought my dress weeks ago" said Claudia excitedly.

The girls met up and Carlton drove them to the hall. Cheryl arrived soon afterwards alone. She quickly looked around the room before heading straight towards Claudia. "Hi Claudia, do you like my cat suit?" Cheryl asked showing off her outfit. Claudia pretended to like it. "Yes that really looks good on you." replied Claudia.

Trevor, Candice and the rest of the crew entered the hall and Claudia introduced Cheryl to her friends. They then got there drinks and began to enjoy the night.

The DJ excited everyone by playing their favourite songs and then suddenly, Cheryl broke away from the crowd and began dancing very provocatively, in the middle of the dance floor. Her eyes were closed and she was singing, very loudly, out of tune.

"Oh my god, what is she doing?" asked Candice in disgust. "Claudia, talk to your friend." Trevor said, teasing Claudia. "I'm not responsible for her, let her do her thing." defended Claudia.

The last hour of the night was devoted to playing the soft, slow music. Candice and Marcia danced with their boyfriends, Trevor grabbed his girlfriend and Claudia, well surprise, surprise she didn't have a dance partner.

Claudia turned around and saw a handsome guy walking

towards her. She became excited and wondered if that special moment in her life had come, where she would be asked to dance?

When the guy got to Claudia, he didn't stop, he kept on walking, then he opened out his arms and held on to another girl. That girl was Cheryl. Claudia's heart sank.

Even Cheryl had somebody to dance with. Men had been walking straight past her for so long now, that it was as if Claudia was invisible. Claudia wasn't a hateful person but she knew that she didn't look as bad as Cheryl did.

Claudia left the party feeling confused. She wondered why she constantly failed to get male attention each and every time she went out. Even when she went on holiday with her cousins, it didn't happen for her and usually if anyone is having trouble meeting someone, they can be guaranteed a holiday romance, because the locals always love the foreigners.

In the coming weeks, Claudia reluctantly found herself spending more and more time with Cheryl and less time with her other friends. It seemed like Cheryl was beginning to take advantage of Claudia's kind nature.

Evidently, Cheryl was a lonely girl with little friends and because she lived on her own, she regularly invited Claudia into her home after university.

Whenever Claudia was not seeing Cheryl at university, she would be speaking to Cheryl on the phone. It seemed like there was no getting away from her. Claudia pitied Cheryl and because of this, she continued to tolerate their incompatible friendship.

Even though Cheryl became quite serious with the guy she danced with at the student union party, she still relied on Claudia. At times Claudia wanted to say no to her demands, but she could not bring herself to say it. Strangely, it seemed like Cheryl had some sort of hold over Claudia.

Chapter 4

WHAT RELATIONS?

"JUST MEET HIM." Cheryl insisted. "I'm not interested." Claudia replied down the phone "Look, he seems like a nice guy. I met him when I was leaving a party last Saturday night." Cheryl explained.

Claudia sighed, "What's his name?" she asked reluctantly. "His name is Ricardo, I didn't ask him his age but he looks a couple of years older than us." Cheryl replied.

Claudia paused, she was puzzled that Cheryl was so keen to set her up on a blind date with this stranger. Then she thought again. Even though Cheryl had her own boyfriend, she cared enough to help Claudia sort out her love life.

"And where does he live?" Claudia asked as she continued to fire questions at Cheryl. "I'm not sure but you can ask him that when you see him." Cheryl said in a persuasive tone. "Well, I'm not interested. You don't know anything about him. He could be a serial murderer for all I know." Claudia said wearily.

Cheryl laughed, "Claudia, whenever anyone meets someone new, they too could be meeting up with a maniac. But sometimes in life, you have to take a chance. Look I mentioned your name to him and he is very keen to meet up with you." she said persuasively.

Over the next few weeks, Cheryl continued to pester Claudia into meeting this man. Whenever there was an opportunity, it would be Ricardo this and Ricardo that and what a lovely person Ricardo was. Cheryl highly decorated the eligibility of this man.

By now, Claudia had graduated in law and was training to be a Solicitor. She was still single and had come to the point in her life that she was very ready for marriage and children.

After much deliberation with herself and a lot of convincing from Cheryl, Claudia reluctantly agreed to meet with Ricardo. She vowed that she would never meet someone on a blind date, but she felt justified because of her long-term singleness.

"Okay I'll meet him, if it will make you shut up." Claudia said in agreement. "Well it makes sense, as you're not dating anyone. After all, what harm can it do?" Cheryl said excitedly.

Cheryl went ahead with the arrangements. Claudia was to meet Ricardo outside her workplace the following day. Although Claudia was excited at the prospect of meeting this guy, she felt nervous, wondering what he looked like, whether he'd have a nice personality and more importantly will she like him.

The next day at work, Claudia felt uneasy. She was watching the clock throughout the day as it approached home time. It was now 4:30pm. Claudia went to the bathroom to re-apply her make-up and when she returned to her desk, her mobile phone rang. It was a number she didn't recognise.

She let the phone ring for a while and then she picked it up. "Hello." said Claudia curiously. "Hello, is this Claudia?" The voice replied. "Yes, who's this?" asked Claudia, even though she knew who it was. "It's Ricardo, Cheryl's friend. We're supposed to meet today. I'm parked outside."

Claudia got up and quickly went over to the window. It was dark outside but she noticed a parked car with white lights on. Claudia nervously replied, "Oh, I'll be there in a few minutes." She shut down her computer and said goodbye to her colleagues, then she ran back into the bathroom to make sure she looked okay before leaving the building.

She walked towards a green car parked across the road with the engine running. As she got closer to the car, the man behind the wheel wound down the window. "Are you Claudia?" he asked. "Yes." she replied. While Claudia overlooked him, she accepted an invitation to sit in his car.

This was very unlike Claudia. Obviously, she wouldn't normally sit in a stranger's car and give them the opportunity to lock the doors and drive off. This man could be dangerous, however, on this occasion, this did not concern her. Claudia gracefully sat down on the front passenger seat, giving her a clear view of Ricardo. She noticed how handsome he was and how well-dressed and smooth shaven he was.

"So Ricardo, why was you so desperate to meet me?" Claudia asked. This was the first of many questions that she had stored up for him. "Well after all the positive things Cheryl said about you, I thought you were worth meeting." Ricardo responded impressively.

"But you were asking about me for weeks. Most guys would have lost interest and met someone else in that time."

Ricardo paused, "It's easy to meet women, but I only want to meet a certain type of woman. I am not interested in those girls who are brash and common. You know the ones who are unladylike, rude and not very ambitious. You just sounded different and now that I've met you, you are definitely not that kind of girl." Ricardo explained.

Claudia nodded her head in agreement. She was impressed with how he spoke and he appeared to be a serious kind of guy.

Ricardo turned and leaned towards Claudia "So tell me about you?" he asked, as he studied every part of her. "Well I'm in my twenties. I don't give out my age, but if we stay in contact you'll know it. I'm a Solicitor . . ." at that point Ricardo's eyebrows lifted, impressed with what he was hearing.

"I'm currently single because I'm a bit like you, quite choosy. I like funny, intelligent, ambitious guys, who are easy going, but serious when they need to be." Claudia explained, giving Ricardo a reason for being on her own.

Ricardo then leaned back in his seat and nodded. "Interesting." he said "So, what do you do for a living?" asked Claudia. "Well I work with computers. I visit companies, installing software packages and suggesting ways of improvement." he explained.

They spent a few more hours talking to get to know each other and the first meeting went so well, they decided to meet up again.

As Claudia left in her car, Cheryl called her. "Yes, Cheryl." Claudia said tiredly. "Come on, Come on, don't leave me in suspense. What do you think of Ricardo? Do you like him?" Cheryl asked anxiously. "Yes. I met him. He seems alright." replied Claudia trying to play it cool. "So, are you going to see him again?" asked Cheryl. "Maybe, well yes. I'm seeing him this weekend." admitted Claudia. "That's good, I knew you would like him."

Cheryl continued, "When you have the babies I want to be the godmother." Cheryl stated. "Whoa, relax." Claudia said. This was typical of Cheryl to jump ahead of herself and be her usual bossy controlling self. Aren't you supposed to wait for the parents to ask you to be a godmother, thought Claudia. "Girl, I've just met him, slow down." Claudia said. "Just, keep me updated." Cheryl said with excitement.

As the months went by, Claudia and Ricardo's relationship blossomed. For Ricardo, it seemed like he was totally in love. For Claudia, it wasn't like Ricardo was the man of her dreams, but he was a nice enough man and he treated her well, so Claudia decided to give the relationship a chance to see where it would go.

In addition, Ricardo was extremely quiet and his lack of objectiveness, meant that arguments were non-existent in their relationship.

One day, Claudia decided to invite Ricardo to her parent's house to meet them for the first time. Her parents liked Ricardo and approved of their relationship. But, whenever Ricardo was in the company of Claudia's family, he would often remain very quiet and seemed too shy to join in the conversations.

Claudia's mother would say, "He doesn't talk much. Remember the quiet ones are the dangerous ones. Because they keep their thoughts to themselves, you can't work out what is on their mind."

However, Claudia didn't mind him being quiet, because it made their relationship easy.

Ricardo also introduced Claudia to his family. He had five brothers. His father was a friendly man and because they both studied Law, Claudia and Ricardo's father had something in common and Law would be the subject of their conversations every time Claudia went to visit.

On the other hand, Claudia felt like Ricardo's mother did not like her. Most of the time, his mother would sit in front of the television with a vexed expression on her face and either she would speak to Claudia in an unfriendly tone or act like she wasn't there at all. Claudia often wondered why a nice man like Ricardo's father could marry such a horrible woman.

One day when Claudia was over at Ricardo's parent's house, Claudia noticed that his mother was more miserable than she usually was. By now it was 11pm and Claudia was watching a film with Ricardo in the dining room, when Ricardo's mother came in. "It's time for your friend to leave." she hollered abruptly. "What did you say?" Ricardo was stunned. "I said, it's time for your friend to leave." his mother repeated. "How could you say that to my girlfriend?" Ricardo said angrily.

Claudia felt hurt. She immediately got up and put on her coat, leaving the house without saying a word. "Look what you've done. You've offended Claudia and now she's gone." fumed Ricardo.

"I don't care. Haven't you noticed the time, it's late." defended his mother. "The time has nothing to do with it. You just don't like Claudia. You make it so obvious, ignoring her when she visits. I know what you are trying to do. You're trying to split us up but it is not going to work. I'm embarrassed and ashamed of the way you have behaved." said Ricardo as he slammed the front door behind him.

Ricardo was devastated that his mother could insult the love of his life in this way. He ran after Claudia and knocked on her car window. They sat quietly in the car for a while.

"I'm sorry." Ricardo said regrettably. "It's not you that should be apologising." Claudia said softly. "The only thing I am going to say is that, I will never go back to your parent's house again and that's a promise." Claudia said with conviction. There was no conversation on the way home, but an uncomfortable silence in the air.

Chapter 5

SURPRISE

IT WAS NEW Years Eve. Claudia stirred and blindly switched off the alarm clock that woke her up at 7.30am. She was exhausted after having had a terrible night wrestling with a severe migraine.

"Brrring, brring." the phone rang. "Hello." Claudia said sleepily "Good morning, can I speak to the account holder of this telephone line." said a voice down the phone. "Oh go away." Claudia said in an irritated tone, as she slammed down the phone.

She quickly showered, had a cup of black coffee and made her way to Felecia's house to help her plan her party. Claudia parked up and knocked on the door. Felecia greeted Claudia with a hat from the Christmas cracker and an apron.

"Girl, there is so much to do before the guests arrive." Felecia said anxiously. "I've hired a sound system and my brother-in-laws friend has agreed to play the music, they'll be here about 6:30pm to set up. I haven't even seasoned the meat which I should have done last night, I still need to decorate the living room with balloons and banners, Janet can't come until tonight because she's at work and Mum and Dad are visiting a sick friend, so I don't have much help."

Felecia stopped to gasp for breath and then she started rambling some more. "Relax." Claudia said reassuringly. "This is why I am here early. Anyway because I can cook better than you, leave it all to me." Claudia joked. "Oi" Felecia said a she lightly slapped Claudia on the back of her head. "Ow, what was that for?" Claudia grinned. "That was for being cheeky, missy." Felecia smiled as she walked into the kitchen.

Claudia followed her and introduced the menu for the evening. "I'm going to cook lamb curry, white rice, fried chicken and salad." revealed Claudia. "Ummm," Felecia was impressed. "Sounds nice, but what will my vegetarian guests eat?" Felecia asked.

"They can have the rice and the salad." Claudia suggested in jest. Felecia looked at Claudia and was not impressed. "Oh please Felecia, do you really have veggies in your circle of friends? Because I don't. I couldn't cope living a life without meat, anyway." Claudia said with an attitude. "Yes, well there will be four vegetarians coming, so you better stretch your menu to cater for them, ok." Felecia ordered.

Claudia felt silly after Felecia put her in her place. "I can make some macaroni cheese and fried fish, providing there are no vegans coming." Claudia said sarcastically. "Well there's one vegan." Felecia confirmed. "Oh for god sake, then I'll do a potato curry as well, happy now? Anyway, do you have all the ingredients I need?" asked Claudia. "I may need some more salad stuff, so I'll pop down to the greengrocers later." explained Felecia as she took all the things needed from the fridge and laid them out for Claudia.

As the day past, the pair sang along to some sweet soul

melodies, while Claudia prepared the food and Felecia tidied up the house.

The time went by and now it was 5:30pm. The food was ready, the house was spotless and they were ready to party. The girls decided it was time to prepare to look glam for the night ahead.

The doorbell rang. It was Janet. "Hey Janet." Claudia said, as she greeted Janet with a hug. The girls got ready and they looked sexy in their outfits.

The doorbell rang again. "I'll get it." said Janet. Three men arrived to set up the sound system. Janet directed them into the living room and rushed back upstairs. "Oh my god, one of the guys downstairs is too nice." Janet said excitedly. "What's his name then?" asked Felecia. "I don't know, but don't worry ladies, I'll have plenty of time to get his identification later on."

The music was playing and the guests had begun to arrive. Felecia had a good turn out of people.

As Claudia mingled with the crowd, she noticed a strong smell. It was a horrible scent, almost like cooked cabbage that had gone stale, so she decided to find out where the smell was coming from. She made her way past the dancing guests and pushed the chair forward slightly to look behind it, but she found nothing.

Every so often, this scent would come and go throughout the night, which puzzled her, as it appeared that nobody else could smell this sickening scent but her.

As midnight approached, the girls gave out party poppers and glasses of champagne to their guests. "Right party goers," said the DJ, "We are 30 seconds away from midnight, make sure you all have your glasses filled to toast the New Year. 15 seconds to go, right let's do the count down." The guests joined the DJ in counting from ten to one. "Happy New Year" everyone cheered as the 1st January arrived.

"Claudia," Felecia said beckoning her to the kitchen, "We better start serving the food because I don't want it wasted. Let's serve the DJ's and the elders first." instructed Felecia. The girls proceeded to give out the food to the guests.

"Hey everyone," the DJ announced, "This food is wickedly good, it's as good as restaurant standards. Everyone, let's applaud the master chef. Well done Claudia." The crowd cheered and complimented Claudia on her cooking skills. "Claudia, thank you for all your help." Felecia said gratefully. "Well, that's what cousins are for." she replied.

As the DJ winded down the evening with his slow jams, Ricardo grabbed Claudia to dance to their favourite song. "Excuse me, I need to interrupt you lovebirds." Cheryl said. "I'm getting married next year." Cheryl announced. "That's great news, congratulations." Claudia said as she hugged Cheryl. By now, Cheryl had her children and the couple were ready to cement their relationship.

"Have you enjoyed your evening?" Ricardo asked. "It's been lovely." Claudia replied. Ricardo serenaded her as they danced the rest of the evening together.

When the party ended, the guests began to empty the rooms and even though the girls were exhausted, they decided to clean up before they went to bed.

The next day, Claudia's mother got up at 6am and went into the girls bedroom. "Good Morning mum, you're up early." Claudia said. "Yes, I had a dream last night." said Maureen. "Ladies," Claudia interrupted. "Let me warn you, my mother likes to tell us about her dreams because they usually have some kind of meaning behind it." explained Claudia.

"Anyway," Maureen proceeded, "I dreamt that I was

swimming in the sea with these massive silvery type fish, do you know what that means?" her mother asked, staring into the eyes of each of the girls, waiting for one of them to make an admission.

It was common knowledge, that when someone dreams about fish, it usually means that someone close to you is going to have a baby.

"Well, I've been a good girl." Felecia stated. "Well it isn't me because I'm single at the moment." Janet confirmed. Then everyone turned to look at Claudia. "I think it's me." Claudia declared sheepishly.

Claudia continued, "I suspected I was pregnant a couple of weeks ago and more recently I have been very sensitive to certain smells, even yesterday at the party I kept smelling this strong scent of stale cabbage. I was convinced that this smell was real, to the point that I was trying to find out where it was coming from." Claudia explained.

As Claudia continued talking, everyone had a big smile of approval on their faces. They all hugged Claudia with feelings of excitement and happiness in their hearts. The rest of the day was filled with baby talk and broodiness for everyone except Claudia's mother, of course.

The next morning, Ricardo got up early to go to work, but Claudia was so exhausted she didn't stir, even with all the noise Ricardo was making in the house. "See you later." Ricardo hollered as he left the house. Claudia didn't reply, she was still enjoying her sleep.

She finally rose out of bed a few minutes after 12 noon. But she woke up feeling extremely nauseous and quickly ran to the bathroom.

"Aarrgghh." Claudia moaned. She was not having an easy time with the morning sickness. So many things put her off. Firstly, she wasn't able to tolerate strong sweet smells, so

Ricardo had to avoid using aftershave. One smell of this and Claudia would go crazy.

Dairy products were a big no, no. Although it was good for the baby, it made her morning sickness worse. In fact, it wasn't just restricted to mornings, it was more like morning, noon and night sickness.

Claudia's diet now consisted of breakfast with hot pepper sauce, lunch with hot pepper sauce and dinner with hot pepper sauce, actually the hotter the better. Her drinks were strictly limited to tropical juice and energy drinks, which had to be chilled before consuming.

Claudia made herself a cup of ginger tea, apparently, the ginger eases the nausea and it appeared to work for Claudia.

After work, Claudia met up with her family at Mr Nelson's house to celebrate his birthday. Everyone greeted Mr Nelson with birthday wishes and presents.

As the party progressed, Mr Nelson kept looking over at Claudia in a concerned way. Unable to keep his thoughts to himself any longer he approached Claudia and invited her into the back room so he could have a word with her.

"Claudia, I had a vision just now." Claudia was nervous, she had always felt a slight fear of Mr Nelson because of his mysterious powers. But, most of all she was afraid of looking into his eyes as they were not a typical colour. His pupils were an unusual shade of grey which she had not seen in any other person before.

Claudia stayed silent as Mr Nelson continued. "I can see that when you have your baby, you will experience a lot of problems in your relationship." Mr Nelson looked worried but Claudia wasn't concerned at all because she thought that his prediction was ridiculous.

"But Mr Nelson, Ricardo doesn't cause me any problems, actually he's quiet and very easy going." Claudia explained. Mr

Nelson made a suggestion. "Claudia, you and Ricardo need to come and see me so that I can pray for you." Claudia nodded and returned to the party.

She easily put the conversation that she had with Mr Nelson, to the back of her mind. It was not something Claudia would have taken seriously, as she still didn't believe in that sort of thing. When the party ended, Claudia said her goodbyes and left.

Cheryl's wedding day was approaching. Claudia really didn't want to drive because her pregnant belly had really swelled up recently. But she had no choice because Ricardo had already told Claudia that he wasn't going to be able to come to the wedding until later on in the evening.

Claudia found it very strange that Ricardo did not try to make more of an effort to attend the wedding of the girl who got them together. What could be more important? Claudia thought.

She decided to phone Ricardo to convince him to take her and her mother to the wedding. "Ricardo, look, please come to the wedding. Can't you just drop us to the venue and then come back for us later on?" persuaded Claudia. "Sorry babes, I told you that I need to do a job for my brother. Anyway it'll be extra cash which I'll give to you, so that you can buy yourself something nice." Ricardo said trying to soften her up, which worked because she temporarily let him off the hook.

On the day of the wedding, Claudia decided to get dressed, early. She put on her floral orange dress with a matching shawl. However, she didn't feel at all happy with the way she looked. "I feel so frumpy and unattractive in this dress." Claudia said to herself.

She looked in the mirror and saw someone looking back at her that she did not recognise. This person was a double chinned, fat person with swollen ankles. Claudia wasn't just round on the tummy but she was round everywhere.

"You're not supposed to be eating for two." the doctor would say when she attended her appointments, commenting on her rapid weight gain. "You're allowed to increase your calorie intake, but you're not supposed to double it. It may be quite difficult to get back to your pre-pregnancy weight if you don't control your eating habits now." her doctor would advise.

Claudia herself was also worried about the mammoth amount of weight she had put on recently, which was a stark contrast to her fitness days when she would go to the gym at least 3 times a week and follow a healthy diet.

Claudia stopped working out when she fell pregnant because she feared that she would harm the baby, but since then she has ballooned. The doctor did recommend that a non-impact exercise such as swimming would be safe, so Claudia decided that she would start next week.

"Mum I'll wait for you in the car." said Claudia. She struggled to squeeze herself behind the wheel of the car, twisting and turning until she got comfortable.

Her mother arrived shortly afterwards and sat in the front passenger seat. Her mother didn't have a licence, but if she had she would have offered to drive. "You don't have much space. Are you okay to drive?" her mother asked in a concerned way. "Barely and this useless man that I've got just doesn't care." Claudia said angrily.

Thankfully, the journey to the church was not far and they soon arrived. They were a bit late but they settled down in the pew at the back of the church, just before the bride arrived. Cheryl came up the aisle, with four bridesmaids and one pageboy. After they exchanged wedding vows and sung a few hymns, everyone made their way to the reception hall.

The guests sat at their designated table and waited for the newly weds to arrive.

As the bride and groom came through the entrance doors, everyone clapped, and cheered for them. "This is the best I've ever seen Cheryl." one guest said. "This is the slimmest I have ever seen Cheryl." her friend replied, as she laughed.

When the important speeches had finished, there was an opportunity for the rest of the guests to say a few words, but nobody volunteered. Cheryl then began to call upon random people to come forward to say a few words. "Please give that lady over there the mike, her name is Claudia." Cheryl said to the host. Claudia began to blush.

As Claudia struggled to stand up, she quickly tried to find something to say. "Well I've known Cheryl for a few years now. We became friends at university. I would just like to congratulate you both on your wedding day and I wish you a long happy marriage." Claudia said shyly. Everyone clapped and Claudia quickly sat down, relieved that it was over.

The night progressed quickly with good music and plenty of food and drinks. Half an hour before the night ended, Ricardo decided to stroll through the door. "Oh, look who's here." Claudia's mother said pointing over at Ricardo. He casually walked towards Claudia, but he wasn't dressed for a wedding and he looked sheepish as he greeted everyone.

Claudia looked back at Ricardo, she had an unimpressed look on her face as she checked the time on her watch. "You shouldn't have bothered." Claudia snapped. Ricardo held his head down as if he was a naughty child that was guilty of something. "Well, I had to show my face." Ricardo replied.

"Well done. Let's give Ricardo a round of applause for making such a great effort to come to our special friends wedding." Claudia said sarcastically as she tried not to raise her voice. "This isn't the time or place to argue, so when we get home, you better explain to me why you're acting so weird." Claudia then turned her chair away from him.

After the night ended, they dropped Claudia's mother to her house and then they drove on home. As Ricardo put the key through the door, Claudia was about to state her grievances, but then she changed her mind.

"All I'm going to say is this. It was disrespectful to make a last minute appearance at the wedding of the girl who did so much for us. I am pregnant and I could have done without having to drive today, not that you cared."

Claudia continued, "Your behaviour was strange today. You seemed uncomfortable and I don't understand why. At times I feel like I'm single because we don't attend parties together, we should have at least gone to Cheryl's wedding together as a couple." Claudia said and then she went to bed.

Ricardo on the other hand, didn't defend himself and although he felt bad, he was relieved that he did not have to explain his actions.

As Claudia's pregnancy progressed, the arguments began, which became more frequent as time went on. As the cracks in the relationship appeared, toleration of each other was no longer in their vocabulary.

Many women go off there partners during pregnancy, Claudia's mother would say and Claudia definitely had.

Chapter 6

GIFT OF LIFE

CLAUDIA WOKE UP with a dull ache in her abdomen. "I think this is it, the baby's on its way." Claudia announced to Ricardo. "Are you in pain?" Ricardo asked with a blank expression. "Yes, I think I'm feeling mild contractions, I'm going to call the hospital."

While Claudia telephoned the midwife, Ricardo ran around the house in a panic getting together the hospital case and Claudia's other belongings. "Ricardo, I need to go to the hospital straight away." Claudia said nervously. "Why, isn't it too early? I thought you would have to wait until your contractions became more frequent." Ricardo said, recalling on what he had learnt at the pregnancy classes. "Well, I can't feel any movement from the baby, so the nurse said that I should come to the hospital to monitor the baby's heart beat." explained Claudia.

Ricardo was concerned. "That's serious isn't it?" he asked. "Well they just want to be on the safe side, the baby's probably sleeping and that's why it's so still." Claudia said re-assuringly even though she herself was very worried.

Ricardo took Claudia's things to the car while Claudia waddled behind him, cradling her stomach every time she felt a contraction. Claudia phoned her mother to tell her they were on the way to the hospital.

When they arrived, they took the lift to the second floor where the midwife greeted them. They entered the labour room and Claudia climbed up onto the bed. The midwife connected Claudia to the machine to monitor the baby's heart beat.

Claudia's mother soon arrived. "Hey mum, thanks for coming." Claudia said cheerfully. "Well I have to be here to support my daughter. Hi Ricardo how are you?" her mother asked, but Ricardo barely spoke and mumbled a feeble response.

Claudia noticed that Ricardo had walked over to sit in the chair furtherest away from her bed, which she found unusual.

Claudia's contractions became progressively stronger and her mother was right there to comfort her. Hours had past by and Claudia's pains were becoming unbearable, however Claudia's mother was there to rub her back and reassure her when the pains got rough.

As for Ricardo, he didn't move a muscle and even when Claudia decided to lie down on the floor to cool down, he remained motionless in the chair. "Help Me." her mother shouted over to Ricardo. "What?" Ricardo said with surprise. "Look, can't you see that Claudia's on the floor. Help me to get her back on the bed." her mother said abruptly.

Ricardo finally reacted and got up to help Claudia back onto the bed. "Ricardo, what's wrong with you? You're doing too much day dreaming and not enough concentrating." Claudia's mother said.

Claudia shouted out in pain, as she experienced the strongest contraction of all. "Can you give her something for the pain?" her mother asked the midwife. The midwife agreed and subsequently injected pain relief into Claudia's thigh.

A few minutes later, Claudia became sleepy, which made her more comfortable. "Claudia, how are you feeling?" asked her mother.

But Claudia was too drowsy to respond. She then began to mumble some unusual things, "I'm going to be late for school, I need to meet Deena at the bus stop." Claudia said in a daze. "Oh my god she has gone back to remembering her past." her mother said as she turned to Ricardo, but again he didn't react, he just remained expressionless.

Hours had past by and Claudia was almost ready to give birth. Claudia's mother decided to go and get some refreshments downstairs. "Ricardo, look after Claudia, I'll be back soon." her mother instructed.

As soon as Claudia's mother left the labour room, Ricardo immediately got up from the chair and walked over to Claudia's bed. She smiled as he came closer and she was ready to embrace him.

"I can't even get to rub your back." Ricardo blurted out. Claudia was taken by surprise at Ricardo's outburst. She was still in a haze because of the medication so she wasn't able to give him a deserving response.

"I am in labour, do you know what that means?" Claudia said faintly. "It means that I am experiencing the most excruciating pain I have ever felt and all you can do is say, I can't get to rub your back." Claudia said as she imitated him. "Gosh, the extent of your insensitivity is disgusting, you haven't even asked me how I'm feeling." Claudia said angrily. "Ow" Claudia wailed as the contraction peaked. Ricardo began to rub Claudia's back. "Is that better?" Ricardo asked.

These were his first kind words since Claudia arrived at the hospital. "You need to rub the lower part of my back." Claudia said frustratingly.

Ricardo did as Claudia asked and moved his hand down her spine and then attempted to rub her back again. However, it was more like the stroking of a cat than something that would make any difference. "You're not doing it properly, just stop." Claudia snapped, still angry over his selfish comment.

This was definitely not the behaviour of a man who was about to witness his first child being born, but more like a man possessed by demons. Claudia's mother soon returned to the room, unaware of what had just happened and Ricardo returned to his favourite seat at the other end of the room.

They put aside all the negative feelings when Claudia finally gave birth to a baby girl in the 15th hour. Everyone was overjoyed at the new arrival. "The baby looks like you, Ricardo." Claudia's mother said.

Ricardo smiled proudly. "Well I knew she would look like Ricardo, because they do say that the baby will look like the father if you both argue during the pregnancy." her mother explained. "Anyway, I'm going to call your father and your brother." her mother said as she left the room. Ricardo also went to give his family the good news.

Claudia was exhausted, she thanked god for blessing her with a healthy child and sat back to admire her beautiful daughter. Thankfully, after a smooth birth and no complications, Claudia was able to leave the hospital, the next day.

The next morning, Claudia was packed and ready to go. Ricardo soon arrived with the car seat. They thanked the nurses before leaving the hospital.

Claudia was still angry with Ricardo for his selfish behaviour in the labour ward and she wondered whether his weird reaction was because he was so overwhelmed about the responsibility of being a father. Can men suffer postnatal depression, if so does Ricardo have it? Claudia wondered.

For the next few hours, Claudia's responses to Ricardo's questions were one word answers. This was definitely not the time for small talk. Quite strangely, Ricardo acted as if he had done nothing wrong and looked at Claudia in a way that made him wonder why Claudia was upset.

Claudia was happy with her baby. However, the baby was only one day old and already she felt that she chose the wrong person to be her baby's father.

By the time they arrived home, the phone rang and Ricardo answered it. After a short while he passed the phone to Claudia. "My mum's on the phone." Ricardo said. "I'm not talking to her." Claudia snapped.

Ricardo quickly put the phone on mute to prevent his mother from hearing their conversation. "Why is she calling now? She missed her chance when she failed to contact me to apologise for kicking me out of her house all those months ago." Claudia fumed.

"She didn't even phone to congratulate me when I was pregnant either. She should have at least attempted to reconcile then, knowing that I wasn't just going to be a passing girlfriend in your life. I am the mother of her granddaughter and if she wants to be in the baby's life, she has to get on with me." Claudia said furiously.

Ricardo took the phone off mute. "Mum, Claudia can't come to the phone right now because she's feeding the baby. Call back later." explained Ricardo. "She said she'll call back in half an hour." stated Ricardo. "You shouldn't lie for me. Why didn't you tell her what I said? I'm not interested in talking to her." Claudia said calmly so as not to alarm the baby. "I don't want to look like an idiot when she calls, so you better talk to her." ordered Ricardo.

Claudia bathed the baby and put her to bed and then she returned to the front room to rest. After a short while, the phone rang again. "That must be my mother," Ricardo said anxiously. "Yes mum. I'll give the phone to Claudia." he said as he waved the phone in front of Claudia's face. Claudia paused for a while, trying to decide whether to accept or reject the call.

She thought it would be better to talk to her because even if she refused now, she would probably have to speak to her eventually and even though the stubborn old goat will never apologise, she did swallow her pride and make the first move. So Claudia thought that it would be better for everyone if the lines of communication were open.

Claudia reluctantly took the phone from Ricardo. "Hello, yes the birth went well. No, we haven't decided yet. Anyway I have to go, bye." Claudia then replaced the handset. "What did she say?" asked Ricardo. "She asked me about the labour and whether we have named her yet." replied Claudia. "Yes. We need to decide on a name." said Ricardo. "What do you like then?" asked Ricardo. "I like Courtney. It's a cute name," said Claudia. Ricardo remained silent. "and what middle name shall we give her?" asked Claudia. "I don't know, I'll think about it." Ricardo said in a stern tone that Claudia had not noticed.

Ricardo left the room, but returned shortly afterwards with his mobile phone in his hand. "Cheryl's on the phone, she says that she doesn't like the name we've given to the baby and she wants us to change it." Ricardo said in a displeased way. Claudia was shocked.

How dare Cheryl have the audacity? Just because she got

them together, does not give her the right to voice her opinion over the name they have given to their daughter.

After all, Claudia didn't like the name Cheryl had given to her children, but it would have been rude to say so. That's why Claudia kept her opinion to herself and Cheryl should have done the same.

"I don't think you really want me to speak to Cheryl, because I think she will be really offended by what I have to say to her. Why didn't you tell her to mind her business?" Claudia said sharply. Funnily enough, neither Cheryl nor Claudia brought up the subject about the name, again.

Chapter 7

PRECARIOUS TIMES

CLAUDIA AND RICARDO took to parenthood like a duck to water. Family and friends regularly visited and Claudia's mother was very supportive by dropping off home cooked meals for them, as she knew how tiring it was to be looking after a young baby.

One evening, Ricardo came home to find Claudia and her mother serving the food. "Hey, you're just in time for dinner." Claudia's mother said to Ricardo. Ricardo faked a smile and went into the bedroom.

Claudia wondered what his problem was, so she decided to follow him. "Is there something wrong?" asked Claudia. "Everywhere I turn, I see your family. Why is your mum always here?" Ricardo said angrily. Claudia was stunned, she couldn't believe what she was hearing.

She felt hurt by Ricardo's comments, knowing that her mother was just trying to be helpful. "Mum has been very good to us, why do you have a problem with that? She only comes around three times a week anyway. It's not like she's here everyday so don't exaggerate, Ricardo." defended Claudia.

"Well we need space and time to be on our own as a family. You don't even realise that my special moment of seeing my first daughter being born was taken away from me, because your mother was there in the labour ward." revealed Ricardo.

"Well my special moment was taken away from me when you stressed me out during the labour because of your selfish comments." Claudia said in defence. "Look, when Courtney grows up and has her own children, as long as she asks me, I will be there for her when she gives birth and if you loved and cared about me, you would have done everything to make sure that I was happy on that important day. I was the one in pain, so my feelings should have taken precedence over yours." Claudia said angrily.

"You know what your problem is, Ricardo? You're jealous. So I'll warn you now, whatever issues you have, you better deal with them quickly. Otherwise I can't see how this relationship can work." advised Claudia angrily, before she returned to the front room to eat her dinner.

"I was wondering why you took so long, your dinner is getting cold." said Claudia's mother. "Is Ricardo going to eat now?" her mother asked. "No, he's not hungry right now." replied Claudia.

Her mother could see that Claudia was not happy, but she hoped that things would soon blow over.

One day, Ricardo was sitting in the front room with a concerned look on his face. "What's wrong?" Claudia asked. "Well my mother has been asking me when she is going to see the baby." he revealed. "Excuse me. Why is it that your brothers and your father have come to our house to see

Courtney, but your mother hasn't? I have never told her that she isn't welcome here, she's the one who told me to leave her house." Claudia said abruptly.

"Look, she's not going to come round here, because she feels ashamed. She would prefer us to visit her." Ricardo said desperately. "Well, I don't care what she would prefer, that's your mum's problem. She kicked me out of the house, hoping we would break up." Claudia fumed. "She never thought we would have a baby together, that's why she has to try to be nice to me, if she wants to see her granddaughter." she explained.

"Nothings changed, she still doesn't like me, she just realises that she has to tolerate me. She behaved worst than a child when she wanted me to leave her house and she still hasn't apologised. Sorry, if she wants to see this little girl, she has to see her here at our house or forget it." Claudia said angrily.

However, Ricardo was not going to let it go and over the next few weeks, he continued to bring up this issue and every time he did, it would end in an argument.

Claudia finally gave in, because holding out over this situation was draining her. "Just tell your mother that we will be there tomorrow about 2pm. Tell her not to cook because I won't be eating from her." Claudia said reluctantly. Ricardo was happy and phoned his mother to give her the good news.

The next day, Ricardo drove the family to his parent's house. Ricardo's mother opened the door and invited them inside. She immediately took hold of the baby chair and stared a long stare at Courtney. "She looks just like you Ricardo." his mother said.

With the low regard Ricardo's mother had for Claudia, if the baby didn't look like her son, she probably would have claimed that he wasn't the father.

"Where's Dad?" asked Ricardo. "Oh he's gone to visit

Uncle Frank. He'll be back later." explained his mother. "Claudia, you look well." Ricardo's mother said with gritted teeth. Ricardo's mother bent down and lifted Courtney out of her chair, she took off her coat and sat Courtney on her lap.

"Hi Courtney," she said, as she played with her, "It's taken 5 months for me to see you, you've grown so much, since I saw you in that picture when you were born." his mother said sarcastically. Claudia discreetly shook her head.

She quickly regretted her decision to give Ricardo's mother a second chance. It soon became clear to Claudia that his mother had no intentions of making amends. Her plan was to gloat, embarrass her and make her life a misery.

Ricardo's mother knew that if Claudia didn't agree to visit them, Ricardo will give Claudia a hard time about it and now that Claudia has agreed to visit, his mother has and will continue to make Claudia feel unwelcome. Either way Claudia felt trapped.

"Do you want a drink?" asked his mother. "Yes please." replied Ricardo. "No thanks." said Claudia. Claudia stood to her word and vowed never to eat and drink from someone who did not like her.

As his mother left the room to get the drinks, Ricardo began to moan. "Why didn't you accept the drink from my mother? She's trying to make an effort you know." Ricardo said angrily. "My god, there's no pleasing you is there? It was not easy for me to swallow my pride and agree to come here today and look, you are still not happy. You have nothing to complain about so why are you complaining?" fumed Claudia, trying her best to lower her tone so that his mother would not hear.

Ricardo's mother soon returned with the drinks. Then she went over and took Courtney out of Ricardo's arms. "So, I hope you're giving the baby water as well as milk." said his mother, purposely insulting Claudia's ability to care for Courtney. Ricardo could see that Claudia was offended and quickly responded. "Yes we do give her water, mum."

Courtney began to gurgle and swing her arms around her head. On a few occasions, Courtney's hands had caught his mother's face. "You must try and stop the baby from hitting." his mother reacted. Claudia could not believe the ridiculous comment she had made and refused to give a response.

After a while Claudia became fed up with all the nasty comments his mother was making and she stood up and took Courtney out of her arms. "Ricardo, we should go now because it's getting late." said Claudia. "It's only 5pm, why are you going so early? Ricardo, your father would have liked to see his grandbaby." his mother said. "Well it's getting dark and I want to give Courtney her bath and put her to bed." explained Claudia, as she put on Courtney's coat.

"So when are you bringing the baby back to see me?" asked his mother, intentionally putting the pair on the spot and forcing them to make a date. "We might visit next weekend." Ricardo said, eager to please his mother.

"Well, I can't promise about next week. We will let you know." responded Claudia, as she gave Ricardo a foul look.

Claudia quickly gathered Courtney's things and hurried through the front door. "We'll call you and let you know." reassured Ricardo as he patted his mother on the back and then they left.

Courtney was growing up quickly and they wanted to have her blessed before her first birthday. So, Ricardo and Claudia began to plan Courtney's christening.

One day when they were visiting Ricardo's parent's, Ricardo mentioned to his mother that they had hired a hall to have the christening party. She immediately reacted, "Why are you having a hall? It's not a wedding." his mother said sarcastically.

Claudia struggled to stay silent, which was a regular thing she had to do in the presence of Ricardo's mother.

Shockingly Ricardo reacted in a way that Claudia was not expecting. "Mum, that's true." he said, then he turned towards Claudia. "It would have been cheaper if we held the party at home." suggested Ricardo, Claudia felt humiliated. Lately she had to deal with too many negative surprises from Ricardo and she was becoming tired with it all.

"Hold on a minute. We both went to the hall and booked the date. You didn't mention to me that you had a problem with renting a hall. Why are you against it now?" asked Claudia, trying her best to hide her anger, but she failed.

The pair soon left the house and had a blazing argument in the car. "How could you turn against me? And you did it in front of your mother. She's going to be so happy about that." fumed Claudia. "But it's true. my mother has a point. We could have saved that money." Ricardo said, stupidly trying to justify his point.

"Why didn't you tell me that you were this idiotic when I met you? I would have ran many miles away from you, if I knew you were like this." said Claudia sadly.

"You've got everything back to front, inside out and upside down. When there isn't a problem, like my mother being in the labour ward and cooking for us 3 days a week, you see it as a problem and when there is definitely a problem, you think everything is fine." Claudia fumed.

"You don't see anything wrong with your mother making negative comments towards me. There's nothing wrong with your jealousy, and it's okay for you to go against me and side with your mother over the hall for the christening, when you paid the bloody deposit remember?" Claudia explained as she tried to stay calm.

"Please tell me that you're suffering some short term memory loss, because at least there would be a proper reason for your ridiculous antics." Claudia said, she was livid.

Ricardo on the other hand did not defend himself and chose to leave the flat to give Claudia time to cool down.

It was the day of the christening. Claudia got little sleep after being up all night cooking with her family. It was a mad rush to make it to the church on time.

All the Godparents and other relatives had arrived before them. As they walked in, they were pleased to see that both their families had filled up the church. Courtney was the first of the four babies to be christened and the hymns that followed made a lovely ceremony

In the evening, Claudia's family arrived at the hall early to decorate it before the guests arrived. Shortly afterwards the DJ came and connected the sound system.

It was a lovely atmosphere in the hall as the music played and the guests strolled in. Courtney went from hand to hand as everybody fussed over her.

"Hi Deena, Hi Janet, What's up Felecia, Nice to see you Mr Nelson." Claudia said as she greeted her guests on arrival.

As the evening progressed, Claudia noticed that Ricardo and his family were taking pictures with Courtney. It had angered Claudia that Ricardo did not invite her to take pictures with his family. However, this was neither the time nor the place to complain, so she put her feelings aside and mingled with her guests.

Mr Nelson came up to Claudia and discreetly pointed in the direction of Ricardo's mother, who excluded herself from everyone else and positioned herself at the far end of the hall on her own. "Is that lady over there Ricardo's mother?" asked

Mr Nelson. "Yes" replied Claudia. "She is definitely doing spells in her room, to make you and Ricardo separate. That is why you two are always arguing. She is an evil woman." explained Mr Nelson.

Claudia realised that there was some substance in what Mr Nelson was saying. He did say problems will start after she had the baby, which was true and Claudia knew that Ricardo's mother would prefer her not to be with her son. But Claudia didn't really believe that a spell could actually cause a couple to fight and split up. So, Claudia dismissed what Mr Nelson had told her.

During the course of the evening she prepared to feed Courtney and in her attempt to find Courtney, she noticed Ricardo's mother in her same spot at the far end of the room, but this time Courtney was in her lap.

Claudia was not happy that Ricardo's mother would keep Courtney away from all the other guests, so Claudia walked towards Ricardo's mother. "Courtney needs to be fed." Claudia said as she lifted Courtney out of her arms.

After drinking her bottle, Courtney fell asleep. Claudia placed her in her pushchair and left her mother to keep an eye on her. The night soon ended and a few helpers stayed behind to tidy the hall before they locked up and returned the keys to the caretaker.

As Ricardo drove home, he really wanted to say something and after a while, he could no longer keep quiet. As soon as they arrived home, he let it all out. "It wasn't very nice to take Courtney away from my mother." said Ricardo. Claudia sighed, exhausted by his constant complaints and his incapability of resisting an argument.

"Remind me who gave birth to Courtney. Did your mother tell you, that I took Courtney so that I could feed her? Now I know where you get your childish stupid behaviour from." Claudia said angrily. "Well what's wrong with my mother feeding her?" defended Ricardo. "It's always your family. Felecia baked the christening cake; Janet fried the chicken, your mum . . ."

Claudia interrupted, "Stop right there. Are you upset because I never asked your mother for any help? This is nothing to complain about. I should be the one to complain, because your mother kept Courtney away from all the other guests and don't think I didn't see you and your family taking pictures with Courtney, without me." said Claudia furiously.

"You are forcing me to decide between you and my family. If you put me to the test and you want me to choose then you will lose. I should be able to have both." Claudia warned.

"My family treat you with kindness, if my mother treated you the way your mother treats me then you would have something to complain about. I'm tired, I'm not doing this now." shouted Claudia. Ricardo stormed out of the house and drove off.

Claudia began to weep. Since she had the baby, she really wasn't enjoying her relationship with Ricardo. His behaviour had changed dramatically since the day Courtney was born.

She knew that she wasn't perfect but she wanted the old Ricardo back. The placid, easygoing guy, not the rottweiler that he is today.

Chapter 8

FRESH START

RICARDO WOKE UP early the next morning to go to work. As soon as he left, Claudia called her mother. "I'm going to end the relationship with Ricardo." Claudia declared. "Are you sure? I know you haven't been happy lately but you could wait to see if things improve. Courtney is still very young and it's not easy being a single parent." advised her mother.

"No mum, I've made up my mind. He picks arguments all the time, he is always miserable. It's hard work being with him and it's affecting my happiness. I find him boring and predictable. We argue almost everyday and that is not an exaggeration. I'm always angry when he's around me and I shout a lot because of him. I was never like that before. I don't like the person he has turned me into." explained Claudia.

"Well his mother will be happy if your relationship ends. Mr Nelson said that she is trying to destroy your relationship." said Claudia's mother.

"I don't believe in those things." Claudia snapped. "How

can someone change another persons mind and force two people to argue with each other? This is my own mind and no one has the power to control it, except Ricardo, who right now is driving me crazy." Claudia continued, "I can't imagine spending the rest of my life with this man. He obviously doesn't love me and he definitely doesn't want the relationship to work, otherwise he wouldn't find stupid things to moan about. No, I've made up my mind. I'm definitely ready to end this joke of a relationship." Claudia said with conviction.

"I just want the best for you Claudia." her mother said softly. "Well getting Ricardo out of my life, once and for all, will be the best thing for me. I'll talk to you later."

Now, this was not the first time Claudia had finished the relationship with Ricardo. However, this was the first time she had told her mother, which meant she was serious about finishing it for good and this time she wasn't going to take him back as she had in the past.

It wasn't an easy decision for Claudia, but when she remembered all the silly arguments Ricardo brought to the table, including the time when he complained that Claudia's parents had not given him a Christmas card, Claudia felt very much justified in ending this ridiculous partnership.

Claudia got ready and went to the shops. She pushed Courtney around the mall looking to buy something that would cheer her up. But, nothing tickled her fancy so she returned home.

Courtney fell asleep, so she picked her out of the car seat and lay her down in her cot. Then she went in the kitchen to pour herself one glass of wine to give her the courage to end it.

Claudia sat in front of the television and waited patiently for Ricardo to come home. She could hear Ricardo's keys jingling as he opened the door. Claudia sat up straight and breathed deeply as she prepared for what she was about to say.

"Hi babe." Ricardo said with a smile on his face. Then he looked at Claudia's expression. "You look serious, has something happened?" asked Ricardo in a concerned way. "Well, I've noticed that for the past few months, you haven't been happy. I haven't been happy either." explained Claudia. "Yeah, but things will improve." Ricardo casually replied as he warmed up his dinner in the microwave.

Claudia followed Ricardo into the kitchen. "You keep saying things will improve, but things can't improve unless you improve." explained Claudia. "It's sad that you want to destroy our relationship over silly arguments. It almost seems like you initiate the arguments on purpose so that you can have an excuse to leave." said Claudia.

"No, you're wrong. I really want this to work." admitted Ricardo. "Well I feel the opposite. I am not perfect, but I can't see us having a future. We are both always angry at each other. I have come to the end of the road in this relationship and there is nowhere else for it to go. We just don't make each other happy." declared Claudia sadly.

"You make me happy and we have a lovely daughter." said Ricardo. "No the idea of a family makes you happy. However, the reality is that it doesn't, because you are obsessed, over protective and controlling and this is not doing any of us any good, especially Courtney."

Claudia continued, "In her short life, she has heard too many arguments and it is not fair on her. You need some sort of help, because your behaviour is definitely not normal." Claudia said emotionally. "You keep saying you want to end it, but Courtney is only a baby. It wouldn't be fair for her to grow up without her father." said Ricardo.

For Claudia, it was not about the presence of a father in

the home, the important thing was that a parent should enrich the life of their child and be somebody that their child would want to aspire to be.

Of course, Claudia wanted Courtney to be raised with both parents, but with Ricardo's unresolved issues, the idea of a two parent family was now impossible.

Ricardo's mother probably nurtured the attitude Ricardo has today, because she herself also had a twisted mind. Claudia did not want Courtney to be raised in a dysfunctional environment, as she feared that Courtney could also have big issues in her adult life. For Claudia, the cycle had to be broken.

"Whatever happens she will not grow up without you, she'll know who her father is." reassured Claudia. "It's not the same. Look I can see that you're fed up, so I'll go. I'll be at my parents house." Ricardo suggested.

As Ricardo packed a bag and left, Claudia thought it would have been more difficult than that to end the relationship with a volatile person like Ricardo. But actually, he left the house without putting up a fight.

A few hours after Ricardo had gone, Cheryl telephoned her. "Hello Cheryl." Claudia sighed. "Ricardo told me what happened." Cheryl said. "Yes" Claudia replied, waiting for Cheryl to make it her business to lecture her.

"Well you two should try to work it out for the baby's sake. My husband and I argue too. Why don't you go away on holiday? That may help to make things better." Cheryl suggested.

Mrs no it all, Cheryl, really didn't know much about their relationship at all. She meant well, but Ricardo's inability to change will just make it impossible to be with him.

"He tells me that you're always arguing and he keeps calling me, complaining about your family. I'm getting pretty tired of it all, actually." Cheryl revealed. "What has he been saying about my family?" Claudia asked curiously. "Well I don't think that I should betray his trust." Cheryl said.

Claudia wasn't in the mood to persuade Cheryl to tell her what Ricardo had been saying about her family, neither did she want to argue with her, for keeping this information back. So Claudia made an excuse to get Cheryl off the phone.

Claudia thought it strange that she had only just ended it with Ricardo, and he had already told Cheryl.

In the coming weeks, Claudia hired a childminder to look after Courtney, so that she could go back to work. A weight had been lifted off her shoulders when she ended it with Ricardo. She was free, she was no longer controlled and she now felt relaxed when her family visited and happier within herself.

To stay close to Courtney, Ricardo would meet Claudia at the childminders every day. One day after she safely secured Courtney into her car seat, Ricardo quickly opened the door on the front passenger side and sat down in Claudia's car.

"Claudia, we have had a long enough break now and it's time we got back together." Ricardo announced unexpectedly. Claudia couldn't believe what she was hearing. She thought that Ricardo understood that the relationship was over and it seemed like he was beginning to move on with his life.

At that point, Claudia realised that getting Ricardo out of her life for good was going to be more difficult than she had first thought. "Ricardo, this is not the best time to discuss this. It's cold and I really want to get home." Claudia explained, avoiding a confrontation.

"When then, when can we talk about us?" Ricardo asked anxiously. She wanted to remind him that there was no us, but instead she told him that she would call him, to make arrangements. However, she never contacted him, which fuelled Ricardo's anger.

So the same thing happened again and Ricardo sat in Claudia's car a couple of days later. "I'm not moving until you talk to me right now, about this relationship." demanded Ricardo. "You've been messing me around, saying that you will find time for us to talk. But you haven't." Ricardo said as he raised his voice. Claudia suddenly became agitated when she realised how angry he became, she wondered how she could get out of this difficult situation. But on the other hand, she felt that she should be honest with him.

"Okay Ricardo. I think you need to get some professional help for your insecurities, it's not normal for you to want me to cut my family out of my life to please you, they are here to stay and you complain far too much." explained Claudia. "I'll change." Ricardo said unconvincingly.

"No amount of begging and pleading will make me take you back. The sad realisation is that you are you and you cannot change without help." Claudia said softly.

Ricardo got out of the car and slammed the door. "You're going to be sorry you've done this." he threatened, as he pointed his finger at her. Claudia immediately locked all the doors and sped off.

By the time she got home and settled Courtney, Claudia's mobile rang. She noticed Cheryl's number, had come up on her phone. "Yes Cheryl." Claudia said, she was beginning to get tired of Cheryl. "I think you should try and give Ricardo another chance. He called me and told me what happened today. He really wants things to be different. Won't you give him another chance?" pleaded Cheryl.

"Why does he keep running to you every time we have a problem? Does he think that you can get us back together? Listen, if you were in a relationship with him, you would not be telling me to go back to him. Anyway I've got to go, bye." said Claudia angrily as she ended the call.

As the months passed by Ricardo left Claudia alone, but Claudia didn't trust him. She began to see less of Ricardo, which worried her. What was he planning? When will he explode? Claudia wondered. Then she remembered again, what her mother used to say, "The quiet ones are the dangerous ones."

Courtney's first birthday had arrived. Claudia decided to drop her to the childminders and celebrate by having a small party later on in the evening.

She was unable to take the day off work, because she had to appear in court in the afternoon and she couldn't ask a colleague to stand in for her because nobody else was familiar with the case.

After the case had finished, Claudia checked her phone and realised that Betty the childminder, had telephoned her more than fifteen times. Claudia was worried that something bad had happened and desperately returned Betty's call. Betty answered the phone with a distressed tone.

Claudia put her phone on loudspeaker as she frantically drove to Betty's house. "Claudia, Courtney's dad came to the house saying that he had a birthday present for Courtney. He then asked me if he could see her." sobbed Betty.

"I told him to speak to you to arrange a visit, but then he got angry and he started to raise his voice, telling me that Courtney is his blood and how dare I prevent him from seeing his own daughter." explained Betty.

"And what did he do next?" Claudia asked anxiously. Betty continued, "Well, I slowly began to close the front door and I pleaded with him to discuss the matter with you. It seemed like when I closed the door, it angered him more, because he kicked the door into my face. I fell backwards and landed on the floor." Betty explained as she continued to sob.

Claudia soon arrived at Betty's house and raced to the door. As Betty pulled opened the door, Claudia could see that Betty had swelling on the right side of her face and bruising around the eye.

"Oh Betty, I'm so sorry." Claudia said sympathetically as she embraced her. "What did he do after that?" Claudia asked anxiously. "Well it seemed like he got scared. After he realised what he'd done, he ran off." said Betty.

Betty's injuries were a cause for concern. Claudia strapped Courtney into the car and insisted that she drive Betty to the hospital. The doctor confirmed that she was not suffering with concussion and her injuries were only superficial, which would heal in a few days.

Claudia subsequently drove Betty back home. "Betty, I'm ashamed that Ricardo did this to you, I am very very sorry that you suffered like this. I don't want to put you in anymore danger, so I think it would be best if I placed Courtney with another childminder." explained Claudia.

"But, you don't have to do that. I'll miss Courtney, she's a lovely baby." Betty said with tears running down her face. "Look I'll pay you for the rest of this month and the whole of next month to tie you over until you find another baby to mind." Claudia offered, understanding Betty's financial concerns. Betty appreciated Claudia's kindness.

"I'm going to tell that no good man not to bother coming back to your house, because Courtney won't be coming here anymore. Now will you be okay?" asked Claudia. "Yes I'll be fine, you get Courtney home to bed." Betty said bravely.

Claudia was enraged when she left Betty's house and she couldn't wait to confront Ricardo about his appalling behaviour. As soon as she got Courtney out of the car and into the house, she immediately telephoned Ricardo but he didn't answer, it went into voicemail.

She repeatedly called Ricardo and each time he failed to answer. So the next time she called, she left a message. "Ricardo, you should be ashamed of yourself, harming a defenceless lady while she was looking after our daughter. How could you kick the door into her face? What if Courtney was behind the door? You could have killed her. You've left Betty with a blood shot eye and bruising."

Claudia continued, "and then you cowardly, ran away. If Betty became unconscious, who would have been there to care for the child that you proclaim to love so much. By the way, from tomorrow Courtney will be going to another childminder, so don't you ever go back to Betties house again." Claudia said angrily, then she slammed the phone down.

Shortly afterwards, Claudia's parents came over and her mother helped her to prepare the food for Courtney's birthday party. Then, Clint and his wife arrived. "Hi, come in, how are you?" asked Claudia. "I'm fine. You look stressed are you okay sis?" asked Clint. "Yes, I've been so busy at work." replied Claudia.

Claudia decided to keep today's events to herself. It was Courtney's first birthday and she did not want Ricardo's behaviour to tarnish the celebrations.

The number of guests that turned up was more than Claudia had expected, but it was not a problem as she had prepared plenty of food. Felecia and her kids, Cheryl and her family and her old school friend Deena came with her kids.

Claudia was happy to be back in touch with Deena after bumping into her a few months ago when she was out on a shopping trip. It was a lovely evening, with nursery songs and party games. "Hey Felecia, how is Uncle Max? I miss him, when is he coming back over?" asked Claudia. "Well he won't be, he's all loved up now and enjoying his second chance of happiness." Felecia joked. "Well say hello to him when you speak to him next."

Claudia then left to go into the kitchen to cut up the birthday cake, but Clint got there first. Clint then turned towards Claudia.

"He wasn't good enough for you, you know?" he revealed. "It may be hard, but you're better off without him. The next one will be the right one, I'll make sure of that." Clint said.

This was Clint's way of letting Claudia know that her big brother cared.

Claudia stayed quiet and arranged the cake neatly on the tray. Then she carried it into the front room to offer it to the guests. The party ended early which was good for Claudia because after a difficult day, she really could not wait to get to bed.

Claudia took one week's dependency leave from work while she searched for a suitable childminder. She thanked her boss for being understanding towards her personal crisis and for accepting her requested leave at short notice.

A couple of months passed before Ricardo raised his ugly head. He knocked on Claudia's door early on a bright Saturday morning. Claudia was reluctant to let him in, but for Courtney's sake, she did. "I don't want to talk about what I did." Ricardo said sheepishly as he stepped into the flat,

"Well I'm going to talk about what you did. You are lucky she didn't put the law on you. Imagine if she were minding other children on that day. She could have lost her livelihood." Claudia said with disappointment. "Ricardo you are many things, but I never had you as a person that would hurt a woman. You're here to see Courtney, then?" Claudia asked. "Yes, I miss my daughter." Ricardo replied. "Yes and you've missed a few child maintenance payments as well." Claudia reminded him.

She left the room and soon returned with Courtney in her arms. She was talking her baby talk and shaking the plastic bunch of keys in her hand.

"Oh, you look pretty in your yellow dress." Ricardo said as he gently lifted Courtney up. Courtney quickly struggled to get out of Ricardo's arms and she held onto Claudia's shirt, wanting Claudia to take her back. Courtney then set her face up to cry, but her frown didn't develop into tears.

Ricardo threw Courtney up in the air and tickled her. After a while, Courtney became comfortable with her feelings and began to smile with Ricardo.

He spent a few hours with Courtney before he was ready to leave. "We need to make firm arrangements for when you get to see Courtney." suggested Claudia. "Okay, I'll call you." Ricardo replied.

Claudia was lenient with Ricardo, because she wanted Courtney to know her father. Although she did not want to under estimate Ricardo's actions towards Betty, but rather she saw it as an insight into how far Ricardo was prepared to go in anger.

If he could do that to Betty, he could possibly do worse to her, Claudia thought. Ricardo clearly was volatile and unstable and while Claudia effectively dealt with Ricardo in a way that would help him to remain calm, it will be inevitable that a situation will occur in the future that will challenge his ability to control his temper, like when Claudia begins dating again.

Claudia decided that moving to a new home would give her the fresh start that she needed, but she decided that Ricardo shouldn't know her new address.

Claudia started the ball rolling by giving her requirements

to the Estate Agents who began searching for properties on her behalf. After a number of viewings, she found her dream home. A lovely four bedroom two bathroom, semi detached house, situated on a quiet residential street, with off street parking and a large south facing garden.

The owner wanted a quick sale, so Claudia being the businesswoman that she was, took the opportunity to propose a price that was 10% below the asking price. Her offer was accepted and Claudia quickly moved into her new home.

Claudia was a woman of many talents and she wasn't afraid of getting her hands dirty. Assisted by her father and her brother, she greatly contributed to the interior design of the rooms. Her ideas and eye for detail gave her a home that she was proud of.

Ricardo kept in regular contact with Courtney, visiting her once every two weeks. It seemed like he had accepted that their relationship was over and everything appeared to be pretty good in Claudia's life.

But one thing she was concerned about was that although she wanted to be a single lady for the time being, she definitely would not want to be on her own forever and eventually in the future she would like to have a relationship with the right person. However, she feared that this incessant lack of male attention would cause her to be single by force and not by choice.

Chapter 9

IT'S SHOWTIME

THE 5TH ANNUAL Disc Jockey competition was fast approaching. Where DJ's near and far have an opportunity to present their skills to a five hundred strong crowd. Supported by famous artists and talented acts it's always the place to be.

Deena called around at Claudia's house to invite her to the event. "Claudia, you know it's the DJ competition showdown this Saturday and girlfriend we need to be part of this night. Shall I get some tickets?" Deena asked. Claudia screwed up her face, "I'm not really interested and it's too far, maybe if it was nearer . . ." Deena interrupted. "It's only in the next town." Deena said positively. "Yeah I know," Claudia sighed, "but, I'm busy this weekend and I've got work on Monday morning." Claudia explained.

"Yeah, yeah, yeah I get the message." said Deena. "I'm definitely getting a ticket. Claudia imagine, there's going to be bear men up there. You should come, you may find your husband." Deena and Claudia giggled. "Anyway, I've got to go." Deena said, as she dashed out the door and quickly sped off down the road.

Claudia could not be bothered to attend the big night. The thought of a 2 hour drive back home while the rest of the crew sleep off their hangover in the car was very off putting. Anyway, Claudia was still trying to shake off Ricardo, there was no way she was interested in picking up another man, right now.

It was Saturday night, as Claudia prepared for an early night, Deena and her friend, Clarissa were dressed up to the nines and had set out on their journey. As they pulled up outside the club, there were plenty of posh cars and queues of people dressed up like film stars.

"OMG" said Deena. "What?" Clarissa said. "It means, Oh My God, you should know what it means by now, everyone says it." Deena explained. "Damm, look at the talent over there." Clarissa said excitedly.

The girls quickly found a parking space. They presented their tickets to the bouncers and elegantly walked into the main hall, as if they were walking down the catwalk. They wanted to be seen and they were definitely seen.

After getting their drinks, the girls made their way to the massive white sofa that they had reserved. They didn't want their seven-inch heels to be pinching their toes into the night, so a seat was a must.

As the crowds gathered, the MC opened the night. "Good evening everyone. Welcome to the 5th Annual DJ showdown. Your evening will include performances from ten DJ's who will do a series of mixing, scratching and chatting on the mike. The winner will win the latest sound system, £5000 in cash and a trip to New York to work with a number of talented DJ's over there." The MC revealed.

"OooohhhhHH." the crowd cheered and hollered, impressed with the prize on offer. "Also you will be entertained by a number of great artists, who were kind enough to come and support our show," explained the MC.

The evening began and the crowd applauded the first of the ten DJ's, as he came on to the stage. He did a good performance as he entertained the crowd.

Each DJ was welcomed and applauded as they attempted to out do each other. "They all seem so good, I think the judges will find it hard to pick a winner." said Clarissa.

Finally, it was time for the last DJ to perform. "Please welcome DJ Ricky." As DJ Ricky walked on to the stage, all the girls were going crazy. DJ Ricky was a newcomer to the scene, he was good looking, well dressed and talented.

DJ Ricky threw the latest track onto the turntables and scratched it. He then placed another track on the other table and mixed the two. The crowd were going crazy and then he entered into a rap. "DJ Ricky, DJ Ricky in da house tonight, which one of you lovely ladies wanna get with me tonight?"

All the girls hollered and screamed, all putting up their hands and begging to be the one. There was a good vibe in the place and as DJ Ricky's last track faded out, the crowd were alive.

The MC returned to the stage, "Well folks, you have just seen all ten of the DJ performances. The judges will confer and we will announce the winner at the end of the evening." he explained. "For the second part of the night there will be dinner and dancing. The dancing will be held in this hall and all the guests who will be attending the dinner, please go to the hall on my left. I wish you all an enjoyable evening."

The DJ turned up the volume of the music and everyone was dancing and enjoying the vibe. The girls were drinking cocktails and singing along to the tracks.

"DJ Ricky is a talented brother, but you know what? There's no point chasing a man like that. They always say that DJ's have a bad reputation for picking up a girl at every party they go to." said Deena.

Before the end of the night, The MC returned to the stage to reveal the most talented DJ of all the ten contestants. "Ladies and Gentlemen, we are about to announce the winner of tonight's competition. Who will be that lucky person to win £5000, a brand new sound system and a trip to New York? Firstly, let us reveal the runners up. In third place it's DJ Mix It, Please give it up for DJ Mix It." The crowd clapped as DJ Mix It came to collect his prize of £1000 in cash.

The MC continued, "In second place, we have DJ Chatty. Please give him around of applause." DJ Chatty bowed as he came on stage to receive his £2000 prize.

"And for the moment we have all been waiting for, the winner of this year's most talented DJ in town, is, wait for it." The MC deliberately paused for another few minutes, teasing the crowd by making them wait in anticipation for the winner to be announced. "Give it up for DJ Ricky?"

The crowd roared like thunder. People stamped their feet, flickered their lighters and blew their whistles in appreciation. The chanting drowned out the MC's voice. DJ Ricky came on stage with his stylish walk, nodding his head and raising his hands up in the air.

The ladies were going crazy and shouted out his name. The MC gave DJ Ricky the mike. "To the crowd, I wanna thank you for being a great audience. I hope you all enjoyed your night of entertainment. To the judges, you made the right decision." DJ Ricky said cheekily.

DJ Ricky closed the show by playing some of his favourite tunes, but before he began, he did an encore of his famous one-liner. "DJ Ricky, DJ Ricky in da house tonight. Which one of you lovely ladies wanna get with me tonight?" The evening ended on a high note, it was an enjoyable evening, thought by all.

Outside, DJ Ricky hugged the ladies and shook hands with the guys. Nearly all were in agreement with the judge's decision of selecting DJ Ricky as the winner.

The party continued outside, with music blaring from the car speakers. The guys were chatting up the women, telephone numbers were exchanged and champagne was flowing.

The remoteness of the location, allowed the extended outdoor party to carry on until the early hours, without disturbing the local residents.

DJ Ricky proudly lapped up all the attention. Clarissa tried to draw DJ Ricky's attention, by pushing through the crowd to get to the front and then using her curves to draw his attraction, but unfortunately she was up against some fierce competition.

"Oh lets go?" grumbled Clarissa. "There's no point. Who wants to go out with a guy who is prettier than you are anyway? All the attention he'd be getting, it would drive any woman crazy if they had a man like that." Clarissa decided to cut her losses and the pair drove the long journey home.

The party was still in full swing. As DJ Ricky talked to the ladies, he could not help but notice a girl standing alone leaning against her car while talking on her mobile phone.

She was tall and slim, well dressed with long hair. She was quite a plain Jane, pretty straight up and down as opposed to curvaceous and sexy, which is DJ Ricky's usual type.

Although she was the complete opposite of DJ Ricky's preference in women, she caught his eye. "So DJ Ricky, are you married?" one fan asked. "Oh, no I'm definitely not married." DJ Ricky replied, still distracted by this girl, who was still talking on her phone. But at the same time, she made sure that she kept DJ Ricky on her radar, scanning his whereabouts and admiring him from a distance.

"Excuse me for a minute, ladies." DJ Ricky said politely as he squeezed through the crowd and made his way over to the girl.

"Hello, nice lady. What's your name?" DJ Ricky said charmingly as he approached the girl. "My name is Annette." she replied shyly, flattered that this man she liked for so long would pull himself away from a bunch of pretty women and choose to talk to her.

After years of being a loyal fan, she could not believe that DJ Ricky was finally in her sphere. "And you're DJ Ricky?." Annette stated. "Yeah, but just call me Ricky." he clarified.

Ricky looked perplexed. "You know, you really look familiar to me. Do I know you from somewhere?" Ricky asked. "Well, I used to go to Frank's house, years ago when he used to have his summer barbecue's." revealed Annette. "Ok, yes it's coming back to me now. I remember I grabbed you to dance with me and then we kissed. Silly young teen, I was back then." Ricky said embarrassingly.

Annette nodded, "yeah, then you disappeared. I wondered where you got to. I later found out from your cousin that you drank too much and ended up vomiting on the bedroom floor." Annette stated, taking great pleasure to embarrass him further. "Oh yeah, that's shameful. But since that day, I haven't touched a drop of alcohol." confirmed Ricky.

"Anyway, Annette, my boys are beeping the car horn, seems like they're ready to go. You know Annette, I would like it if we could meet up again sometime. Here's my card, my number's there, call me." said Ricky as he gave Annette his business card. "Ok, I will." Annette said excitedly as Ricky got into a BMW and drove off.

Well as far as Annette was concerned, the evening ended on a perfect note. I can't believe I have DJ Ricky's number, she thought as she drove home, exhilarated.

Annette had endured a difficult journey in her life. Past boyfriends had hurt her and she never really knew what it was like to beloved by a man. Fearon, her first boyfriend, never introduced her to his family and friends. He denied their relationship, claiming the attraction was one sided on her part. Unrequited love had destroyed her.

Gavin, well he was like a booty call but he just forgot to tell Annette that. It was not love, just sex and then there was Ray, her last boyfriend, who beat her and raped her. This was a perfect storm, which would eventually create feelings of worthlessness, ugliness and obsessive tendencies.

Annette also experienced a series of deaths amongst her circle of friends. Lydia was Annette's childhood friend and they remained close throughout the years. Lydia was a tall attractive young woman. Her skin was flawless and her figure was something to die for. She gave off an amazing aura, which everybody loved, especially the guys. She was in the prime of her modelling career when she sadly died in a fatal car crash at the age of 21.

Then Annette's friend Julianne sadly passed away at the age of 25, she left two sons that she adored. Fearon, Annette's boyfriend at the time once made a pass at Julianne and Julianne was so horrified, she told Annette and advised her to find a new boyfriend.

Soon after Julianne became very depressed. The only thing Julianne was happy about was the fact that her complexion had changed to a darker skin tone, in the months leading up to her death.

One day, while Julianne was out shopping, she suddenly collapsed on the floor and began frothing at the mouth.

The post mortem concluded that she died of natural causes, whatever that meant.

Anyway, Annette was now ready to bury her past, revamp herself and return to the land of the living. She was a thirty something, single woman who was childless and desperate to start a family. So much so, that although her relationships were far from okay, she was prepared to raise a child on her own. As she desperately wanted to give love to somebody that would love her back.

Unfortunately, as the years rolled by nothing happened and her concerns led her to see her doctor. They revealed that she was suffering from endometriosis, which would cause her debilitating pain at times. The doctors had suggested a hysterectomy but there was no way Annette was going to destroy her chances of conceiving. She continued to live in hope, praying and patiently waiting for a miracle.

Two days had gone by and Annette still had not called Ricky. She was too nervous to phone him, cancelling the call after each attempt. What do I say when I call him? Annette thought.

On day three, she finally plucked up the courage to make contact, by sending him a text. The message read, "Sorry that I took some time to contact you, I miss placed your number. Anyway, are you busy this weekend?" Then she patiently waited for a reply and within 5 minutes, she received a text back saying, "Hey, I wondered what happened to you. Are you free this evening?"

Annette thought about turning Ricky down and arranging another date, as she didn't want to seem too keen. Then she thought again. She had waited so long for this day to come, that she refused to wait any longer. She keenly accepted the invitation and Ricky arranged to collect Annette at 8pm that night.

They had their first date and many more dates were to follow. This unlikely relationship, which was expected to die a sudden death, had conversely begun to develop into something more long term. After years of being DJ Ricky's biggest admirer, Annette finally had her man and she felt like the luckiest girl alive.

Chapter 10

LOVE AND MARRIAGE?

EVERY TIME RICKY would go to collect his kids, Annette's feelings of jealousy would grow. If he's seeing his kids, he's seeing his ex-girlfriend, Annette thought and as she allowed her imagination to run wild, her jealousy grew.

"How are the kids?" Annette would ask sarcastically. "They're good." Ricky would reply, oblivious to the fact that she had concerns about his former partner who she felt was very much present in their lives. "Why can't I see your children more often? I've only seen them a few times. Look how long we have been together. You've kept them away from me for too long now." Annette would say angrily.

These kinds of situations would bring back thoughts of not being worthy and all of Annette's complexities would manifest. She would draw upon her experiences, when her former partners would keep their relationship a secret. Although Annette was Ricky's girlfriend, she longed for the day that he would publicly give her that title.

As time went on their relationship blossomed and eventually Ricky decided to move in with her. The accommodation was not ideal for Ricky.

Her one bedroom flat was on the second floor, on a rundown, drug fuelled estate. It had a tiny kitchen, the walls needed painting and the ceiling needed plastering. With the mismatch of furniture and the tacky old carpet, the place looked dull and dirty.

Ricky liked nice things, but unfortunately he didn't earn an income that would maintain the lifestyle that he desired. Clearly, Annette neglected her home in order to support Ricky. Nevertheless, Annette had met her man, the one she wanted to be with forever.

As the months passed, Annette felt that the time had come in their relationship, where she wanted commitment from Ricky.

She wasn't getting any younger, her body clock was ticking and she was getting more and more worried because secretly she had wanted to conceive. But the last thing Ricky wanted was another difficult baby mother to deal with.

One night, Annette decided to have a sincere talk with Ricky. "I really want us to try for a baby." confessed Annette. "Nah, I'm not ready for that." replied Ricky in an aggressive tone. He then composed himself and calmly stated, "Listen, I'm enjoying our time together and sometimes when you bring a baby into the mix, things can fall apart. I've been there." he admitted.

Annette felt hurt by his remarks. "If you think I am just going to let you use me, then you're mistaken." Annette said angrily. "Not good enough to be your wife, hey? Am I not up to that standard to bear your child?" she said, getting up close to him and shouting in his face. "Look woman, calm down. Why are you acting like this? You're going to spoil things if you carry on like this, I'm happy the way things are. I'm going out." Ricky said furiously as he slammed the door behind him.

Many hours went by and Ricky still had not come home. She called him numerous times, but his phone was switched off. Annette had left dozens of messages on his voicemail, but Ricky never returned her calls.

She was so devastated, that she decided to call her pastor at 1am. "Hi, Pastor John." Annette said. Pastor John could tell that Annette was upset. "Annette, I'm surprised to hear from you at this time. Is something wrong?" he said sleepily.

"Oh Pastor, I'm very sorry if I woke you up, but I've just had a terrible argument with Ricky. It seems like he is not serious about our relationship. I know God wants me to be married and I really want this relationship to work, but Ricky seems reluctant." explained Annette.

"The devil is interfering in your relationship. You need to bring Ricky to church so that I can pray for both of you." the Pastor declared. "That's going to be hard, but I'll try my best to convince him. Thank you for your time Pastor John."

Usually Annette would wait up for Ricky, she never liked going to sleep on an argument but tonight she was too exhausted, so she left the light on in the hallway and went to bed.

Getting Ricky to agree to go to church with her, was difficult. She had to give him a reason to attend without disclosing the truth.

"Ricky, there will be two christenings at church this Sunday and it would be nice if you could come along with me." Annette persuaded. "Ermm, I'm not sure. You know I'm not really into the church thing." Ricky announced. "But sweetheart, the parishioners are always asking me, when are they going to meet you. They'll soon think that I am lying about having a boyfriend. Please babes." Annette pleaded. "Alright, I'll go on this occasion." Ricky said reluctantly.

So it was agreed, Annette would finally introduce Ricky to Pastor John, so that he can pray from them and perform a miracle to improve their relationship and get them down the aisle.

Over the next few days, Annette thought about the Sunday service that was fast approaching. She felt good that she was going to attend church with her man beside her, which would never have happened with her former partners.

It was 8am on Sunday morning. Annette brought some coffee in to Ricky who was still sleeping. "Ricky wake up." Annette said, vigorously shaking him. Annette was worried, she didn't want any excuses from Ricky about not being able to attend, even though she prepared herself for them.

"Babes, I came in about 4:30am." groaned Ricky. "Well, who told you to go out Djing, when you knew you had to get up early today, you idiot." Annette said angrily.

"Oh, you know what? I'm just going to get up now and get ready, because I'm not in any mood to argue with you." and with that Ricky got out of bed, took a couple of sips of his coffee and went into the shower.

"I've ironed your shirt and trousers." Annette said eagerly. "Which shirt?" Ricky shouted from the bathroom. "The China blue poplin Classic Shirt." replied Annette.

Annette knew that Ricky would definitely be happy with her choice. She knows how fussy Ricky is with his clothes, he had very expensive taste and the shirt was a pricy present Annette had bought for him.

"Ricky, get a move on." Annette said, hurrying him up so that they wouldn't be without a seat, in this regularly over packed church.

The two quickly left in Ricky's car. As they entered the church, Pastor John greeted them. "Good morning Annette." Pastor John smiled. "Hello Pastor, please meet my partner Ricky." Annette said proudly.

"Hello Ricky, welcome to our church." Pastor John said as he shook Ricky's hand. "Please come in." The Pastor guided the couple to the seats at the front of the church.

The pair sat down and listened to the service. "So do you know the families that are having the christenings?" Ricky whispered. "No, they are new to the church." Annette admitted. "What? You were acting like you knew them. Why was it so important for me to attend the christenings of families that you don't even know, I could be in bed catching up on some sleep." Ricky said loudly. "Shhh Ricky, you're here now, just enjoy it."

The service progressed with the wetting of the babies head at the font and ended with a popular hymn. As the parishioners congregated for refreshments, Pastor John discreetly beckoned Annette over. Annette gently grabbed Ricky's arm and guided him to where Pastor John was sitting.

"Did you enjoy the service?" asked Pastor John. "Yes it was nice." Ricky replied, feeling uncomfortable. "Well I hope we will see more of you. Please fill in this visitors form with your details. We like to stay close to our churchgoers so that we can provide guidance and support to them in the future." said Pastor John, as he pushed a white piece of paper and a pen, in his face.

"Oh, I'm not sure if I'm ready to pass over my details yet." said Ricky as he looked over at Annette for help.

He remembered how in the past, the church used to telephone his mother all the time trying to persuade her to attend.

"Don't worry Sir, we are very careful in keeping your

details confidential." Pastor John explained, making a second attempt to encourage Ricky to complete the form.

Ricky felt uneasy about giving out his personal information, but he didn't want to insult the Pastor.

After he returned the form, the Pastor announced that he would like to pray for the couple. "Please come into this room, so that I can bless you."

The pair followed Pastor John into a small room and he placed his hands on to their head. "I ask God to guide and protect this couple, may they receive your blessings in abundance and may they fulfil the purpose that you have for their lives as you bind them together, Amen." Pastor John said. "Thank you, Pastor John." Annette said gratefully.

Annette said her goodbyes to her fellow friends and they left. But there was silence in the car. Ricky was not happy, but he tried to disguise it, as he didn't want to burst Annette's bubble of happiness.

Ricky has never been interested in church and as far as he was concerned, he was never going to be a regular churchgoer. He also wondered why the pastor would pray for them to be bound together. This made him slightly suspicious.

As they got home, Ricky changed his clothes and went to visit his parents while Annette made herself some lunch and made a phone call.

"Hi Pastor John." Annette said happily. "Hi Annette, it was good to meet Ricky today. He seems like a nice chap." Pastor John said. "I just called to say thank you for your prayer. I need blessings in my life and I hope this works." Annette said anxiously.

"Well, Annette. It was good that Ricky filled in the form, because now I have his full name and date of birth written in his own handwriting. This will make the prayer stronger." Pastor John revealed. "What I will do is put your forms together and place them on my alter and pray that you will marry and have children in the future." he announced.

"Oh Pastor, I thank you for all that you have done for me and may god continue to bless you in your life." Annette said in appreciation. Annette was happy and looked forward to a great future with Ricky.

As time went by, Annette and Ricky settled into their relationship. Ricky continued with his DJ work, playing music for all different types of events, but the money he earned from this wasn't great.

Because Annette worked full time, she regularly paid Ricardo's half of the bills when there was a shortfall. Actually, you could say she ran the household on her own and she happily obliged. Why? Because Ricky did not beat her or rape her and he remembered her birthday. As far as she was concerned, he was the best boyfriend she ever had.

As time went on, she noticed that Pastor John's prayers were beginning to manifest itself in her life. Ricky seemed ready to settle down with her, slowly coming around to the idea of marriage and babies.

Annette was now in a good place in her life, but her happiness was clouded by her inability to conceive naturally. Month after month, her cycle would present itself and during those rare times that she was late, she would excitedly run to the chemist and purchase a pregnancy test kit. But each time, the result would be negative.

Her endometriosis was still causing her pain but through faith and belief, she waited for a miraculous conception.

"Babes, I'm going to take my kids to see my parents," said Ricky. When he said that, the anger began to boil up in Annette. She was about to complain that he never involves her in his children's lives when he said, "then I'm going to bring the kids here, afterwards." Ricky smiled, knowing that this would make Annette happy.

Annette was pleased. "Great, shall I cook for them?" she said excitedly. "Oh no it's okay, I'll probably take them out to eat. But you can provide some snacks for them. They like popcorn and chocolate." replied Ricky as he left.

Annette was excited that she was finally going to spend some quality time with Ricky's kids. She believed that Ricky was keeping them away from her because she didn't have kids of her own.

Annette went to the shops to buy lots of goodies in preparation for their visit and she laid everything out on the dining table.

She sat down with a glass of red wine and watched the hours tick by. She was about to pour herself a second glass of wine when she stopped herself, thinking that maybe it wasn't a good idea to be drinking if she was going to be in the company of the children.

Shortly afterwards, Ricky's car pulled up outside. They all got out of the car and ran up the communal stairs to the flat. Annette greeted the kids at the front door. "Hey kids, meet my girlfriend." Ricky announced. "Honey, meet my kids. Wayne and Louise." Annette briefly glanced at Wayne, then she quickly turned to Louise and smiled at her, holding her gaze for a while. "Hello, I am very pleased to meet you, I've got some treats over there on the table, help yourselves." Annette said, as she guided them to the dining area. "Thank you." the kids said, as they went over to the table and began eating the snacks.

Annette leaned over and kissed Ricky on the cheek. "This is nice. Thank you for letting me spend time with your children." Annette said in appreciation. "Well we are going to get married someday. So you need to get to know them, because I'd like them to be apart of the wedding." Ricky declared.

Annette smiled, feeling proud that for the first time, Ricky reminded her of his commitment to her. They spent the rest of the evening watching movies and playing games, with Annette trying to build up a positive relationship with her stepchildren.

As time went on Annette's maternal instincts were being exercised and before long, she was accompanying Ricky and the children on their days out. Sometimes she took them out on her own.

She was getting a real taste of motherhood to prepare her for when she has her own children.

More recently, Louise would visit without her big brother. He was a teenager now and found spending time with all these females boring. As Annette bonded with Louise, she gradually became more and more controlling.

One day, Louise was searching through Annette's dvd collection to find an interesting movie to watch. "Annette." Louise shouted out, but there was no reply. Louise hollered again. "Annette." again there was no reply.

Annette was in the kitchen. She remained silent and started to become quite angry. Annette thought it was disrespectful for Louise to call her by her first name after all this time.

Annette felt like a second mother to Louise after all the time she spent with her over the past few months. Annette would regularly spend her money on Louise, taking her to her favourite restaurants and treating her to her favourite toys.

"It's time this little girl addressed me in the manner that I deserve." Annette mumbled to herself. She contained her anger and slowly walked to the front room, where Louise was sitting.

"Louise," Annette said in a soft, pretentious voice. "one

day, I'm going to marry your father and when that happens, I will become your stepmother. But you calling me stepmother, doesn't sound right." Annette said sarcastically. "So, I think you should call me mum." she declared.

Louise was startled and jumped up. She was shocked and unimpressed by Annette's suggestion.

"But, I have a mum." Louise said nervously. "Well aren't you the lucky one. How many of your friends can say they have two mums, like you? It's more polite to call me mum, now that we are going to be family." Annette said sternly and then she quickly smiled to correct her negative expression.

Louise felt confused and not at all pleased with her request. She didn't want to upset Annette, but she knew her mother would be extremely angry if she found out.

"My mum won't be happy if she knew I was calling you mum." Louise explained, hoping that Annette would understand. Annette leant towards Louise and whispered in her ear. "Don't worry, this will be our little secret." and she got up and gave Louise a menacing smile before leaving the room.

Ricky came home a little while later. "How's my little girl?" Ricky asked Louise as he picked her up. "I'm fine, dad." Louise replied as she buried her head in his shoulder and squeezed him tight. "Did you have a good day with Annette?" Ricky asked. "Yes" Louise said reluctantly.

She couldn't stop thinking about what Annette had said. Everything was fine until Annette asked her to call her mum.

Ricky left the front room and went into the kitchen where Annette was serving dinner. "Lets, set a date for the wedding." Annette suggested with excitement, as she stepped forward to kiss Ricardo. "What's the rush babes?" Ricky asked, shocked at her sudden request.

"Well we've been together for a while now and we have a good relationship, don't we? We're not getting any younger, so it's time we got serious." persuaded Annette. "Isn't the man supposed to propose to the woman?" Ricky asked in jest. "Yes, but it's a leap year, so I'm allowed to ask you." Annette said justifying her proposal.

"I'm sure you're supposed to propose on 29th February." Ricky said making a comeback. "Well, you were taking too long about it. So someone had to take the lead." Annette replied, as she hugged him and stroked the nape of his neck. "We'll talk about it after I drop Louise off." said Ricky.

As they got in the car, Ricky turned to Courtney. "Remember, you mustn't tell your mother that you've been spending time with Annette, because she will get sad and you don't want mummy to be sad do you?" Courtney shook her head and then stayed quiet, as Ricardo drove her to her mother.

After they left, Annette decided to set a date for the wedding. So she reached over and took down the calendar and she began to turn the pages, wondering whether she should get married in the spring or the summer.

Then she turned the page to the month of Ricky's birthday and waited patiently for Ricky to return.

As she heard the key turning in the door, Annette ran to meet him. "Can I suggest a date for the wedding?" said Annette impatiently. "Okay." Ricky replied. He was flabbergasted that she had set a date already.

"Let's have our wedding day on your birthday." Annette said excitedly. "On my birthday?" a surprised Ricky replied. "Yes, your birthday falls on a Saturday this year. That day would be perfect and also there would be no reason for you to ever forget the date of our wedding anniversary." chuckled Annette. "Okay," Ricky said, agreeing to her proposal.

As the months passed by, Annette was busy involving her

friends and family with the wedding plans. Whereas Ricky was doing what he did best, being a DJ.

It was a bright cold Saturday morning and the wedding was only a few months away. "I'm going to pick up the kids, so we can buy them their wedding outfits today." Ricky said as he headed out the door.

Meanwhile Annette made a couple of phone calls to the florist and the photographer. Shortly afterwards Ricky returned with Louise only. "Where's Wayne?" asked Annette. "I just remembered he's gone to Europe on a school trip. Never mind, I'll take him with me, when I buy my own suit." explained Ricky.

Annette turned towards Louise. "Hi Sweetie, how are you?" smiled Annette. "I'm fine." Louise replied. She purposely avoided saying her name, because she knew that as soon as she called her Annette, she would highlight the fact that Louise did not call her mum.

"Louise, today we are going shopping to buy you a nice white princess dress." Ricky explained.

Ricky and Annette purposely kept the wedding a secret from the kids, so Ricky had to give Louise a reason why they would be buying her such a pretty dress. "Yippee" Louise said. "Thank you Daddy, I would love to have another princess dress." Louise said excitedly.

They went from shop to shop, had a spot of lunch and then continued shopping. However, Louise did not like any of the outfits she saw. "Louise, honey you need to decide on a dress because there are not much shops left for us to go into." Ricky explained.

Ricky and Annette were getting impatient and walked past the last few shops on that street. "Dad, dad look over there, I love that one." Louise pointed. As they walked into the shop, Louise's eyes lit up as she admired the long white frilly dress on the mannequin. "I want that one dad, can I try it on?" Louise asked. Ricky and Annette waited until Louise emerged from the changing room wearing the beautiful satin dress.

"Ohhhh, doesn't my girl look pretty?" Ricky said. "We'll take it." Annette said to the shop assistant, expecting Ricky to pay for it.

"Babes, could you buy the dress and I'll pay you back next week?" Ricky asked. "Okay" Annette said reluctantly, worried that the price of the dress was more than her budget.

She knew that she would never see that money again, because when Ricky says he is going to pay her back, his words are just an empty promise.

Louise was happy with her dress and held her bag close to her for the whole journey home. As they arrived back at the flat, Ricky took the bag from Louise and put it in the bedroom. Louise was puzzled and followed her Dad. She wondered why he had hung up her dress in his wardrobe.

"Dad, why are you putting it in there? I want to take it home." Louise moaned. "Listen sweetheart, you've got lots of dressing up clothes at home and you should have some here too. If you're a good girl, daddy will buy you another pretty dress." reassured Ricky. Louise was not happy, but she accepted her dad's explanation.

Chapter 11

HELL ON EARTH

CLAUDIA MET RICARDO in the shopping centre so that he could take Courtney for some lunch. While Claudia went to the cash machine to withdraw some money, she noticed a flash of light at the corner of her eye. When she turned around, she realised that Ricardo had secretly taken a picture of her.

"Hey, what are you doing?" Claudia shouted as she ran over to him. "Delete the picture that you just took of me." Claudia ordered as she wrestled with Ricardo to get the phone off him. However, Ricardo just laughed, as he raised his arm higher and kept hold of his phone even tighter.

Eventually, Claudia gave up. She then realised that Ricardo probably still had not got over her after all these years. For him to go to such great lengths to obtain a picture of her was enough evidence for Claudia that Ricardo still liked her.

Now that Courtney was growing up, Claudia recently made the decision to relax her strictness over Courtney and allow Ricardo more freedom with her. Also, he seemed like he had matured over the years, so recently she allows Ricardo to take Courtney out on his own.

"Where are you taking Courtney today?" Claudia asked Ricardo. "Well she hasn't seen my parents in a while." Ricardo replied. "I think Courtney will be extremely bored, if that's going to be the highlight of her day." Claudia said disappointingly. "I'll take her to the park, afterwards." Ricardo said trying to compensate for his pathetic suggestion. "Is that because it won't cost you any money, I mean parks are free? Anyway got to go, bye." Claudia said as she hurried back to her car, preventing Ricardo from responding to her sarcastic comment.

Claudia spent the day shopping. Buying jewellery, garments and Courtney's favourite things. Well why not, I work hard enough, Claudia thought as she tried to justify her overspending. She was so engrossed in her shopping trip that she hadn't realised the time.

When she pulled up in her car, she saw Ricardo's car parked up. "Mum, where did you go? We've been waiting ages for you." Courtney said, grumpily. "Sorry sweetie, never mind look at all the stuff I bought for you." said Claudia, opening the bag for Courtney to examine the contents. Ricardo on the other hand was so angry that he drove off without saying goodbye.

As they walked into the house, Courtney told Claudia about her day. "Daddy and his girlfriend took me to the park and then I went to Grandma's house." Courtney revealed.

Claudia was taken by surprise. "Oh, so what's daddy's girlfriend's name?" Claudia asked. "Well, Grandma calls her Lucinda . . . ." Claudia then interrupted. "Is she nice?" Claudia asked curiously. "Yes, but she's not as nice as you mummy." Courtney said sweetly.

Claudia wondered why Ricardo had not told her that

he was dating, because he should have known by now that Claudia would be okay with it.

It was now clear that Ricardo didn't like her in that way after all. But then why did Ricardo take a picture of her in the first place? In any case it was good for Claudia, that Ricardo had a girlfriend because she was keen for Ricardo to start a new relationship and finally be somebody else's problem.

During the evening, Courtney started crying out in pain. "What's wrong sweetie?" Claudia asked in a concerned way. "My tummy hurts and I've got a headache." Courtney wailed as Claudia cradled her head. "Let me give you some medicine." Claudia said as she went into the kitchen to fetch the bottle. Claudia gave Courtney two doses and then placed Courtney's head in her lap.

Courtney began to whimper and fidget. "Don't worry, it will work soon. See the medicine is trying to find out where the pain is. It has checked your arm and realises that the pain is not there, so now it's travelling to your leg, then it will eventually reach your tummy and your head and then the pain will disappear like magic." Claudia said reassuringly.

Unfortunately, Courtney was not better and when Monday arrived, she had to take a day off school.

Later in the day, Ricardo called to find out how Courtney was. "Hi, can you call me back, I don't have much credit?" Ricardo asked. When Claudia called Ricardo back, she explained that Courtney was unwell. He wanted to speak to Courtney, so Claudia passed the phone to her. "Hi my little princess, your mum told me that you are not well." said Ricardo. "Yes Daddy, I have a headache and a tummyache." Courtney explained, feeling sorry for herself. "Well I hope you get better soon. I'll see you at the weekend." said Ricardo.

Claudia made sure Courtney was comfortable and she eventually fell asleep, which allowed Claudia to catch up on some housework. As Claudia pulled back the sofa to sweep behind it, she saw the long tail and the hind legs of a rat that quickly disappeared.

Claudia froze and then she let out a muffled screamed, as she did not want to wake Courtney. Claudia held onto the broom tightly and attempted to find the rat. Even though she was scared, she began to tap the broom against the wall to frighten the rat away.

She proceeded to try to find the hole that the rat may be hiding in, because if she found the hole, she could then block it and eliminate the problem.

However, she couldn't find any holes, which confused her. She wondered how the rat could have got into the house. Then she realised that the patio doors were open. Claudia assumed that it was a stray rat, that had disappeared back into the garden.

Courtney woke up a few hours later feeling a bit better. "Mum I'm hungry." Courtney said to her mother. "I can see you're better then. What would you like to eat?" smiled Claudia. "Umm, well I want chocolate, lots and lots of chocolate." Courtney joked as she rubbed her tummy. "Oh you little comedian." Claudia said and she went into the kitchen to make something to eat.

As they sat down at the table to eat, Claudia's mobile phone rang. "Yes Ricardo, what's up?" an irritated Claudia asked. "Can you call me back? I don't have much credit." he asked. "No, I'm not calling you back. Why should I pay to speak to you. Just talk, Ricardo." Claudia said angrily.

"I'd like to take Courtney out this Saturday, if that's okay?" asked Ricardo. "Well I don't know. You usually see her every two weeks, which means your next visiting day is the following Saturday. Why do you want to see her this week, anything special happening?" Claudia asked curiously.

"No, it's just that Courtney's growing up quickly and I want to start spending more time with her." explained Ricardo. "Okay, pick her up about 1:30pm." Claudia said suspiciously. "Great, thanks, bye."

It was 12:30pm on a breezy Saturday afternoon. "Will dad collect me every Saturday from now on?" Courtney asked, as Claudia brushed Courtney's hair. "Well maybe, he said that he wants to spend more time with you." explained Claudia.

Claudia and Courtney left the house to go and meet Ricardo. She waited in the car on the high street for Ricardo to turn up. He arrived promptly in a brand new vehicle. "Where is he going, driving new wheels, when he doesn't work anywhere?" Claudia mumbled to herself.

Claudia switched off the engine and got out of the car with Courtney. Ricardo also got out and met them half way. "Do you like my new car?" Ricardo boasted. "Not bad." Claudia replied, as she effectively resisted calling him a selfish low life scumbag, who fails to pay maintenance for his child.

Claudia quickly changed the subject. "Bring her back for 7:00pm." Claudia suggested. "Okay, see you." Ricardo said, as he strapped Courtney into the seat.

Claudia decided to spend the day pampering herself again. She got her nails done, treated herself to a new hair do and she had just enough time, upon her return home, to relax in a nice bubble bath.

After her bath, Claudia quickly got dressed and went to pick Courtney up. Ricardo parked up parallel to Claudia to ensure that she got a good look at his car. "Hi mum, I like your hair." Courtney said, excited to see Claudia.

Ricardo looked at Claudia up and down as if to admire her appearance, but he didn't compliment her. "Bye dad." Courtney waved as she got out of Ricardo's car. "Bye darling,

I'll come and see you the same time next Saturday." declared Ricardo.

"Is this going to be a weekly thing?" asked Claudia. She was puzzled over his increasing interest in his daughter. "Well, probably, but bear in mind that sometimes on a Saturday I may need to help out my brother at his company." Ricardo explained.

As soon as Claudia put her key in the door, Courtney bent over clutching her stomach. "Ow mum, my tummy is hurting me again." moaned Courtney. "Oh dear, are you not well again, Courtney?" Claudia asked as she guided her to the chair. "It hurts a lot mummy." Courtney cried. "You weren't well last week either." Claudia said with concern.

Claudia fetched a basin and put it by Courtney's side. Then she gave her a warm drink that she sipped slowly. Suddenly Courtney started heaving.

Claudia quickly grabbed the basin and placed it under Courtney's chin. Courtney began to vomit violently. Then she lay down and had a short nap and by the time she woke up, she felt a bit better, although she wasn't well enough to go to school on Monday.

Ricardo continued to pick Courtney up every week and Claudia realised that nearly every time Ricardo took Courtney out on his own, she would come back sick, which caused Courtney to be regularly absent from school.

Courtney's 100% attendance and punctuality was now a thing of the past and within the first two months, Courtney had clocked up 10 days off from school.

The school highlighted this problem to Claudia and warned her that if Courtney's record does not improve, they may consider reporting her to the Education Board.

One day Claudia decided to challenge Ricardo. She

phoned him to express her concerns. "Ricardo, I have noticed that 9 times out of 10, Courtney comes back home sick after she has been with you." revealed Claudia. "What are you trying to say?" Ricardo snapped, getting all defensive. "What do you give her to eat, then? Because it's not agreeing with her." asked Claudia. "I take her out to eat at the restaurant." Ricardo replied.

"Wrong, maybe your girlfriend can't cook, she could be poisoning Courtney for all I know." accused Claudia. "How dare you accuse my girlfriend of poisoning Courtney? She loves her." Ricardo said defensively.

"Protecting your girlfriend are you? Well I am protecting my child. You are going to have to take me to court, if you want unsupervised access because I'm not allowing you to take her out on your own anymore. Do you understand? You're up to something, Ricardo." Claudia said suspiciously. Ricardo immediately put the phone down on her.

Claudia then decided to log onto the computer to check her bank balance online. She was shocked when she saw that her balance was substantially less than what she was expecting. "What, I don't understand. Where has all my money gone?" Claudia exclaimed. "This can't be right. I must be a victim of identity fraud."

Claudia viewed the individual transactions that had debited her account. She analysed each one looking for items she didn't recognise. Then she checked her statement again, desperately trying to find anything unusual, but unfortunately, all of her transactions were legitimate payments that she had made herself. Claudia was overcome with confusion and worry.

Claudia was always good with money and even when she was a college girl, her fellow student friends would ask her to lend them money because she was always the one with the cash.

However, two weeks after being paid, Claudia didn't even have enough money to see her through to the next payday. The balance remaining in her account would probably only last her another week at the most.

Nevertheless, Claudia assumed that it was due to an overspend on her part and next month she would have to tighten up the purse strings and spend less on luxuries.

The weekend had arrived and Claudia had invited Ricardo to see their daughter perform at the local church. Ricardo wasn't happy that Claudia stopped him from taking Courtney out on his own, but he had no choice but to adhere to her rules.

Ricardo phoned her when they were getting ready. "Hi Claudia, can you call me back because I have no credit." he asked. She was irritated by his request but agreed to return his call.

"So what time should I meet you at the church?" Ricardo asked. "Well the show starts at 1:30pm, so at least get there 5 minutes before." replied Claudia. "Okay, I just need to visit my parents first and then I'll come by." explained Ricardo.

Ricardo came late as usual and arrived just when Courtney was about to dance. There were lots of cheering in the audience as Courtney and the rest of the dancers did their famous heel toe movement while dancing to a gospel song. A round of applause followed as the girls went on to perform their play.

After the show ended, they left the church hall. As they were walking to the car, a strange feeling came over Claudia. She suddenly started to feel anxious and extremely nervous. Claudia wondered why she was feeling this way.

She looked over at Ricardo, but he wasn't the Ricardo

she had come to know and dislike. Suddenly, right before her eyes was the man of her dreams. Weirdly, her emotions were such, that she instantaneously felt a strong connection towards Ricardo, stronger than she had ever felt before, almost like love.

While in the car park Ricardo received a call from his girlfriend and for the first time, Claudia felt an overwhelming sense of jealousy. "Why would I feel this way?" Claudia wondered.

It didn't make sense. Claudia had been separated from Ricardo for so many years now and not once within that time and during her singleness did she find him attractive or consider getting back with him. So why would she want a reconciliation now?

Although Claudia played down her feelings and waved goodbye to Ricardo, she was scared of what she was feeling. As the days went by, Claudia became anxious, nervous and depressed and gradually what she felt became unbearable to cope with. To her family and friends Claudia was fine but as time went on, she was unable to sleep, unable to eat and cried when she was alone.

After a time, her family could see she was not herself. Her placid, kind nature was replaced with an impatient, intolerant, frustrated person. The strength of her emotions was so powerful that she had a breakdown at her brother Clint's house one Sunday afternoon following a family meal.

She cried and cried and began to shake uncontrollably on Clint's bed. Her worried family had crowded around her and Claudia could faintly hear her dad saying, "Maybe we should call an ambulance." "No," Claudia's mother quickly replied, "They may admit her into the mental hospital. She could lose her job and her child. No, I will look after her." Her family consoled her, until Claudia was able to manage her emotions a bit better.

Claudia had a difficult week and now today was the first time that she was going to see Ricardo since she developed those love feelings for him. She met him at the musical shop so that he could treat their daughter to a new instrument.

On the way home Claudia, unexpectedly said to Ricardo. "Would you like to come in?" This was shocking for Courtney because for so many years, Claudia kept her home address a secret from Ricardo and Courtney was told to do the same.

"Mum" whispered Courtney, "I, thought my dad's not supposed to know where we live. What are you doing?" she asked. "Don't worry Courtney." Claudia tried to reassure her daughter. "It will be alright." Ricardo instantly accepted the invitation.

Ricardo was happy that he was finally coming to see where his daughter was living. As Ricardo stepped into the hallway, his eyes widened and brows lifted. He entered the large front room and was impressed by the decor.

He mentally graded her house as being highly impressive. Comparable to the homes of the rich and famous with the high ceilings, expensive paintings and dark wooden floors. There was a lovely floral feature wall, with a large oval mirror and a granite fireplace below.

"You're not just a pretty face." Ricardo complimented. "Seems like interior designing is your thing." Ricardo said, truly surprised that Claudia had acquired such an amazing home as a single woman.

"Well I actually painted the walls and laid the flooring myself, I might do a short designing course at college to enhance my talent. I really enjoyed the experience." Claudia said proudly. "This house is really nice. It reminds me of those show homes." Ricardo said with envy, as he rested back into the recliner chair.

Courtney's feelings were on the fence, she was happy that her dad was finally going to see her pretty pink bedroom, but then she thought maybe it was not a good idea that her dad knew where they lived.

"Come on Courtney. Show me all your toys." Ricardo said excitedly "Ok dad, I'll race you upstairs." As the pair made their way up the stairs, Claudia decided to sit outside in the garden.

She noticed a couple of plastic bags on the grass and wondered whether the neighbour's children had thrown them over the fence. She quickly gathered them up and put them in the bin. Then she sat back down and breathed a sigh of peace. She felt complete. In her mind, the concept of an intact family was suddenly important to her, even though it had never bothered her before.

When Claudia ended the relationship with Ricardo, she thought they had come to the end of the road and at the time, she felt that she had made the right decision that one happy single mother was better for Courtney than to have two miserable parents living together, in a relationship fuelled by intimidation and jealousy.

Although at times things were challenging because of Ricardo's erratic behaviour, Claudia still made sure that Courtney had contact with her father, as she feared that by preventing visits at a young age would result in Courtney growing up not knowing anything about her father.

Maintaining contact would allow Courtney to see for herself the good and the bad in Ricardo.

That was the sensible Claudia, but now Claudia had adopted such a ridiculously naive point of view and her new ideology was such that she believed if a woman makes a choice to have a child with a man, they should stick with their partner whether the man was good or bad.

When Ricardo and Courtney came downstairs into the dining area, Courtney suddenly screamed. "There's a rat, there's a rat." she said as she jumped onto the chair. "Ricardo, quick catch it." Claudia said in a panic.

Ricardo looked around the room, but could not find the rat. "It probably ran back into its hole." said Ricardo calmly. "But there aren't any holes in my house. I have looked everywhere, even the floorboards are secured. I can't figure out how they are getting in." Claudia said in a puzzled way. "Never mind, it's gone now." Ricardo said casually.

Claudia began to serve the dinner. "This is what I always wanted, to live with my daughter and to be a family." Ricardo said regrettably. "Ricardo, I love you, I want to be back with you. Come and live with us." Claudia declared. Ricardo appeared surprised by Claudia's unexpected revelation.

"I really wanted our relationship to be successful, but you never gave it a chance. All this time I have been away from Courtney, I can't get that time back. Spending time with her at weekends, is never as good as living with her and seeing her everyday." explained Ricardo in an overt way.

He portrayed himself as a victim, with an unblemished character and passed all blame on to Claudia. "Ricardo, why don't we talk about this another time? Let's just enjoy the meal." said Claudia bluntly.

However, Claudia's special moment had come to an abrupt end after Ricardo's outburst. They spent the rest of the evening in silence with Claudia also blaming herself for the broken relationship.

At the end of the evening, just before Claudia said goodbye to Ricardo, he told her to give him a few months and then he will leave his girlfriend.

Claudia had mixed emotions, she was elated that Ricardo wanted to be back with her but she felt like crap after he left, because she missed him terribly.

After she put Courtney to bed, she collapsed in a sea of tears. She felt Ricardo's pain and believed that she had caused it.

Claudia was no longer able to keep her feelings about Ricardo to herself and like an adder who spits out its poison, now was the time for Claudia to blurt out all her emotions to her mother.

"Mum" Claudia, screamed down the phone. "Why didn't you tell me to give my relationship with Ricardo another chance, when I ended it? You didn't give me any advice about how to handle relationships, you never told me that you got to take the rough with the smooth, I know that now, but it could be too late." sobbed Claudia, making senseless accusations.

Claudia's mother was confused that Claudia would say this now, many years after her relationship had ended with Ricardo. However, she was sympathetic. "Claudia, I wanted you to try again." explained her mother. "Remember, I said to you that if you end it, his mother would be happy because she didn't want to see you two together? But you knew that Ricardo wasn't right for you. He was a difficult person to please and he did not want you to have anything to do with your family"

Claudia's mother continued, "Ricardo was not worth holding on to. If you had stayed with him, you wouldn't have been happy. It makes sense now. This was the reason why you had a breakdown at Clint's house. I'm so sorry to see you hurting like this." her mother said softly.

The grief prevented Claudia from speaking. She slammed down the phone and sat motionless. She then entered into denial. She chose to believe that she was going to get her man back eventually, but he was just playing hard to get because he was scared of getting hurt again.

Hours after Ricardo left, Claudia's depression disappeared. Why? Because as Claudia had developed a deep love for Ricardo, she imagined Ricardo as her man. She was now 100% sure that she wanted to get back with Ricardo and based on what Ricardo was saying he wanted the same.

For the first time in weeks, as Claudia thought about her life with Ricardo, she had the most peaceful sleep or so she thought. "Arrrgh" Claudia suddenly woke up at 4am screaming and crying.

She was so tormented, that she got her penknife and began to stab the wall, slash the bed sheets and attack everything around her. She was in a frenzied state, as her ability to cope with this hell was now becoming impossible.

Every time Claudia saw Ricardo, her depression lifted. Ricardo was not employed, so whenever she took Courtney to see him, Ricardo would take advantage of Claudia, because of the love she had for him.

She would end up paying for the restaurant meals, his petrol and even his groceries. For as long as Claudia new Ricardo, she always demanded he pay monthly maintenance. So how could Claudia now expect to receive regular contributions for Courtney when she was maintaining him?

Sadly, Claudia was so blinded by love. She could not see that every time he said he would leave his girlfriend to be with her, he was only giving Claudia false hope.

As the weeks and the months rolled by, Claudia became more and more tired, weaker and weaker and thinner and thinner and Ricardo still had not left his girlfriend.

Suicidal thoughts had now entered Claudia's mind. She would drag herself to work with the world on her shoulders, but fortunately, her depression did not affect her ability to win her clients court cases and maintain her knowledge of the law changes.

Claudia could not understand why the urge to commit suicide was too strong to handle. Why did she want to end it? It seemed like she could not imagine living without Ricardo in her life. How crazy could this be?

Claudia became vulnerable and confided more and more in her friends to the point that she would sound like a broken record. She constantly repeated herself.

"Claudia what's happened to you, how can you be paying money to this guy?" her girlfriends would say. "I remember how you used to protect your address with your life. Now you've got this guy coming into your house and turning up whenever he likes, he's taking advantage of you."

Claudia thought about the comments people had made and she decided that it was time she took control of her life. Claudia didn't want unfinished business to contaminate any future relationship she may have.

This may be the reason why I am single, thought Claudia. I must be giving off a vibe to the guys that I am in a relationship, because my mind is always on Ricardo. But I must try to forget him, because I really am a single woman. Claudia thought trying to convince herself.

It was Saturday evening and while she reflected on her lonely existence, she shouted. "'I'm fed up of being on my own, fed up of going to sleep alone and fed up of being unloved. I've been single ever since I finished with Ricardo. Am I that unattractive, that I should be ignored?" Claudia mumbled.

"If the man isn't coming to me, I am going to find the man." she declared and with that, Claudia spontaneously got up, glamorised herself, got on the train and headed for the singles club in the city. The one that her friends had encouraged her to go to on numerous occasions.

As she arrived, Claudia nervously entered the front doors of the club and walked up to the reception desk. "Good evening, can I have your name?" the woman behind the desk asked. "Well, I'm Claudia." she replied.

The woman looked up her name on the computer. "I'm sorry, but we don't appear to have you on the list. Just take a seat, while I check the diary in the office." Claudia sat down on the brown leather sofa, expecting to be told that she had to leave, because she had not booked in advance.

As she walked to her office, the reception lady looked around the room until her eyes stopped on a well dressed neatly shaven guy. "Sir" the receptionist shouted over to the man. "Please can I pair you up with this lady right here?" she asked as she pointed to Claudia.

The man smiled and walked over to where Claudia was sitting. "Hello, may I" the gentleman said as he sat down next to Claudia. "Sure, take a seat." Claudia said cheerfully. "So what's your name?" he asked. "My name is Claudia" she replied.

She was very impressed with the man's appearance and thought something could develop from this meeting. "And what's your name?" "I'm Ric." he replied. Then he paused. "Well my name is Ricardo, but everyone calls me Ric."

Claudia was shocked, she gulped and placed her hand over her mouth, as she tried to hide her devastation. Then, she began to tremble and the palms of her hands started to sweat.

There's Claudia trying her very best to get Ricardo out of her head and what happens? An unlikely nightmare of a situation occurs, where a new potential partner holds the very same name as that slime ball.

"Miss, good news we have a few spaces for this evening . . ."

Ignoring the woman, Claudia got up and raced out of the building. She ran and ran, aimlessly between office blocks, dodging the busy night traffic with tears rolling down her eyes, which blurred her vision.

She darted left into a side street and continued down the long road into a park, she headed for a bench and flopped herself down. Breathless and suffering uncontrollable grief, she wept like a baby as the rain came down on her.

She allowed herself to get drenched right through, not caring that her nicely curled hair was now flat and stuck to her face and the hair gel had started to drip and mix with her tears, which caused her eyes to sting.

Claudia checked her phone and noticed that her mother had called her 15 times. Claudia knows that her mother gets worried about her, if she doesn't hear from her, so she had to reassure her mother that she was okay.

Claudia calmed herself down and telephoned her mother. "Claudia, where have you been?" her mother asked, relieved that Claudia had made contact with her. "Mum, I went to a singles club and I met this guy." Claudia wailed. "Really, do you like him?" Claudia's mother asked excitedly. "Mum no I didn't, well actually he was okay, but guess what? His name is Ricardo." and Claudia began to weep again.

"Mum, why can't I get away from him. I feel like he is haunting me. I want to move on with my life and somehow in this crazy abyss I can't." sobbed Claudia. "Don't worry, text me the exact location of where you are and I'll come and get you. I'll leave Courtney with your father. You stay strong." her mother said softly.

Half an hour later, Claudia's mother arrived. She wrapped a blanket around Claudia and gave her a well needed Starbucks cappuccino, to warm her up. Then they walked to the car and went home.

As they got into the house, the phone rang. It was Claudia's brother Clint. "Hi Claudia, mum has been telling me how you've been doing."

Claudia snapped. "Yes, Clint and where have you been over the months? You haven't come to see me. You couldn't even pick up the phone." Claudia said abruptly.

"I know Claudia, I have to admit that I kept my distance because I couldn't cope with the way you were behaving and I didn't understand why you would want to be back with a worthless scumbag like Ricardo." admitted Clint.

"I judged you, but I now realise, who am I to judge. You didn't judge me when I was down and out and going through my challenges. You supported me, you walked by my side and I will never forget that. Families need to stick together and I know your big brother has let you down, but now I'm going to be there for you." explained Clint.

There was a long silence, then Claudia began to express her feelings. "I appreciate what you are saying but you hurt me when you turned your back on me. I am depressed but I don't know why, I want Ricardo back and I don't know why. Deep down I know it is wrong. It seems like there is this invisible force or spell that is controlling me and making me do things I don't want to do, it sounds mad I know." Claudia said emotionally.

"Well sis, do you remember my friend Jaz, the guy in America? He's an author, and he is having a launch party for his latest book in Manhattan at the end of this month. He wants to invite me over for the event, all expenses paid because he is loaded. Anyway, the wife can't go due to work commitments, so I thought I'd invite you." Clint explained.

Claudia smiled with acceptance. "Well I don't like being second best, but yeah, I'll go with you. I think a break will do me good." said Claudia. "Great that's sorted, I'll let him know that we need two tickets." confirmed Clint.

Claudia was happy about the holiday. She was really looking forward to getting away and she thought that a different environment might help her to get on the path of recovery. She also felt happy that her brother was back in her life again.

As the days and weeks went by, Claudia couldn't bear to open the post. She would step over the letters piling up at the front door, too scared to open them. She obtained loans and exhausted her credit cards and now Claudia's debts had spiralled out of control.

Her monthly salary, turned into a fortnightly salary leaving her penniless for the next two weeks, before her payday. As a solicitor, she was well paid and up until recently, Claudia lived comfortably on the money she was earning.

Nowadays month after month, she noticed that her salary was consistently disappearing and she didn't know where it was going or why it was happening.

Fearing the bailiffs and the county court judgements, she buried her head in the sand rather than facing the truth. However, through her depression, Claudia never forgot about God. She would always call upon him, praying for him to make her well again and to bless her in her finances and her love life.

Claudia felt like she was locked in an invisible cage, with no way of escaping. She decided to go out in the car and drive to the countryside to smell the pollution free air.

She stayed there for a while and then stopped at the petrol station to buy a drink and a newspaper. "I'm sorry, but your card has been declined." informed the man behind the counter. At that point, her world began to cave in.

Claudia's depression was bad enough and now she didn't

have any money, how much worse could it get for Claudia? She quickly ran out of the shop and raced off in her car. As she drove, her phone rang. She didn't recognised the number, but she decided to answer it anyway. "Hello" Claudia said curiously. "Hi Claudia, its Shari." the voice replied.

Claudia couldn't believe that Shari had called her and she felt so happy to hear her old school friend's voice, for the first time since she left to go on her travels. "Shari, when did you get back? Did you enjoy your trip?" Claudia asked excitedly. "Yes, lovely food, great weather and gorgeous men. It was fantastic." Shari explained.

"I missed you, girl. Things have not been great with me lately. I'm just not in a good place right now." Claudia said sadly. "Well I know about what you're going through. As soon as I got back, I saw your mother. She told me everything. That you want your daughter's father back and that you're massively depressed. I'm worried about you." explained Shari.

"Shari, I want to switch from surviving to true living, because I know I am wasting my life, being stuck in this depression. I feel worried, scared and lonely all the time." Claudia explained. "I want some light at the end of the tunnel, and I look forward to the day that I will experience inner peace and a loving relationship with a special person." Claudia spoke passionately.

"Exactly, a special person. Ricardo is not that person. You deserve so much more and one day you will get it. I will come and see you soon. but in the meantime, stay strong." Shari said empathetically.

Claudia enjoyed speaking to her old friend Shari, she had uplifted her and with Deena already back in her life, it felt like old times.

Chapter 12

MORE HELL

IT WAS THE day of the holiday. Claudia checked the house and was about to lock the patio doors, when she noticed that there were plastic bags in her garden again. She cleared them up and thought about talking to her neighbours, on her return.

She then left rat poison in every room. She didn't want to return from her holiday to find another rat problem in her house.

Claudia said her goodbyes to Courtney and her parents and made her way to the airport, where she met Clint.

They boarded the plane at midday, the flying time was 6 hours and they were due to land in New York, early afternoon.

During the flight Claudia was agitated, but she was looking forward to the holiday. She had taken a couple of sleeping tablets, which kept her calm throughout the flight.

Clint and Claudia dragged their luggage through arrivals and sat outside to wait for Clint's friend. "There he is, Jaz over here." Clint said as he waved Jaz over. Jaz drove up in his SUV jeep and parked up. "Jaz, this is my sister Claudia." Jaz stretched out his hand. "Yeah, I remember you in the photos." Jaz smiled. "Really?" Claudia blushed as she rejected the handshake and greeted him with a kiss on the cheek instead.

Jaz chauffeured Claudia and Clint to a nice 2 bedroom apartment on the 15th floor. After they checked in at the reception desk, the door attendant greeted them.

"Well, hello and welcome to New York. We are here on hand 24 hours a day, 7 days a week. So, if your lights are not working, I'm the man. If you can't get any hot water, I' m the man. If you're hungry though, you need to check out the restaurants on the main road." he chuckled.

"We will try to make your stay as pleasant and as comfortable as possible. By the way, my name is Lamont." he said with a smile. "Well Lamont, thank you for welcoming us to this fabulous complex. We will see you soon." Jaz replied as he led the way.

Jaz opened the door to the apartment. But actually, it looked more like a mansion than an apartment. Claudia was amazed at how everything was so big.

There was a 50 inch flat screen television in every room. Each bedroom contained a queen-sized bed, a three seater red leather sofa, an ensuite bathroom, plus a coffee making area.

Clint allowed Claudia the room with the best view. As she looked through the window, the scenery amazed her. The dark skies revealed dozens of lights many floors up, with skyscrapers appearing to disappear into the sky.

Those famous yellow cabs were crawling the streets of New York and the sound of the horns were louder than what would have been acceptable back home. But that's cool it's New York.

Claudia took a slow deep breath. However, it wasn't a

sigh of relief. It was to ascertain whether the new scenery and this fabulously great city plus all the good looking men, were enough to cure Claudia of her depression.

Unfortunately, it did not and sadly, Claudia felt the same way as she did when she was back at home. Although unnoticed to others, Claudia still trembled and shook. The force of the depression was still as strong and the feeling of ending it all was still as shockingly powerful as before.

Claudia's brother, Clint, thought that a holiday would fix Claudia's problems. Claudia knew that her brother was not the type of person that could handle her situation, and rather than try to support her through one of the most challenging things that she will probably ever have to deal with in her lifetime, Claudia's brother swept things under the carpet and pretended that everything was okay.

This is not so much to criticize Clint, but to point out that when people face a problem like this, it can either make or break the relationship between the sufferer and the other person, be it sibling, friend or other family members.

Providing support may become too difficult and they may find the sufferers behaviour embarrassing or offensive. Some people had judged Claudia's mental illness but if those people were suffering in the same way, they would not like someone to judge them.

"Hey Sis." Clint hollered from the kitchen, causing Claudia to jump suddenly out of her thoughts. "I'm looking at a few restaurant leaflets stuck up on the fridge. Shall we just order a pizza to keep it simple?" Clint asked. "Yeah, I'll have the margarita thanks." Claudia replied. "Ok and where's your cash Sis? You gotta pay your half. Anyway you earn more money than me, so you should be paying for me too." Clint joked.

Claudia laughed off his suggestion and then she reflected

on the true extent of her money worries. Right now Claudia's financial situation was equivalent to a jobless person living off the state.

In fact it seemed like if she had won a million pounds on the lottery, before she had a chance to invest it, her money would have disappeared into thin air. If recent events were anything to go by.

Soon, the doorbell rang. Claudia opened the door. "Pizza delivery." said the woman behind the massive pizza box. Claudia gave the woman the cash and took the pizza to the table.

"Hey Clint, what size pizza did you order? This will feed about ten of us." Claudia said in amazement. "Well, I did ask for a medium." Clint laughed. "Clint, you should have asked how many people it will feed. When my friend went to Miami, she told me that she had to order a kids meal at burger king, because the regular meal was way too big for her. Anyway enjoy." The siblings ate, drank champagne provided by Jaz and watched cable TV until the early hours.

The next morning, Claudia was woken up by the phone ringing. She could faintly hear Clint on the line, talking to Jaz.

Claudia stretched out and rolled over to the other side of the Queen sized bed and she got up on her knees to look out of the window. Manhattan greeted her with clear blue skies and temperatures reaching 92 degrees.

As she looked around, she noticed a group of tiny hummingbirds gracefully gliding in the sky, adopting a sense of peace and serenity.

Claudia enjoyed their presence and envied their simple life and while she observed their behaviour, for a moment she was magically taken away from all her troubles.

Clint knocked on the door and came into Claudia's room. "Hey Claude, that was Jaz on the phone. He's having a dinner party over at his place tonight at 8pm." Clint announced. "Really, okay. It should be a nice evening. I think I'll go down to the shopping mall to see what I can find to wear." Claudia said excitedly.

Claudia was looking forward to seeing Jaz again because for the short time she was in his presence, he had made her feel alive and normal again. Quite oddly, when Jaz occupied her mind, she would very easily forget about Ricardo.

Claudia was puzzled by this. If she was so desperately in love with Ricardo, to the point that she feels that life was not worth living without him, then there should be no other man that could interest her. Because Jaz did interest her, she questioned whether what she felt for Ricardo was really love at all.

Claudia showered, dressed and said bye to Clint. As she left the elevator, she could smell a sweet aroma of mouth watering cinnamon buns. Claudia couldn't resist picking up a bag on the way.

As she fought through the busy streets, she appreciated the diversity of the city, the variety of languages spoken and the New York tones.

Claudia continued down the road, but she began to walk erratically on the street, carelessly walking in front of the cars to get to the other side of the road. Suddenly a horn beeped as the tyre of a car skidded to avoid hitting her. "Hey lady, are you crazy? You should be arrested for jay walking." the angry driver shouted. Claudia jumped back.

She was in such a daze and in her own thoughts, that she wasn't aware of what was happening around her.

As Claudia entered the shopping mall, there was a wide choice of shops, from casual wear to designer wear. Claudia walked into the shop that had four floors of gear.

"Ohhh, that's nice." Claudia said to the assistant, as she

pointed to a silver top on the rack. "Yes, this style came in just last week and it's one of our best buys." the assistant explained.

Claudia thanked the assistant and continued down the aisle, but Claudia was not just looking for clothes, she was scanning the area to see if there were any nice looking guys.

Claudia was mentally trying to move on from Ricardo and she needed to see that there were other eligible men out there in the world.

For many years since she left Ricardo, she very much wanted to start a new relationship and experience a healthy normal partnership but it never happened.

Nobody had approached her but she thought maybe, just maybe this big city with lots of people and a lot more choice will make her lucky in love.

Unfortunately, Claudia quickly came to the realisation that it was going be the same thing, on a different day, in a different country. Along the way, she saw attractive men and she smiled at them. They looked at her but then they looked away. There were no second glances happening here. Good looking or not, these guys were definitely not interested in Claudia.

This endless loneliness would cause her to remember the time when she had that premonition at thirteen years old, about it being hard for her to meet a boyfriend in the future.

Those words continued to haunt Claudia and as much as this message was not important to Claudia when she was a young teen, this message was now the main cause of her unhappiness.

Claudia began to feel scared again, the thought of growing old alone filled her with fear and anxiety. She then began to shake uncontrollably, her heart began to beat quickly and she struggled to breathe.

Everywhere started spinning around her and Claudia collapsed on the floor in the middle of the mall. The fear of dying shocked Claudia into unconsciousness.

Claudia could hear people shouting, "Call the paramedics." "This lady needs help." "Put her in the recovery position." "What's wrong with her, has she had a seizure, is she breathing?" "Help fire." a woman shouted.

A man looked at the woman and asked. "Why are you shouting fire? There's no fire." The woman replied. "Well if you shout fire, you're more likely to get people's attention."

The ambulance soon arrived and Claudia was taken to the hospital. Shortly afterwards, she began to come around. Claudia slowly opened her eyes and became confused about her surroundings.

She realised that she was not back at home and the room didn't look like the apartment she was staying in so Claudia was wondering where she could be.

She saw a man with a white coat entering the room. Claudia was not fully awake but she was stirring. "Claudia how are you feeling, there's nothing to worry about, you just had a panic attack. We have given you some medication to calm your nerves?" The doctor explained. "Is there anyone that we can call to collect you?" asked the doctor.

Claudia opened her eyes fully. "Doctor, I felt a very strong pain in my chest. I thought I was having a heart attack," Claudia said anxiously.

The doctor smiled. "Well, there's not much chance of you having a heart attack at your age, but your panic attack was pretty strong. You're okay now but you may want to find out the reason why you had the attack in the first place, to prevent it from recurring." The doctor advised.

"No, no I'm absolutely fine." Claudia said, trying to convince herself that she was okay. "I probably just got myself into a state, because I was trying to find an outfit for an important evening tonight. Oh my god what's the time, I can't be late for the dinner." Claudia began to panic. She got up rushing around the room to gather her belongings.

"Claudia, please calm down," the doctor said, gently placing his hand on Claudia's arm and guiding her to the chair. "If you give me the number of someone who can pick you up, I'll call them right away. In the meantime drink some water." The doctor said as he poured Claudia some water.

Claudia wrote down Clint's number and gave it to the doctor. She then lay down on the bed and closed her eyes. "What's happening to me?" she thought.

She reached into her handbag and pulled out her mobile phone. She knew that she shouldn't use her phone in the hospital but she wanted to check to see if her brother had tried to call her.

When she turned on her phone, she saw 16 missed calls from Clint. Poor Clint must have been so worried about Claudia, knowing that he let his depressed little sister out on her own in a big strange city.

The doctor soon returned to Claudia's room. "I spoke to Clint, he's been very worried about you. He is on his way. Now do you have travel insurance? If you do, then you will not need to pay for your treatment." the doctor explained.

"When you leave the hospital, please give the receptionist your details and don't let me see you back here in the hospital. Take care of yourself and enjoy the rest of your stay." the doctor said as he smiled and left the room.

Claudia took her things and made her way down the elevator to the ground floor. She gave the cashier her particulars then she sat in the waiting room until Clint arrived.

Claudia hoped that Clint would hurry up because she was freezing cold. She looked up towards the ceiling and realised that she was sitting directly underneath the air conditioning vent, which was on high. Claudia decided to telephone Clint to see where he was. "Clint" Claudia said impatiently. "Where are you? Oh, you've just parked up. Okay I'll meet you outside."

Claudia picked up her bags and headed for the exit. Feelings of excitement came over her, when she realised that Jaz was so kind to come with Clint to collect her. Claudia felt so special.

As she approached the car, Clint and Jaz came out to greet her. "Claudia," Clint said, relieved that his sister was safe. "You worried the hell out of me. I called you so many times and couldn't get hold of you. Jaz suggested I call the hospital. Thankfully, the doctor got in contact with me and told me what happened to you. Come here, sis." Clint gently grabbed Claudia and gave her a big hug.

"Here, take this," said Jaz. "You must be cold, Claudia." Jaz kindly wrapped his jacket around Claudia's shoulders to warm up her goose pimpled arms.

Claudia was mesmerised by Jaz's deep sexy voice. He was a well-built, 6ft stature of a man. "You really gave us a fright when we didn't hear from you." Jaz explained.

"Now, I'm the one that invited you guys over to America and I don't want anything to happen to you out here. So from now on I will be your chauffeur, your tour guide, whatever you want. I just want to make sure that as my guest, you enjoy your vacation." Jaz explained.

Well Claudia definitely had no objections with this new arrangement and looked forward to spending more time with him.

Claudia got in the car and Jaz drove them back to their apartment. The rear of the car was cosy with luxurious seats.

Jaz pulled up outside the apartment building within

minutes. It was a shame that Claudia's enjoyment of her surroundings had to be cut short.

As they entered the apartment, Claudia flopped down on the bed with exhaustion. "Guys, you know what. I think I am going to stay home and rest. But make sure you two have a great time this evening." Claudia said. "Ahhh sis, I would have liked you to join us, but I understand. You rest." replied Clint. "Well if you can't make the dinner, I'm gonna have to take you out for a meal tomorrow night." said Jaz, making a great effort to cheer Claudia up. "That's a date." Claudia agreed.

As Clint and Jaz got ready, Claudia made a quick meal and sat out on the balcony to experience the busy city on a Saturday night.

The streets were jammed with cars, as if it was rush hour and the people looked like a docile swarm of bees, with no particular place to go.

Claudia had noticed that during the holiday, Clint was in denial about her problems and Jaz was obviously oblivious to her condition. Claudia barely heard them say bye to her, as the voices in her head took over her mind.

"Life is pointless without Ricardo in it, you're never gonna be happy. Why carry on with this endless suffering. The pressure is too much for you now. Just end it. All you have to do is jump off this balcony. It will be over in seconds." said the devil in her mind.

"You can't kill yourself. How would Clint cope if you committed suicide? Imagine how difficult it would be for him to break the devastating news to your parents and then having to make the harrowing journey back home with your body, and what about your child, think about your daughter?" Claudia reasoned with herself.

She then imagined herself in a coffin and then she began

to weep, as if she was crying at her own funeral. Then Claudia heard a voice calling her name. "Claudia." the voice whispered.

Claudia jumped up, wondering where the voice was coming from. "Claudia, over here." Claudia followed the voice as if she was hypnotised.

The voice led Claudia to walk towards the wall of the balcony. She slowly stepped onto a chair and climbed up, balancing her feet on the edge. "Just finish it, you'd be happier on the other side." the voice said.

As the voice continued to explain to Claudia why jumping would be the best thing for her, she nodded in agreement.

She opened her eyes and she no longer saw those gigantic skyscrapers, but she saw her ancestors before her.

A strong sense of peace came over her as she made up her mind. She drew in a few deep breaths as she prepared to stretch out her arms and fly like a bird and now she was ready, ready to be free and then she fell.

Crash, bang, wallop. "Arrgh." Claudia hollered, crumpled on the floor of the balcony with a sore head. Instead of falling forward into the street, something forced her to fall backwards onto the balcony floor.

A righteous voice told her that she cannot put her family through such devastation. They say that good conquers evil and today it definitely did because something out there saved Claudia's life.

As she digested what had just happened, Claudia gained inner strength to hold on to life, even though the temptation to harm herself was still shockingly powerful and stronger than ever.

Claudia wondered why she had this urge to do away with herself more so now on holiday than when she was back home. She had never actually attempted to harm herself back home the way she did just a moment ago.

Then she realised that she felt comfortable, expressing her feelings to her mother, but now her mother was not there. Clint was there, but he was in denial because he pretended that she was fine.

Obviously, he wouldn't want to be listening to Claudia going on about her former boyfriend, the man that Clint despised. Therefore, it would be difficult for Clint to show Claudia compassion and understanding under the circumstances.

Because Claudia had nobody to talk to, she then had to fight to keep her feelings in. She worked out that constantly talking about her love for Ricardo had become the crutch to hold her up.

Now that she wasn't able to talk about him and express herself, the burden became heavier than ever and she felt that she no longer had the strength to fight any more. The sooner she got back home to her mother the better.

The next morning, Claudia woke up early, she showered and got dressed. She didn't hear Clint come in last night so she went to his room to see if he was there. She heard Clint, before she could see him, because the loud snoring coming from his room sounded like a car engine revving up.

There was a knock at the front door. "Who is it?" yelled Claudia. "It's Jaz." Claudia became excited and checked herself in the mirror before she opened the door. "Hi Jaz." Claudia said enthusiastically. "Good morning, I hope it's not too early for me to come around." said Jaz. "No not at all. Come in and take a seat." Claudia said as she directed Jaz to the living room.

"So how are you feeling after yesterday?" asked Jaz. "Yes, I'm much better now. I think the heat got to me." Claudia replied, shrugging it off. "So where's Clint, hasn't he recovered yet?" laughed Jaz. "Seems like he's hungover. He's still in bed."

Claudia replied. "What, I'm older than he is and I'm alright. Your brother is a light weight." Jaz teased.

"Jaz, do you want some coffee?" Claudia asked. "No thanks, I'm cool." Clint eventually got up looking rough. "Hey man, you ain't looking too good." said Jaz. Clint laughed. "Big man. You're used to this lifestyle, I'm not." Jaz smiled.

"Anyway I want to take you guys across the road for some lunch. It's on me." Jaz offered. "Right now, I'm not able to eat a thing, my friend." Clint said in an ill tone. "Here's some coffee with lemon. That should help you feel better." said Claudia, as she handed Clint the cup.

"Well, it seems like it will be just the two of us." Jaz said as he turned towards Claudia. "Oh okay, I'll just get my bag." Claudia said as she went to fetch it. "Yeah and I'll call up the elevator."

As Jaz left the apartment, Claudia went into the living room to apply some lip-gloss and comb her hair.

"I've seen the way you look at Jaz." Clint revealed. "I'm not looking at him in any particular way." Claudia said defensively. "I'm glad you're interested in other guys, instead of worrying over Ricardo. But I thought I should let you know, Jaz has a lady." Clint revealed. "Well I'm not surprised, obviously a nice guy like Jaz is gonna be in a relationship isn't he?" Claudia replied in a sharp tone.

It irritated her that Clint had dampened the excitement she was feeling. Although the time she will be spending with Jaz will soon be over, she was looking forward to being distracted by him, which will take her away from her reality. "The elevator is here." Jaz hollered. "See you later bro. Wish you better."

Claudia ran out of the apartment to catch the lift, before it filled up with the other guests. They left the elevator on the ground floor and walked through reception. "See you later

Jaz and Claudia. Have a lovely day." said Lamont, the door attendant. "You too." replied Claudia.

"There must be hundreds of guests staying in this hotel. It's amazing that he remembers everybody's name." said Claudia.

They walked the short journey to the restaurant. "Whoa, how can you just step into the road like that?" Jaz said as he grabbed hold of Claudia's hand. "Don't worry, I'm okay." reassured Claudia. "You need to be careful when you're crossing the road. You'll kill yourself one day." Jaz told her, as he guided her safely across the road.

"Table for two." Jaz confirmed to the waiter, when they arrived at the restaurant. They followed the waiter up the stairs to a table next to the window.

"Wow, this place is massive and look at the view out there." said Claudia, as she admired the scenery. "Yeah well as you can see from the menu, they serve a variety of dishes from Chinese, Italian, Indian and Caribbean, which makes this restaurant very popular." explained Jaz. Claudia chose the Italian cuisine and they subsequently placed their order.

"So you're a lawyer?" Jaz asked impressively. "Yes, but back home we call ourselves solicitors." teased Claudia. "I should know that, because my girlfriend comes from your part of the world. I love the way you guys speak." Jaz explained. "Anyway, it makes more sense to call a law graduate a lawyer. Where does the word solicitor come from? It bears no likeness to the word law. Anyway you're giving me the evil eye so I better shut up." said Jaz, pretending to be scared. Claudia smiled.

"So why did you choose to study law?" asked Jaz. "Well I got a taste of business law at college. I found the acts of parliament interesting and the cases fascinating. The evolution of the laws over the years was because of some of those historical cases." explained Claudia.

"I can strongly sense the passion you have for your work," Jaz said proudly. "I admire you and I like talking to you. Why don't you write a book?" Jaz suggested. "Well your book was a good read. But a writer needs to have something interesting to say, otherwise there's no point." explained Claudia. "Although Jaz, you have inspired me so I'll never say never. Anyway how's your pizza?" asked Claudia. "It's lovely and I can see that you're enjoying your pasta?" Jaz said. Claudia nodded.

The pair enjoyed their lunch and headed back to the hotel. As they walked past the donut stand, Jaz couldn't resist picking up a bag of cinnamon buns.

"Want one?" asked Jaz. "A moment on the lips is a life time on the hips and the legs and the butt for that matter. I better not." resisted Claudia. Jaz laughed. "Hi Lamont." Claudia said as they entered the lobby. "Hi, how was your afternoon?" asked Lamont. "Great."

As they headed towards the elevator, Jaz's phone rang. "Hello," answered Jaz. "Who? Where? Now? Okay, I'm coming. Bye." Jaz said down the phone. "Look Claudia, I need to go. But I'll be back this evening, because I want to take you and Clint to a charity concert. I'll call you about 5pm with more details." Jaz explained as he rushed out of the hotel. "Well I hope everything is okay." Claudia shouted but Jaz didn't hear her.

As soon as Jaz left, she missed him. Or rather, she missed the way he made her feel. As she travelled up the elevator, she realised that for the whole time she was with Jaz, she didn't talk about Ricardo, she didn't even think about him.

Again, Claudia was confused by this. Why did she want to kill herself over Ricardo, when on the rare occasion that she got some male attention, Ricardo would immediately disappear from her radar?

To Claudia, it almost seemed like the love wasn't really there. True love should be constant this love was not, it was different. One that was changeable according to current situations.

"Clint, I'm back," shouted Claudia. Clint came out of the bathroom looking worse for wear. "You look more terrible now than when we left you." Claudia said in a concerned way. "Well I'm feeling a lot better now, I just need to rest." said Clint, as he flopped down on the sofa.

"Does that mean you won't be coming to the concert that Jaz will be taking us to later on?" asked Claudia. "Oh no. But it's nice of Jaz to arrange this for us." replied Clint. "Never mind, just get yourself well. You don't have time to be sick. We've only got two days left before we go back home." explained Claudia. "I know, the time has gone by so quickly." thought Clint.

Claudia went to her room and looked through her suitcase to find an outfit for the concert. She tried on a variety of clothes, until she found the one she was happy with. She chose a lovely midnight blue, satin midi dress with matching shoes.

She then showered and ate. She remembered that Jaz said he was going to ring her at 5pm, so she sat and waited patiently for Jaz to call.

5pm came and went, but still no phone call. However, Jaz didn't keep Claudia waiting too long. He called Claudia a few minutes later. "Hello" Claudia said, excited that Jaz had called her as he promised.

"Hi it's Jaz. Listen, I am really sorry. I can't make the concert." Jaz said sadly. "That crisis call I received earlier is taking longer than I expected to sort out. I feel bad, because I know you guys are leaving the day after tomorrow. But we will definitely hang out before you go back home." explained Jaz. "Okay Jaz. Don't worry about it. Take Care." Claudia said bravely.

Claudia tried her best to disguise her disappointment. However, her illness made her sensitive and her emotions were so overwhelming, that as soon as she came off the phone, she broke down in tears, making sure that she sobbed quietly, so that Clint wouldn't hear her. If she were back home, she would be free to let it all out. She wouldn't have to cry in secret if her mother was there.

Claudia knew that an uninteresting night at home, would allow her plenty of time for those terrible thoughts to manifest in her mind. Although Jaz was in a relationship and she was not interested in him on a sexual level, it was clear that being in his company relieved her symptoms.

Just like a person in excruciating pain, who is crying out for morphine. The severity of her suffering was eased by Jaz's presence. The positive feelings she felt when she was with Jaz, made her realise what she was missing by not being in a relationship. Not any relationship, but a relationship with a true gentleman, a total opposite to Ricardo.

As much as her heart ached over her former boyfriend, right now Ricardo seemed like poison, where as Jaz was like a dose of medicine for her.

"Oh God, do I not deserve to be loved?" Claudia cried out in frustration, as she looked up to the ceiling. "Do I really want Ricardo? I know he is no good for me. So why am I making him my world? I don't understand. Please God I need answers."

Claudia cried and exhausted herself so much, she decided to lie down and rest just for a short while, but the morning came before she rose.

Clint knocked on Claudia's door. "Come in." Clint

balanced the tray as he slowly opened her bedroom door. "Good morning Claudia, I have made you a proper American breakfast, we have coffee, pancakes with maple syrup and a bowl of grits . . . ."

Claudia interrupted, "Grits, yuk, take those things out of my room. Just leave me the pancakes. Anyway what's all of this in aid of?" asked Claudia suspiciously. "Don't say it like that. Do I have to have a reason to be kind to my little sister?" asked Clint. "Yes" replied Claudia and they both laughed as Claudia began to tuck into her breakfast.

Clint went into the kitchen to load the dishwasher, when the phone rang. "Hi Clint, how you doing?" asked Jaz. "I'm much better, Jaz?" Clint replied.

"First of all, I need you to tell Claudia that I'm so sorry for not being able to take her our last night. Anyway, I know you guys are leaving tomorrow, so I would like to take you to a dinner and dance evening tonight. You need to wear your best suit." said Jaz.

"But I left my suit back home. I mean, who's going to pack a suit in their case when they are going on holiday? Unless they're going to a wedding or a funeral. Sorry mate, I can't go." Clint explained.

"That's a shame, can you tell Claudia about tonight? If she can't make it, tell her to call me, otherwise I'll pick her up at 7pm." said Clint.

Claudia had just finished her breakfast and she was lying on her bed. She reflected on her stay in New York and she concluded that this was definitely the worst holiday she ever had.

Not because New York isn't a nice city, it's a fabulous place. It was just that she was going through the worst time of her life.

Clint came back into her room. "I have great news, Jaz

wants to take you to a dinner and dance event this evening. He'll come and get you for 7pm. By the way you need to wear your best dress." Clint said and then he left the room.

Claudia had a smile on her face again. Her spirits were lifted and she looked forward to this evening. "Hey Clint, why aren't you coming?" Claudia shouted from her bedroom. "I don't have anything decent to wear. Anyway, I don't want to have an excuse to drink. I need to keep a clear head for the flight tomorrow." explained Clint.

Claudia spent the whole day preparing for her night out. She manicured her nails, put her facemask on and set her hair in rollers. The day flew by quickly and by now it was 6pm. Claudia had showered and prepared to glam herself up.

Claudia started to feel hungry and began to search the kitchen for food. Then she noticed that Clint was eating a pizza, so she attempted to grab a slice. "Oi, go away." Clint said, as he fiercely defended his food. "Don't be so selfish, I'm starving." moaned Claudia. "Well they do say that you enjoy your food more when you are really, really hungry." teased Clint.

Claudia began to sulk as she went back to her room. She had just finished applying her lipstick, when Jaz knocked. Clint opened the door to Jaz, who was dressed in a black tuxedo and polished black shoes.

Claudia came out of her room wearing a long satin black dress, with sparkling high heels and pearl oval earrings. "Your carriage awaits." Jaz said, as he stretched out his arm. "Why thank you, kind sir." replied Claudia, as she wrapped her arm around his.

As they left the hotel, there was a black Mercedes Benz waiting outside. "Oh I feel so special, being chauffeur driven." Claudia teased. "Well I thought I should have a night off from driving." said Jaz.

"So where's your girlfriend? I've heard a lot about her, but I've never seen her." Claudia said curiously.

"Well she's not in town at the moment. She's gone home to spend a couple of weeks with her family." explained Jaz.

They soon arrived at the dance, which was more posh than Claudia had expected. They entered the ballroom and the usher directed them to their seats, a brass band entertained the crowd.

"This is nice, I've never been to anything like this before, back home we attend parties but they are definitely not like this." explained Claudia. "Well I'm glad you're impressed." replied Jaz.

Shortly afterwards, the waiter served the food. "This salmon is very nice." said Claudia. "Really, let's try it." Jaz said as he lent over and helped himself to Claudia's food. "How's your prawns?" asked Claudia. "Nice, it's very tender, would you like some?" Jaz offered. "No thank you, I'm allergic to prawns." replied Claudia.

The waiter came over and regularly topped up there champagne glasses, before it reached half way. "This drink will have to be the last one, because I don't want to have a hangover tomorrow, for the journey back to England." chuckled Claudia.

As the band finished their performance, it was time for the dancing to commence. "May I have this dance?" asked Jaz. "Well since you asked so nicely, of course." replied Claudia. They enjoyed the evening so much, talking to other guests and dancing the night away.

This was the first time in years, she was asked to dance by a man and Jaz was so courteous. Claudia felt protected in the arms of this strapping handsome man.

As they danced, Claudia felt attractive and desirable. The

last song played and it was soon time to go home. "I really had an amazing night, thank you." Claudia said in appreciation.

Even though Claudia and Jaz were just friends, today was her day, a very special day and one that she would cherish forever.

The end of her holiday had come, but Claudia didn't feel so sad. For the whole duration of the holiday, she fought to keep her feelings to herself, which had made her illness worse.

She longed for her mothers listening ear and desperate to have Courtney in her arms again.

Chapter 13

INTO THE ABYSS
AND BEYOND

By THE TIME Claudia had arrived back home from America, the letters had piled up so high, she used the door to slide the mail against the wall to clear the way.

She then noticed a terrible smell in the house. She followed the scent into the kitchen and when she pulled back the oven, she saw two dead rats.

The smell was so bad she began to feel sick. Claudia plucked up the courage to scrape up the rats and dispose of them in a black dustbin bag.

This rat problem, along with her financial worries, plus those suicidal thoughts, caused Claudia to sink further and further into depression.

While Claudia moved out to stay with her parents, Pest Control came in to fumigate the house and fill the holes that were never there in the first place. It was an expensive job, but

Claudia felt re-assured that the rat problem had finally been eradicated for good.

One day Claudia decided to tackle the mountain of letters on her dining table. She took one letter from the middle of the pile and opened it. As she read the first few lines, she almost collapsed with shock. The letter was from the bank, it was a notice to repossess her property because she was behind with her mortgage payments.

Because Claudia had not read her mail or checked her bank statements recently, she had not realised that she had missed four months mortgage payments, which caused massive arrears on her account. All this time, she was unaware of the true extent of her financial situation.

"How can this be?" Claudia asked herself. She had set up a direct debit, to pay her mortgage automatically, on the same day every month. But because her money was disappearing so quickly, by the time the payment was due to be taken from her account, she had no money and to make matters worse, the bank had subsequently charged her every time a direct debit failed, which brought Claudia further into debt.

Claudia always used to pay her mortgage a couple of months in advance and she never struggled with money before. How could her life get this bad, that she faced losing her home? Theoretically, if she was not paying for the roof over her head, then she should have had extra money. But sadly the mortgage wasn't being paid and the money definitely wasn't being saved.

Claudia was in a daze, she nervously dialled her parent's number and her father picked up the receiver. "Hi dad, can I speak to mum?" Claudia said, trying to stop her voice from cracking. She did not want her father to think something was wrong. "Are you ok Claudia?" her father asked in a concerned way. "I'm fine," she said convincingly. "Okay I'll call your mother." "Hello Claudia" her mother said. "Mum, everything's going wrong." As she proceeded to explain her predicament, Claudia broke down in tears. "So Mum, please could you lend me the money to bring my mortgage payments up to date, otherwise the bank will take away my home. Courtney and I will be homeless." Claudia said desperately.

"Don't worry, you won't be homeless. I will bring the money tomorrow. Listen, I heard that if you bathe in blu and salt it will help to get rid of bad energy." her mother revealed.

"What's blu?" Claudia asked curiously. "It's something that whitens your clothes. It helps because the blu makes the water blue and the salt makes the water salty. The two mixed together resembles the sea, which is supposed to help wash away the negative energy. You've been suffering so much lately and I thought this could help you. I'll buy some tomorrow." said her mother.

Claudia was so grateful for the support her family were giving her. She suggested that her mother should write a cheque directly to her bank. Because money was going through Claudia's hands like water, she didn't trust herself to handle this transaction.

Claudia put Courtney to bed and decided to lie down next to her. Although she received terrible news today, she still thanked God for making her open that one letter in particular. If she hadn't then her home would have been taken from under her nose.

It was almost the weekend. Claudia suffered another sleepless night and in the morning, she struggled to get herself and Courtney ready and out of the house on time.

She decided to have a quick bath in the blu and salt her mother had given to her and then she patiently waited for a miracle. However, unfortunately this was not going to resolve her problems. Although she did feel a little bit calmer, the difference was almost insignificant.

"Hurry up Courtney. You're going to be late for school." Claudia was in a rush, as she had to appear in court at 9:30am. Thankfully she came out of court winning a victorious case.

As Claudia drove back to the office, she suddenly found herself gasping for breath. She quickly parked up and telephoned her boss. "Mr Greenway, I'm sorry, but I don't feel at all well, so I'm going to see my doctor. I'll be back in the office tomorrow. By the way, we won the case?"

As she placed the phone in the seat, she suspected she was suffering another panic attack, similar to the one she had experienced when she was in New York. The doctor confirmed this and put Claudia on a course of anti depressants and counselling sessions.

Claudia was not in a good place and she was devastated that her life had reached rock bottom. However, during these challenging times, she never forgot about God and she diligently continued to pray to him, believing that in his own time, at the right time, her pain and suffering will be gone forever.

It was nine o'clock on a dismal November morning and as she was eating her breakfast, she saw her mother's name flashing on her phone. "How are you?" her mother asked. "I don't feel any better, mum. I don't know what's wrong with me. Why am I feeling this way?" Claudia said desperately.

"Have you been bathing in the blu and salt?" asked her mother. "Yes, it makes me feel a little bit more relaxed, but it hasn't really changed my feelings because I'm still depressed." Claudia explained.

"My daughter," her mother said softly. "Where have you gone? You are not the Claudia that I know. Turn to the father above, he can see your pain and he cares for you." Claudia's mother continued, "Your weeping may endure for a night, but joy will come in the morning. Claudia, trust in God and you will have a break through before the end of the year."

The cry water that filled up in Claudia's eyes blurred her vision, while she listened attentively to her mothers comforting words. As Claudia wiped away her tears, she suddenly became angry.

"I'm invisible mum, nobody sees me, there must be something wrong with me. I have been on my own for so many years now and in that time, not one single man has approached me. People form new relationships all the time, so why can't I?" Claudia said emotionally. "Even before I met Ricardo, I was single for a long time. I feel there is something wrong with me. Why do men ignore me? I'm so lonely." Claudia cried.

"My child," her mother was about to reveal something shocking to Claudia. "This new church I am attending, has taught me so much. A few weeks ago, they were talking about curses and they mentioned that people could use your picture and place all different types of curses on you to blight your life. I remember I gave Miss Gloria a picture of you and your cousin Shereen when you were little." her mother revealed.

Claudia interrupted, "Yes mum, but you've given our pictures to so many people. Why would you suspect her of doing anything?" Claudia asked curiously. "When I would visit her, I never saw that picture in her house. This was a professional photograph taken at the studio, so why would she want to hide it away? She was the one who asked me if she could have the picture in the first place. I never offered to give it to her. This is probably the reason why she wanted it." declared her mother.

Her mother continued, "When the pastor mentioned that curses can be put on you in this way, a light switched on in my head. I believe that Miss Gloria put a curse on you, causing you to be single."

Claudia was in a state of shock. This was a ridiculous statement that her mother was making, but what other reason could there be for her singleness.

Her mother proceeded to say. "It's not normal for you to stay on your own for so long. Ever since you ended it with Ricardo, I had hoped you would meet your ideal partner, your soul mate." Claudia's mother admitted. "When it didn't happen, I hoped it would happen the following year. Every year I prayed you would meet someone that would treat you well. We have attended so many weddings over the past few years and I wondered when it would be your turn. Claudia, I believe that what I am saying is true."

Claudia nervously replied, "Mum, I also believe that what you're saying is true. Shereen has not dated anyone for years either and she definitely wants to be married and to have children one day. What you have just told me makes sense. Nearly all my friends are married. Why should Shereen and I be the ones left on the shelf? Now I'm actually beginning to believe in curses."

Then a past memory suddenly came to Claudia's mind. "I've never told you this, but when I was thirteen, I was running to the bus stop after school and I had a premonition that in the future it will be hard for me to meet a boyfriend." Claudia said emotionally.

"Really?" her mother said. "Yes, that could have been the time when this curse was placed on me. I wonder if that spirit I saw when I was younger had something to do with it. I did see it around the same time that I got the premonition." Claudia revealed.

"Well, you were born with your feet first and I was always told that babies that are born in this way, are spiritual beings and they have a strong connection to their inner self. Claudia, you have your own powers within you. It seems like your guardian angel is around you, to warn you and protect you." Claudia's mother explained.

As time went by, nothing changed for Claudia. She was still depressed and she continued to lose more and more weight. It seemed like her problems consumed her body, to the point where there was no space left for food.

She used her anti-depressant tablets haphazardly, taking them today but not tomorrow, as she feared she would get addicted to them and although she would wake up crying most nights, she still had the strength to hold down a stressful demanding job and she did it well.

Claudia's attempt to end her suffering had previously failed, but she was now ready to try for the second time.

But when and how should she do it? Christmas was fast approaching and Claudia made a vow that she did not want the New Year to arrive and still be in this state.

She often told people that she did not want to go into the future. Friends and family could not understand what she meant by that and why she would want to harm herself, over a useless person like Ricardo.

Claudia's father would shout at her and say, "Why would you want to kill yourself? You have a lovely daughter, a nice family, a good job and a lot going for you."

Others who didn't have the ability to cope with Claudia's illness, turned against her. Telling people who knew her, that she was mad.

They became fed up with Claudia going on and on about wanting Ricardo back, so when the going got tough, they got going and eventually they stopped bothering with her all together.

Through her illness, Claudia realised that her support

network had dwindled to a tiny number of people, that included her close family and a few friends. Thankfully those that mattered to her, continued to love and care for her.

Christmas Eve had arrived and everyone was looking forward to Christmas except Claudia. She struggled through Christmas day, making an effort for her daughter's sake.

One day Claudia decided to plan an important event. She took out a piece of paper, which was almost as thick as card and cream in colour. Then she pulled out a new black fountain pen and proceeded to write the following title. "A list of people coming to my funeral." and then Claudia began to write the names of her guests.

A list of people coming to my funeral

Names of Guests	Number of People
Mum and Dad	2
Clint and Wife	2
Felecia, Janet and family	4
Penny and Family	4
Shari and Will	2
Deena and Family	3
Shereen	1

And the list continued.

When Claudia finished, she decided to count the numbers, "one, two . . . ninety three." Claudia looked puzzled and began to count again, but she came back to the same number of people.

"Only ninety three guests?" Claudia sighed. She felt even

more depressed and worthless, when she realised that she wouldn't even have a hundred guests at her funeral.

She folded the list and placed it inside her brief case. Then she opened the draw and gazed at the sleeping pills that she had ordered over the internet. Claudia now felt prepared for the 31st December, New Years Eve. It was to be her last day on earth, to avoid another year of torment.

The next few days leading up to New Years Eve went by in a blur. Thankfully, Courtney spent her Christmas holidays at her Grandparents house, so in the evenings, Claudia would visit and spend some time with Courtney before going home. Her parents had offered to look after Courtney to give Claudia a break, unaware of what Claudia was planning for the last day of the year.

By now, Claudia was not living in the moment, but she was focusing on that day, December 31st, doomsday. She had decided that if she was unable to get better before this day, then she had no option but to go. Three days before the 31st December, Claudia was still hearing the voices in her head instructing her to end it all. Two days to go and the shaking and uncontrollable crying was still occurring. On the penultimate day, her depression was incessant and still in full force.

Decision day had arrived. Claudia woke up on a cold New Years Eve morning, extremely lethargic from the usual lack of sleep. She made herself a strong coffee and had a cold shower to wake herself up.

After she got dressed, she decided to make a mental assessment of her condition. She realised that what she was feeling today, was still as bad as it had always been.

She loved Ricardo but couldn't have him, so Claudia decided that her journey of life had come to the end of the road. The pain of holding on was too much to bear and now it was time to let go.

The phone rang. It was Penny. "Claudia, what are you doing to celebrate New Years Eve?" she asked. "Nothing, I'm not in the mood to go out, I've decided to stay in and spend it with Courtney and my parent's. Clint will probably visit later on in the evening." Claudia replied.

Claudia knew that she could not admit to Penny that she will be at home alone, because Penny would not allow her to spend New Years Eve by herself. "Ok, Claudia." Penny said in acceptance. "I'm having a small party at my place and I thought if you came, it would take your mind off things. Anyway, let me know if you change your mind. Happy New Year and I will call you tomorrow, God Bless."

After Claudia came off the phone, she decided to lie down on the bed to rest. She then began to enter into a meditative state, reminding herself of her sad life. She remembered the good times she had as a child and the difficulties she faced as an adult.

She thought of Courtney, her parents, her brother and her friends. Claudia was sad at the prospect of having to leave her loved ones, but she felt that she'd placed so much stress on her family, it would be better for everyone if she was not around.

She ignored the numerous phone calls and the messages sent to her mobile phone and she remained on her bed for hours and hours in a daze. It seemed like she was psyching herself up, to carry out this murderous self-inflicted act.

It was now 7pm. Claudia's last day flew by quickly. She slowly got up from the bed and got ready to go to her parent's house. As she switched on the car engine, she breathed a few deep breaths to calm herself down. Then she drove the short journey to her parent's house.

When Claudia arrived, Courtney greeted her by waving at her through the window. Courtney was happy to see her mother and she ran outside to meet her. "Hi mummy, I missed you." Courtney said excitedly. Claudia quietly hugged her daughter.

The grief consumed her and she was unable to hold back the few tears that rolled down her face, but she made herself stop, before her eyes turned red. Otherwise everyone would realise that she had been crying. She quickly wiped her eyes, before Courtney looked up at her and then they walked hand in hand into the house.

"Hey mum, hey dad." Claudia said as she kissed them both. She was putting on a brave face and pretending to be happy, but inside the pain was killing her. "Claudia, you've arrived just in time, because I'm serving dinner." said her mother. "Thanks mum." Claudia replied.

The best last supper to have is my mothers home cooking, Claudia thought. As she ate, she didn't talk, she just wanted to appreciate the taste of each and everything on her plate.

"Mummy, when you're finished, can you watch this film with me?" Courtney asked, waving a dvd in Claudia's face. "Perfect timing, because I'm done now, so let's go and watch it." Claudia replied as she cleared the table.

As Courtney put the dvd on, Claudia sat on the bed and looked around the room. Her old bedroom reminded her of her happy childhood.

She recalled her schooldays, when she would dread the maths test the next day. So to avoid going to school, she would fake a tummy ache the night before and then even though she was hungry, she would refuse to eat her breakfast the next morning. Just to make her illness seem more convincing. It always worked.

She remembered how she enjoyed the school holidays going swimming with her friends and creating their own adventure playground, by making swings out of car tyres and using trees as climbing frames.

She remembered how kind and caring she was as a young child, when she would get a drink from the fridge and place two glasses on the table, one for herself and one for Clint.

Then she would pour the drink into both glasses and discreetly and innocently, she would sip down the drink that had the most in the glass, to make sure the amounts were even before offering it to her brother.

And when she would see her mother sprinkle the washing powder into the bath, to wash the clothes, Claudia, being a mischievous 3 year old, would improvise and use the soil from the garden, as her washing powder and pour it into the bath.

Obviously, her mother would wonder why the clothes were getting dirtier and dirtier, but eventually she found out why.

She recalled the fond memories of family days out to the seaside. Having fun on the fairground rides, like, the big wheel and the rollercoaster and enjoying the sensation of the sand between her toes. Those times were the best years of her life.

Then she caught up to the present day, picturing herself trapped in a whirlpool of darkness, sadness and pain.

By the time Claudia had reminisced about her past, the dvd had finished. "Did you enjoy that Mum?" asked Courtney. "Yes, that was great." Claudia said enthusiastically, knowing that the only thing she could remember about the film was the title.

The doorbell rang. It was Clint and his wife. He came in to drop off a box of chocolates and some champagne, but he wasn't staying long because he was attending a dinner and dance evening uptown.

Before he left he called Claudia into the bedroom for a private talk. "Claudia, I know you're still depressed. Mum tells me that you still want to kill yourself." Clint said, built up with emotion. Claudia held her head down.

"Sis, you've been depressed for a long time now and it's clouding your happiness. You're pretending to be okay, I'm pretending that you're okay, but you're not. I wish I could help you, but I can't. Only you can overcome this." Clint said, and then his soft tone turned to anger.

"He's just playing you. Wake up and smell the god dam shit. You need to get over it because he doesn't want you."

Claudia could see that Clint was hurting and she watched him while he unsuccessfully tried to prevent the tears from rolling down his face. Although his comments cut like a knife and she hated him for saying it, she knew he loved her and she knew he was right.

Claudia wiped his eyes with a tissue and squeezed him tight. "Hey, that hurts." Clint squealed. They both chuckled. However, Claudia knew this was going to be the last time she would see her brother, so this was her way of saying goodbye.

Claudia spent the next few hours with Courtney and her parents. Eating chocolates and listening to music. It was coming up to 11pm and Claudia was ready to leave.

"I'm going home now." Claudia announced. "Why are you leaving so soon? I thought you would see in the New Year with us. I hope you're not going home to be alone." her dad said in a worried tone. "No, Penny is having a party at her house, so I'm going home to get ready and then I'll make my way there." explained Claudia. "Sorry, I forgot to tell you."

Claudia then called Courtney into the bedroom. "I've got something for you." said Claudia, as she gave her a present. "Yippee." Courtney said excitedly. Courtney opened the gift and found a box and inside the box, there was a beautiful silver, keepsake necklace with a heart shaped locket.

When Courtney opened the locket, inside she found a tiny photograph of herself and her mother, taken at her last birthday party. "Oh mummy, this is lovely." smiled Courtney as she kissed her. "But mum, I've just had lots of Christmas presents, am I getting another present because I've been extra good?" Courtney asked proudly.

"Yes you've been well behaved, but I'm giving you this present because I love you very much. Whatever happens, I will always be proud of you and I will always be with you." Claudia said emotionally, as she struggled to keep her composure.

They walked back into the front room and Claudia prepared to say goodbye forever. She breathed a few slow deep breaths and tried to sound cheerful.

"Mum, Dad, I've got to go, so happy New Year to you both and I love you very much." as she spoke, she hugged her parents for a long time, then kissed them and said goodbye.

Courtney followed her to the door. "Goodbye my beautiful child, I wish Gods blessings upon you throughout your life, I love you." Claudia wrapped her arms around Courtney one last time and then she quickly left.

As she ran to the car, all her emotions burst out into an ocean of tears and the tissues she used to mop up the cry water were soaked through in seconds.

She quickly got into the car and when she looked up towards the house, she saw Courtney through the window, happily waving and blowing goodbye kisses to her. Unaware that this will be the last time she will see her mother alive.

Claudia couldn't bear to stay any longer, so she waved back at Courtney and beeped the horn before she sped off.

It was 11:30pm when Claudia arrived home and even

though she had half an hour to carryout the act, she felt calm, knowing that the pain was going to be over soon.

Claudia had a quick hot bath and then she wrapped herself in her brand new soft, cream towelling robe. She then made some tea and brought it upstairs.

She decided to put her best throwover on her bed. It was a nice beige satin colour, with brown embroidery around the edge.

Claudia lay down on the bed, enjoying the silky sensation of the bed sheet against her skin and then she shook her body vigorously, so that she would sink deeper into the sheets. She remained motionless for a while looking up at the ceiling.

After a short while, she got up and slowly sipped her drink. She turned around and pulled from the draw, the list of people she would like to attend her funeral and then she retrieved her pills.

She went downstairs, placed both of these on the dining table and looked at them for a while. She saw the pills as her ticket to a peaceful existence and eternal happiness.

She remembered what the pastor had preached at church. "If you kill yourself, you will not go to heaven. Because to take your life or anyone else's life is a sin in the eyes of the lord." however, Claudia didn't care, this was her only way out.

Claudia got up and walked to the kitchen. She retrieved a glass and a jug from the cupboard and filled them up with water. Ensuring that she had plenty of water, to swallow the fifty tablets she was prepared to take.

She returned to the front room, removed each tablet individually and placed them in a bowl and then she put the glass, the jug, the bowl of tablets and the funeral list on a tray. She was now ready to carry out the deed, as she slowly walked upstairs to her death.

New Year's Day had arrived. Courtney woke up early,

because she was eager to speak to her mother. She quickly dialled her home number and the phone rang and rang, but there was no reply.

Courtney ran into the bedroom. "Grandma, Granddad, I called mummy but she didn't pick up the phone." Courtney said anxiously. "Don't worry sweetie, she must have come home late from Penny's party, give her time to rest." Claudia's mother said.

About an hour later, Claudia's mother made several attempts to call her, but to no avail. "I don't know why, but Claudia's not answering her phone. She must have drunk too much." Claudia's mother said to her father.

"But I want to speak to mummy." complained Courtney. "I'll make you some lunch, then we will ring mummy one last time. If there's still no answer, I'll take you home to see her." said Claudia's mother.

The phone rang and Claudia's mother picked it up. "Hi mummy, Happy New Year to you" said the voice on the phone. "Happy New Year to you too. Did you enjoy yourself last night at the party? Claudia's mother asked.

"Yes it was lovely. But I have a slight headache because I drank a bit too much. Mummy, I've been trying to call Claudia but the phone keeps, ringing." Penny said worryingly. Penny always addressed Claudia's mother as mummy.

"We've been trying too, but there's no answer. I'll pop around to her house to see if she's ok. How was Claudia at your party last night?" Claudia's mother asked.

"She didn't come to my party. She said that she was going to spend New Years night with you." Penny declared. "Oh my god, I need to go and see if she's ok. I'll call you later." Claudia's mother said. She quickly got her coat and ran to the bus stop with Courtney. Hoping the bus would not delay her.

When they arrived, Claudia's mother decided to leave

Courtney with a neighbour, before she entered the house. If it was bad news, she didn't want Courtney to be there to witness it.

She slowly turned the key and opened the front door, scared of what she would find inside the house. She ran into every room desperately shouting Claudia's name, but she couldn't find her.

Then she realised that the only room she had not checked was the bathroom. She slowly pushed back the door and found Claudia in a bath full of water, lying motionless with her eyes closed.

Claudia's mother panicked, the shock of seeing her daughter in this state, caused her to struggle for breath. In the extremity of her grief, her knees weakened as she stumbled, leaning against the wall to balance herself.

She knew Claudia was a very sick woman and she wondered how she could miss the signs, that Claudia wanted to harm herself. "Oh my God, Claudia, wake up." she screamed frantically, as she began to violently shake Claudia.

Claudia's eyes opened. "Mum what are you doing? You scared me." said Claudia, as she jumped up and removed the headphones from her ears. "Well I, I." said her mother, as she stuttered her words. "Well you frightened me, I thought you were dead." she said sobbing with relief.

"Mum, don't be silly. I didn't hear you, because I was listening to music." Claudia said calmly. She stepped out of the bath and wrapped her robe around her. Claudia's mother, who was still in shock, followed Claudia into her bedroom. "When you weren't answering your phone and you didn't turn up at Penny's party, I began to worry." explained her mother.

"Well I decided to stay at home and celebrate with a bottle of drink. Don't worry Mum, I'm okay. Now where's Courtney? I want to see her." Claudia said, encouraging her mother to leave the bedroom, as she discreetly used her foot to push the bowl of tablets under the bed. Only leaving the empty bottle in sight.

As her mother left to fetch Courtney, Claudia looked back on the events that occurred, just before she was about to take the tablets.

Instead of swallowing the tablets, she had decided to drink the bottle of rum instead, hoping to numb the pain. The alcohol knocked her out, which was why she never heard the phone ringing.

Claudia didn't carry out the suicidal act, because she listened to that voice reminding her how devastating it would be for Courtney and her family, if she had died.

This was the same voice that spoke to her, when she was about to jump off the balcony in New York.

When Courtney came home, she embraced her and even though Claudia was grateful to be alive, she wondered why the voice of an angel would save her from suicide and prolong her days of suffering, while failing to cure her from her problems once and for all.

Chapter 14

HOPE AND HOPELESSNESS

As MUCH AS Claudia tried to blot Ricardo out of her mind and resist inviting him into her house, she found it impossible. Claudia could see that Ricardo was changing. Before, Ricardo used to tell Claudia to give him sometime and he will leave his girlfriend, to be with her. Nowadays, his sharp tongue and negative comments would destroy Claudia's dreams.

Whenever she would see Ricardo, she would embarrass herself by begging him to come back to her. She would fall at his feet and collapse in a sea of tears. "Pull yourself together, go and take your happy pills." Ricardo would arrogantly say.

"Look at how much time has gone by, I'd be crazy to go back to you, after all the hurt and pain that you caused me. I didn't want us to split up in the first place, I used to beg you to take me back. I'd be on my knees pleading with you, but you weren't interested." Ricardo would say.

He would always play the blame game and refuse to take any responsibility for their failed relationship.

Ricardo's birthday was coming up. Claudia was in denial that Ricardo had a partner and she didn't want to believe his relationship was that serious.

After all, he had only told Claudia about the girl recently, so Claudia presumed it was a very new relationship. With this in mind, she was hoping Ricardo would want to spend his birthday with her and Courtney, together as a family.

Claudia decided to phone Ricardo, to find out his intentions on that day. "Your birthday's coming up, I hope you don't have any plans, because I have lot of things in store for you." Claudia said in her sexy voice.

"Look you stupid woman, I am with someone and she wouldn't be very happy to know that you're talking to me in this way. Anyway, I wanted to know if my mother and I can take Courtney out for dinner on my birthday?" Ricardo said, changing his tone from angry to kind, as he realised that he shouldn't have shouted at Claudia, if he wants to get his way.

However, it was too late, his tactic didn't work because now Claudia was really upset. How dare Ricardo patronise Claudia, saying that he will be dining with just his mother alone. As if Claudia would believe that his girlfriend would not be there.

"Listen, you fool. You're the stupid one not me, so don't think you can out smart me. Obviously, your girlfriend would want to spend time with her man on his birthday. Well you can do what the hell you like, but that bitch will not be going anywhere near my daughter, you got that?" By now, Claudia was seething.

"Who are you calling a bitch? You're the bitch. If it weren't for me, you wouldn't have Courtney. I gave you our daughter." Ricardo said in a feisty, hurtful way. "Oh please. Does an intelligent word ever come out of your mouth? If you had to buy Courtney, you wouldn't have her, because you wouldn't be able to afford her?" Claudia said angrily.

"Why can't Courtney get to know my girlfriend? She's always around your family and your boyfriends." His comment angered Claudia even more.

"How dare you accuse me of being around lots of men? I am a decent, respectable woman and a good mother. You have a cheek to make demands where Courtney is concerned, you don't even pay maintenance. She doesn't live off air, you know?" Claudia shouted.

"Remember, I'm her father, so stop treating me like I'm a stranger. I pay what I can, don't force me to take you to court." threatened Ricardo.

Claudia took a few deep breaths to calm down, recharge her batteries and go for round two of the argument.

"You, a father, that's a joke. You are a sperm donor and nothing more. Don't over rate your stingy contribution. You need to get back into work and be a real man. You waste of space." Claudia said irately.

Ricardo tried to calm down the situation and attempt to butter her up to get his way, so he offered to take them both out on Sunday. "Come on Claudia, my birthday is my special day and I want my daughter by my side." Ricardo said desperately.

"Look Ricardo, why are you playing games with me? One minute you're all over me, then the next, your backing off and treating me badly. Don't mess with me Ricardo."

Claudia wanted Ricardo to see that playing with someone's emotions is a dangerous game. "Ricardo, you're not being fair. When I ended our relationship, I had no intention of getting back with you. So, I made sure that I didn't show you any form of affection, because I didn't want to give you false hope." Claudia explained.

"Anyway, I need to go." Ricardo said in denial. "Look Ricardo, in all the years we split up, you never mentioned that you had a girlfriend. If she is that important to you and she's going to be in your life, then I have a right to meet her, before I allow her to spend time with Courtney." Ricardo didn't answer, he just said goodbye and quickly put down the phone.

Obviously, Claudia wasn't interested in meeting Ricardo's girlfriend and she knew that Ricardo didn't want the two of them to meet either. However, her request wasn't unreasonable.

Claudia decided to take Courtney to the cinema to see the latest animated kid's movie and afterwards they went bowling, where Courtney thrashed Claudia and won the game by far. "That was great mum, I had so much fun today." Courtney said in appreciation.

On the way home, they stopped off at the supermarket to pick up some groceries. Claudia went to the checkout and prepared to pay for the goods.

"Sorry, but your card has been declined." the cashier stated. "I don't understand, I definitely have money on this card. Please try it again, it should go through." Claudia said nervously. Claudia entered her pin number again and waited. "I'm very sorry, but the payment has not been authorised. Do you have another card you can use?" asked the cashier.

To Claudia's horror, she had run out of money and she became extremely embarrassed, as the customers in the queue had become aware of her predicament. "No it's okay, I've got some money at home, I'll just go and get it, I don't live far." Claudia said, trying to act casual about the situation. "Okay I'll leave the groceries at the customer services desk, for when you return." explained the cashier.

Claudia grabbed Courtney's arm and hurried out of the shop in shame. "But mummy, you didn't buy my magazine."

Courtney cried. Unfortunately, she had to do without her shopping, because she didn't have any money at home either.

To make matters worse, the car broke down again. On the sixth attempt, it finally started and she was relieved when she got home safely.

She guided a sleepy Courtney out of the car and into the house. Then the phone rang. "Oh, whose that." Claudia said irritated by the interruption, she herself was tired and wasn't in the mood to answer the phone.

"Hello, who is it?" Claudia asked abruptly. "It's me." Ricardo replied. "My girlfriend want's to talk to you." he declared, but before Claudia could respond, Ricardo put his girlfriend on the line. "Hello," said this female voice down the phone. "I'm Ricardo's girlfriend. When do you want to meet me? Thursday, Friday, When?" she asked in an aggressive muffled tone.

Claudia was wondering who the hell this girl thought she was talking too, so Claudia responded appropriately. "I don't want to meet you, actually I have no intention of meeting you. I am a very busy lady because I actually work for a living. Therefore I have no time in my diary to fit you in." Claudia clarified.

"I work too, anyway my man told me all about you and you're this sad depressed person who's in darkness. He told me that you haven't had a man in years and you're always throwing yourself at him, begging him to take you back." his girlfriend said insultingly.

Obviously, it was true, Claudia has been single for a long time now, but how could Ricardo betray her trust and tell his girlfriend all of her business. Ricardo's true colours had emerged as an untrustworthy, wicked man who had no good intentions towards Claudia.

"Oh please, you don't know me, so how dare you

disrespect me. Do you think you actually have a man in your life? If Ricardo were a real man, then you wouldn't have to look after him. Look at you, paying all his bills, buying his clothes and filling his pockets with money. Your so desperate for a man that you even bought the car he drives. Poor you." Claudia continued, "By the way, he never even mentioned your name to me until now, that is how unimportant you are. Ask your man where he is in the evenings? He spends more time at my house, than he does at home with you, he's just using you." Claudia said angrily.

"He's in your house, really? He just told me that he doesn't even know where you live." shouted the girl and Claudia actually over heard Ricardo saying this in the background.

"Well, your man is a dirty liar. What other lies does he tell you? Remember you are second best and you always will be, because if I never got rid of him, he would not be with you, love." Claudia responded.

It seemed like Claudia's comments towards Ricardo's girlfriend, cut her like a knife. She could no longer bear to listen to the truth, so she slammed the phone down on Claudia.

Claudia was so angry with what Ricardo's girlfriend had told her, but she was more angry with herself, for sinking so low and resorting to arguing with another woman over a man, which she vowed she would never do.

How did Claudia get so weak? She was always a strong person and a fighter. It didn't make any sense. She's the one who creates opportunities and fulfils her ambitions. She's the intelligent professional woman with a good career and a lot going for her.

A woman would not get rid of a good man, so obviously ending it with Ricardo was the right thing to do. Why then would she so desperately want to be back with this evil, jobless, no good man?

Nobody should be that important to someone, to the point that if they can't have that person in their life, then life would not be worth living.

I can do much better, Claudia thought and then she thought again. No, I can't do much better, because if I could have, then I would have, along time ago.

The next day, there was an unexpected knock at the door. Claudia pushed back the curtains and saw Ricardo's car parked on her driveway. She couldn't understand what he wanted with her and what he was trying to achieve, by playing two women off against each other. Ricardo was very persistent and he continued to knock on the door until Claudia opened it.

"Oh, what a surprise. How can you be here at my house when you claim that you don't know where I live? You've got a nerve." Claudia shouted at Ricardo in the doorway.

Ricardo without shame, stepped inside the house and followed Claudia into the living room. "Listen, I had to tell her that I didn't know where you lived. Otherwise she would have given me grief. I don't love her, but at the moment I'm living with her, so I have to keep her happy." Ricardo said trying to soften Claudia up.

"Then why are you still with her? You can move in here with me. There's plenty of room, look how big my house is. I don't understand why you're with someone you don't love, when I have told you that I love you and I want to be with you. I can't deal with all these games Ricardo, it's driving me crazy." Claudia said desperately and clearly still weak over him.

As soon as she said that, Ricardo grabbed her and kissed her on her lips. This act, stupidly gave Claudia the hope she needed to believe that he really wanted her too and someday they would be together.

Ricardo decided to spend the day with Claudia and Courtney. They went to see a film and then they dined out at a restaurant. On the way home, Ricardo stopped at the supermarket and piled a few items into the basket. "Claudia, will you be able to lend me some money to buy these groceries? I'm just a bit short of cash at the moment." Ricardo asked.

Claudia stared at him in a way that showed she was not at all impressed with his request.

"Is this the reason why you're being so nice to me? Because you want to use me for my money?" Claudia asked with raised eyebrows, waiting for him to lie, or say the words that she wanted to hear, which when said, will probably make her back down and give him the money anyway.

"Babes, I would never use you for your money. You're my special girl, you'll always be my number one." Ricardo said convincingly, as he wrapped his arms around her waist.

Claudia smiled. Ricardo did say those words that made Claudia give up all sense of rationalization. In that instant, Ricardo made this insecure woman, feel special and Claudia happily obliged. "Okay, you better not let your girlfriend eat any of the things I buy for you." Claudia said suspiciously.

"Don't be silly, she's allergic to dairy products, so she can't have the cheese or the milk and she hates tuna fish anyway." explained Ricardo. "Here's the money." Claudia said gullibly, as she withdrew some of the cash her mother had transferred into her account, even though she barely had enough money for herself.

Ricardo lifted Courtney up and placed her on his shoulders. When they arrived home, Ricardo kissed Claudia goodbye and left.

After she put Courtney to bed, Claudia reflected on the

recent events and found her handling of the situation to be stupid and ridiculous.

Firstly, Ricardo puts his girlfriend on the phone to curse her, then he turns up at her house the next day, even though he claims that he doesn't know where she lives and then she lets him in.

She ends up kissing him, forgiving him and giving him money she doesn't have. Ricardo walks all over her and disrespects her.

It doesn't matter how bad Ricardo treats Claudia, anything he wants he gets and she can't say no to him, because she loves him. Claudia finally realises that Ricardo is never going to leave his girlfriend.

She then breaks down in tears and becomes so upset that, she phones her mother and tells her all about what has been going on.

"Well Claudia," she said, giving Claudia some motherly advice. "Firstly, a woman shouldn't chase a man. I didn't have to run after your father. Secondly, you must see that Ricardo is no good. You think he has changed but he hasn't. You think you can trust him, but you can't. A leopard does not change their spots."

Claudia's mother continued, "Don't ever let that snake back through your front door. How could he say that he has never been to your house before? The low life even takes your money when you have his daughter to support. I told you before not to give him your cash, because he might be doing things with it, this could be the reason why you don't have any money." her mother said suspiciously.

"Mum, I want to see Mr Nelson. I want him to reveal why I'm feeling this way." Claudia said desperately. "Claudia, didn't I tell you, he's not living in this country anymore." revealed her mother. "See, I can't get anything right. When he was around, I didn't want to see him and now I want to see him, he isn't around." cried Claudia.

"I'm sorry for what happened with Ricardo, but this should open your eyes and see that it's time to walk away. You are destroying yourself over a dirty scoundrel and if you're not careful, this could lead you to a pointless end." her mother said sadly.

Claudia's head was telling her that her mother was right, but even after all that had happened, her heart still had love for Ricardo. However, she tried to fight it and for the first time since her illness, she decided to cut Ricardo out of her life for good?

Chapter 15

I Do

THE DAY OF the wedding was finally here. It was a crazy morning in Annette's mother's house, with everyone running around, trying to find room to do their hair and make up.

The queue for the bathroom grew, but Annette didn't have that problem, because the second bathroom and the back bedroom was strictly only for her.

Annette wasn't an overly glamorous woman, so she opted for simplicity, choosing to style her hair and apply her own make up. Her wedding dress was a no frills strapless satin gown, with a low tiara and a short lace veil.

Meanwhile Ricky spent his last day of being single in the apartment with his brother. He decided to give Louise's mother an early morning call to ask her if he could have his daughter today.

"Hello." said Louise. "Hi Louise, its daddy. Let me speak to mummy." Ricky said anxiously. "Okay, mum, dad wants to speak to you." Louise shouted. Louise's mother came on the phone. "I just want to know if I can spend the day with Louise today?" Ricky asked.

"Well my friend has had a baby, so we're going to visit her today. Why don't you pick her up next week instead? Hello, hello . . ." she said, but there was no reply.

Ricky was so angry that his daughter was not going to be able to come to the wedding and his son was not going to be there either, as Wayne was a semi professional footballer and he couldn't miss his important European away game.

Philip could see that Ricky was upset. "What's wrong?" he asked. "Louise isn't coming to the wedding. Annette spent so much money on her bridesmaid dress, as well. This is the day that I am supposed to see my daughter, anyway. But her evil mother decided to make other plans." Ricky said disappointingly.

"How am I going to break the news to Annette? I don't want her to be upset on her special day. She adores Louise and she will be devastated to know that she won't be there. What a waste of time and money." Ricky fumed.

"Calm down," said Philip. "I know you're upset that none of your children will be at your wedding, but this is your day, try not to let anything or anybody spoil it." Philip advised, reaching out and patting Ricky on the back, to show his understanding of Ricky's pain.

Ricky looked at his watch and began to panic, because he had to be at the church for 1pm and it was already midday. He quickly showered and dressed, choosing to wear a white wedding suit. "This is it bro." Philip said. Ricky breathed a nervous sigh. The brother's hugged and then made there way to the church in Philips car.

As they arrived, Ricky's other brothers and his parent's were standing on the steps of the church entrance. The men were all wearing top hat and tails and his mother was wearing a lemon satin dress with a matching hat.

The day went by without a hitch, with a beautiful service and a small reception. After the speeches, the guests sang birthday wishes to Ricky and just before the night ended, Annette asked Ricky about his daughter. "Louise wasn't allowed to come then?" she asked. "I know, I'm sorry. Her mother made other plan's." Ricky said sadly. "You mean she's still sulking about what happened." Annette said sarcastically.

"Listen don't let her ruin our wedding, lets just dance and enjoy our day." Ricky said as he gently pulled Annette onto the dance floor and she rocked to the music in her husband's arms until the night came to an end.

The couple quickly settled into married life and the more Ricky relied on Annette, the more she felt in control. She believed that if she gave him what he wanted, then he would never leave her.

Ricky began to attend church more often and they were happy, except for one thing. Annette still desperately wanted a child, but continued to find it hard to conceive.

Annette and Ricky would often meet up with Pastor John after the Sunday service. They would tell him of their desires and the Pastor would pray for them and ask god to bless Annette with Ricky's child. "It is not right that she should remain childless. God, I ask you to let her have her wish." Pastor John would say.

Pastor John would regularly repeat that prayer and the couple would often pay money to him, to increase their chances of receiving their blessings. As time went on, although Annette spent time with Ricky's children, she still yearned for a child she could call her own.

Visits to the doctors were useless, they would continue to suggest a hysterectomy, which angered Annette. How many times do I have to tell the doctors that I am willing to endure the pain to give myself every chance of bearing a child in the future? She would say.

This yearning for a child, blighted their relationship. Ricky was also as desperate as Annette, to have a child in the home. They relied on the Pastor to make their dreams come true and he told the couple that they would have a break through on 22nd February.

Chapter 16

GOT TO KEEP MOVING ON

CLAUDIA DID AS her mother had told her and tried to move on from Ricardo. Over the next few days, Ricardo constantly rang her phone and Claudia continued to ignore his endless voicemail messages, until she eventually decided to answer his call.

"What?" Claudia said in an abrupt tone. "Oh, you're alive. Do you know how many times I've been trying to call you? I haven't seen my daughter for weeks and you didn't even have the decency to return my calls? Look, I'm coming down later, so make sure you're home." ordered Ricardo and he went on and on, until Claudia interrupted him.

"Enough. You are really boring me. Who do you think you are?" Claudia said angrily. "Why are you being so horrible to me, what's changed?" asked Ricardo. "I've changed, Ricardo. I'm not interested in playing your games anymore. This has been going on for too long now and I am putting a stop to it. You must have loved it, seeing two women argue over you, with us declaring our undying love for you and throwing our money at you." Claudia explained.

"Well all that has stopped now. I'm not going to be the stupid one anymore. I'm out of the equation now. You can keep your girlfriend, because I don't want you anymore and you better get used to how things are going to be, because everything has changed now." Claudia declared.

"What do you mean everything has changed?" Ricardo said in denial. "Well firstly, you are certainly not coming to my house anymore, because you're not welcome here. Secondly, I am tired of you and your antics and thirdly, stay away from me, Ricardo."

Claudia realised that she had to get Ricardo out of her life, so that she can have a chance of getting on with hers. Of course Ricardo didn't like the new arrangement, because this meant that he was no longer in control. However, Claudia had to show him that he was not important to her anymore and as difficult as it was for Claudia, she decided that it was time to get strong and stop all contact, until she had repaired her emotions.

Claudia was so adamant that she was ready to eliminate him out of her life, that the first thing she did was change her home telephone number. This also made it easier for Claudia to pretend that Ricardo didn't exist.

Claudia tried her best to get over her problems and get on with her life. Her job was very demanding but through the help of God, she continued to deliver first class work, within her challenging role.

It was 22nd February, a cold, chilly Friday morning. Claudia took Courtney to school and then drove to her parent's house, because she was going into town with her mother, to do a bit of retail therapy.

As she was driving down the dual carriage way, without warning, the car suddenly stopped again. It was a good thing Claudia was in the slow lane, which made it easy for her to park up away from the busy traffic.

Claudia's unreliable car was driving her crazy. She had taken it to the mechanic so many times before and each time they claimed, they had fixed the problem and for a while, the car would work ok. But then after a time, the same problem would recur. After a few attempts, she managed to get the car started.

Because the car would break down intermittently, Claudia did not feel safe to drive down the long stretch of the motorway, in case a speeding car crashed into the back of her. Therefore, Claudia usually had to stick to the quiet roads, which would take her longer to get to her destination.

In all her years of driving, she never had so much trouble with her car until now. Her patience was running thin, so she decided that she would drive the car less often.

"Hey parent's." Claudia announced as she arrived at there house. Claudia peeped her head around the bedroom door. "Where's dad?" Claudia asked. "Oh he went out early to get his newspaper." her mother replied.

The pair took the bus into town, but the traffic was so horrendous they had little time to shop. They just had time to have some lunch, before cutting short their shopping trip and rushing back to pick up Courtney. While her mother went home, Claudia made her way to the school.

As she walked through the playground, the secretary, Mrs Hampton called Claudia aside to talk to her privately. "Can I have a word?" Mrs Hampton said softly as she guided Claudia into the office. "Yes, Is Courtney ok?" Claudia asked in a concerned way. "Oh yes, Courtney is doing great. It's just that we had an unexpected phone call from Courtney's father." Mrs Hampton revealed. "Really?" Claudia beamed.

Mrs Hampton continued, "He sounded very concerned about you in particular. It's not my business, but he did mention that you had been feeling a bit low lately and he was worried that something may have happened to you. But due to our rules around confidentiality, I could not disclose any personal information to him." she explained.

Claudia was in a state of happiness and did not really hear everything Mrs Hampton had told her, all that she hung onto was the fact that, because Ricardo didn't have her new phone number, he went to all that effort to telephone the school office, just to see if she was ok.

"Mummy." Courtney shouted as she ran up to Claudia. "Hey gorgeous, did you have a good day?" Claudia asked, squeezing Courtney tightly. "Yes, look I've got a sweetie, because it was Andrew's birthday." Courtney grinned as she popped the sweet into her mouth. "Ohh, lucky you."

They left the school and drove home. By the time Claudia arrived, she looked at the red flashing light on the phone and saw that she had four messages.

As she listened to them, she heard Ricardo's voice. Claudia wondered how Ricardo found out her new number and why he decided to get in touch now, five weeks after she last heard from him. He definitely was making a good effort to track Claudia down.

The message said, "Hi it's Ricardo, I've not seen Courtney in weeks, so I came down to your house to give her some money, but you were out. I was worried about you and Louise, because you haven't been returning my calls. I even contacted the school to find out if you and Courtney were ok. Anyway, I'll be coming down tomorrow afternoon, so see you then."

Claudia was excited and decided to call Ricardo. His phone rang a few times and then he answered. "Hey Claudia, why have you been ignoring my calls? How have you been? Are you well?" he asked. "I'm great" Claudia replied.

"So, you haven't been suffering any illnesses, lately? Because there seems to be a virus going around." Ricardo asked curiously. "No, I'm good." Claudia confirmed, wondering why Ricardo was so interested in her health. "Anyway, I need to go. I'll be around tomorrow." Ricardo said bluntly, as he rushed off the phone. The tone that Ricardo used, sounded like he wasn't happy to hear from Claudia, but Claudia didn't take any notice of that, she was just excited that she had spoken to him. It made her realise how much she had missed him over the weeks.

"Courtney, your dad is coming to see you tomorrow." Claudia shouted upstairs to Courtney.

Claudia had decided a few weeks ago that she needed space away from Ricardo, to give herself the opportunity to heal. There was too much tension between them and the endless arguments was not doing her any good.

Thankfully, although she was still depressed, Claudia was slowly getting a little bit stronger every day. However, because she still had strong feelings for Ricardo, she was happy that he showed he still cared about her. This made her believe that Ricardo still probably loved her and she felt comforted by what she chose to believe.

Claudia began to feel a bit better and she decided to attend the Friday evening bible studies. As usual, the pastor called upon Claudia to read passages from the bible, because he liked the way she read in her soft, clear tone.

When the lesson ended, Penny greeted Claudia with a hug. "Girl, how are you?" Penny asked, hoping that Claudia's depression had past. "I'm still sad, not much has changed unfortunately and to make matters worse, I have no money. I'm in total debt." Claudia admitted.

"Claudia, when I've been to the supermarket with you, I realise that you pick up, one carton of juice, one tin of sweet corn, one of everything. I know you're too scared to spend the money, but it would be better if you buy a least four of everything to fill up your cupboards. That way if you run out of money, at least you will have food to last you a while. Anyway Claudia, I've noticed that your complexion has got darker." Penny said curiously. She was very concerned for Claudia. "I don't know, it must be a sun tan." Claudia joked.

Penny knew that, what Claudia was saying was ridiculous. How could someone get a suntan in the middle of winter? "Claudia, I have to rush because Steve is waiting for me. But I'll call you soon."

Penny ran outside and got into Steve's car, she seemed very worried about Claudia. "Steve, I just saw Claudia. Her skin has become very, very dark since I last saw her and she's still very depressed." Penny said in a panic.

"Penny, you know what that means?" Steve said in a serious tone. Penny did not respond, she stayed silent and just shook her head as Steve sped off into the night.

As soon as Claudia opened her front door, she saw a rat running down the hallway and she watched it as it disappeared into the storage cupboard. The rat moved so quickly, she wondered if she ever saw it at all. Claudia believed that her mind was playing tricks on her, because as far as she was concerned, Pest Control had dealt with the problem.

Still, she decided to open the cupboard and look around. She saw some black small things on the floor and something that looked like a round ball.

When she went up close to inspect it, her worst fears were confirmed. There were fresh droppings and the shrivelled skeleton of a rat on the floor. She stayed strong for Courtney's sake, but after Courtney went to sleep. Claudia sat on the edge of her bed and began to weep.

It was a beautiful morning. The sun pierced through the curtains, but that didn't stop Claudia and Courtney from sleeping in late. By the time they had breakfast and got dressed, the doorbell rang and Courtney opened it. "Mum, its Dad at the door." she said and even though Courtney hadn't spent time with Ricardo in weeks, she didn't seem too excited to see him.

Claudia was quietly pleased that Ricardo had come around, but she was still angry with him for hurting her. She had not seen Ricardo for a while now and she was scared that her feelings for him would become out of control again.

It was important for Claudia to contain her emotions and to show an uncaring demeanour, although she made sure that she looked nice, to remind Ricardo of what he was missing.

Claudia said a weak hello to Ricardo, as she walked down the hallway towards him. "How is it that I've not been able to see my daughter?" Ricardo said sternly. "Don't start Ricardo, I'm a busy lady, your daughter's a busy girl and you're an unreliable man. You're here now so just try and spend some quality time with Courtney, Ok?" Claudia said firmly.

Courtney followed Ricardo to his car, while Claudia looked on. She didn't trust Ricardo with Courtney and had this fear that one day he may try to kidnap her. She thought about the reason why Ricardo continued to keep his address a secret from Claudia and maybe this was it.

"Where are you taking me dad, can we go for a pizza?" Courtney said excitedly. "Sorry sweetie, I can't stay long because I have a job to do, but here's some pocket money." Ricardo said as he dropped some measly coins into Courtney hand. Ricardo seemed miserable and it was strange that he was so eager to get away so quickly.

However, Courtney was happy that she was able to stay and play with her friends, instead of going out with her father. Especially after the lack of effort her father was making with her. Courtney was smart and she knew the value of money, a few coins given to her after many weeks was not good enough and she expressed her dissatisfaction with his inability to pay for her keep.

"Dad, I want paper money, not coins." she said in a disappointed tone. "Don't worry, I'll come back next week and give you some more money and if you're not at home, I'll drop it through the letter box." Ricardo said convincingly. "Okay dad." Courtney said, satisfied with another one of his lies.

"Mum can you give me my pocket money? There's a magazine that I want to buy." Courtney asked. "Ok Courtney, run upstairs and bring me my bag." advised Claudia.

While Courtney was gone, Claudia had an opportunity to talk to Ricardo. "Excuse me. Please do not insult Courtney by giving her the loose change in your pocket. She is worth much more than that. If you carry on doing what you are doing, one day she will insult you by rejecting your offer, as it seems like you're more in need of that money than she is. Get a job. Ricardo." Claudia said angrily.

Even though Claudia's heart was weak over Ricardo, she still had no problem in telling him off when it was necessary.

Ricardo began to get angry, but before he had a chance to respond, Courtney had returned. "Here's your bag Mummy." Courtney said, as Claudia took out her purse and gave Courtney her weekly allowance.

Claudia went back inside the house to get the broom and while Ricardo spoke to Courtney, every so often he would look over at Claudia. Studying her appearance and watching the way her hour glass figure moved from side to side, as she swept the dust away from the door and Claudia, discreetly looked over at Ricardo as she felt his eyes on her.

Ricardo had struggled to let go of their volatile relationship and he moved on into a new relationship on the re-bound. Because of this, Claudia believed that his girlfriend was second best and that she was the one that Ricardo really wanted to be with, but she felt that he was just playing hard to get.

Claudia continued to play it cool and avoided verbally expressing her love to Ricardo and breaking down crying, as she used to do before. Her pain was still evident and his rejection made her feel ugly. But she still made an effort to dress up and take care of her appearance.

Claudia found Ricardo's flying visit strange. It was unusual that he didn't want to spend time with Courtney, since he hadn't seen his daughter for many weeks. Anyway, Courtney hugged her Dad and waved goodbye to him and then Claudia took Courtney to the sweet shop to spend her money.

Later that evening, there was a knock at the door. It was Claudia's mother. "Hi mum, guess what? Ricardo came by to see Courtney." Claudia announced. "He had the audacity to give Courtney some small change for maintenance money." Claudia explained. "I tell you, that man is up to something. One minute, you don't hear from him for weeks and the next he turns up out of the blue, both yesterday and today. Don't trust that man." her mother stated.

"Mum, I don't trust him. In the past, I would have invited him in the house, but now, he has to stay outside." explained Claudia.

"It was hard, but I had to fight it. I've noticed that since I stopped Ricardo coming to my house, I'm starting to get stronger everyday. I'm even putting on a little bit of weight and sleeping better at night." Claudia said positively.

"Well I'm glad to hear that you are getting better day by day." Strangely enough, Ricardo came back to Claudia's house, again, the very next day.

Chapter 17

THE DAY OF REVELATION

THE PHONE RANG early in the morning, causing Claudia to jump out of her sleep. "Hello." Claudia said sleepily. "Claudia, your situation needs to be resolved quickly, it is an emergency. I want you to see someone, who may be able to reveal things to you and give you answers to why you're feeling this way." Penny said anxiously.

Claudia thought about what she was saying and figured that Penny was going to introduce her to a pastor, to talk through her feelings. "What time shall I meet you?" Claudia asked. "Come to my house for 7pm this evening." Penny confirmed.

Claudia was still uncertain as to what to expect. She didn't really want to talk to a stranger about her problems, but she trusted Penny and met her at her house as agreed. She decided not to bring Courtney, leaving her with a neighbour, instead.

Penny's partner, Steve drove them to a terraced house on a busy street. A slim man, with large brown eyes, answered the door. He was wearing jeans and trainers and didn't look at all like a pastor.

Steve did the introduction. "Claudia, meet Merde, Merde meet Claudia." Then Merde invited Claudia into the kitchen. Claudia was a bit nervous because she didn't know what to expect, so she asked Penny to go in with her.

Merde began to pray and when he finished, he produced a pack of cards from his briefcase. He told Claudia to shuffle the pack. Claudia slowly and clumsily did as she was asked. Merde then instructed her to individually pick a card and give them to him. At that point, Claudia realised that Merde was a Psychic and for each card Claudia gave to Merde, he revealed shocking truth's about her life.

Card no 1

"You were born to travel, what are you doing in this country? You should be living in America."

Card no 2

"Your cousin Felecia is a good person."

Card no 3

"You didn't care about your education when you were at school. But, you are intelligent because you graduated in law."

Card no 4

"You should bathe in the blu and salt that your mother told you to do."

Card no 5

"Who is Miss Gloria? She is a witch. She sent a spirit to

walk with you from a young age so that you won't be able to attract a man."

"What? I can't believe this" Claudia blurted out. "I knew there was something wrong. I knew that premonition meant something."

Card no 6

"Your name has been placed on a magic table."

Card no 7

"The girl who introduced you to your daughter's father is no good. She's also a witch." Merde revealed.

"Oh my God, that's Cheryl." said Claudia as she looked over at Penny in disbelief.

"Wait, You said these people are witches. What do you mean?" Claudia asked.

"You're not supposed to interrupt me when I'm reading. What is your definition of a witch?" Merde said, as he threw the question back at her.

"Well a witch is an evil person who puts spells on people." Claudia said simply.

Merde nodded his head and then he continued.

Card no 8

"You've been having many arguments with Ricardo lately."

Card no 9

"Ricardo's girlfriend saved a message you left on the phone and used your voice to put a spell on you"

Card no 10

"Your life is in a mess."

Card no 11

"Why do you want to kill yourself over this man? You love him more than you love yourself."

Card no 12

"The rats that you had in your home was a curse. This is why you couldn't get rid of them."

Card no 13

"Your baby's father has an item of your clothing in his car."

Card no 14

"When they put the spell on you, they spelt your name wrong, which is why the work failed the first time."

Card no 15

"The spirit is tampering with the electrics on your car, causing it to breakdown."

Card no 16

"You are not supposed to have no money, no car, no job or a home. You are even supposed to lose your daughter."

Card no 17

"There is a wreath over your head."

Claudia was unable to react to all these revelations and stood there in a state of shock.

Card no 18

"You have missed death already. But your life was saved, because you were born feet first and because your mother is a spiritual person."

Card no 19

"You're supposed to die, either by a car accident, a stroke or by some other means."

Claudia was astounded. Slowly, she turned over her last card.

Card no 20

"You have an evil spirit around you. It was sent by Ricardo to destroy you, because he wants to take your daughter. The spirit lies down next to you at night and it follows you everywhere you go." Merde revealed.

"No, no, no. Ricardo was so nice to me, I trusted him. How could Ricardo do this to me?" Claudia wailed.

The truth had stared her in the face. All that she was hearing was shocking and unbelievable. "Merde, you have just met me and you know more about my life than I do," said Claudia.

Merde asked Claudia to shuffle the cards again and pull out a card from anywhere in the pack. Claudia was in a daze but she chose a card from the middle of the pack.

When Merde turned over the card, Penny let out a scream. Claudia had chosen the death card, which is a picture of a skeleton.

Claudia was disorientated and she did not understand exactly what was happening around her. Merde asked her to shuffle the pack of cards, for the second time. Claudia did as she was asked and she selected another card from the pack.

Penny began to cry. "What? What?" Claudia said. "What's going on?" Claudia was confused and she really didn't understand the danger she was in. Shockingly, Claudia had chosen the very same death card for the second time.

"I will not even ask you to pick a card for the third time."

Merde said in a concerned tone. Merde knew that Claudia definitely would have chosen the Skeleton card again, because he knew her fate.

Merde explained to Claudia that death was in her midst and she would need to be treated quickly, otherwise she would not survive.

"You missed death already, you know. I can tell you the date they had set for you to pass away." Merde declared.

Claudia quickly stopped him. "No, don't tell me," she shouted. "I don't want to know, I don't want to know." Claudia repeated. "Alright then, I can see that you are scared, so I won't tell you." Merde said reassuringly.

Strangely enough, even though Claudia felt devastated by what was revealed to her, she noticeably felt better. The depression eased, the anxiety disappeared and the shaking stopped. For the first time in months, she felt well again.

Claudia asked Merde why she suddenly felt a lot better, after just one reading. Merde explained, "Claudia, you came to my house with an evil spirit. But because my house is holy, the spirit could not enter through the front door." revealed Merde.

"You became depressed after this evil spirit was sent to you. Because the spirit transferred the suicidal thought into your mind. This is why you had a strong desire to harm yourself. This spirit went everywhere with you, to work, to home, even on your holiday. Eventually you would have killed yourself." Merde explained.

"Therefore, no matter what you did or where you went, the spirit was always there tormenting you. The reason why you would tremble and shake, was because the spirit would enter your body and take over all control of your thoughts and your actions. Throughout your months of suffering, you was depressed 24/7 because the spirit was by your side 24/7." Merde declared.

Claudia remained silent, to give herself time to digest this information. It all made sense, why else would she be so stupid to love Ricardo? She could only ever have those feelings by force.

Merde continued by saying, "The reason why you felt better almost instantly, was because you left the spirit at my front door and you came in on your own. That was the first time you got any break from the spirit and therefore you quickly felt well." Merde explained

"You were ill, because the spirit made you ill. You now feel better because the spirit is not with you, but remember the spirit is waiting for you outside." Merde declared.

Claudia screamed with fear but Merde reassured Claudia. "Don't worry I can help you, we will speak about it tomorrow."

As Merde walked them to the car, Claudia decided to question him about Ricardo. "So, Ricardo really wanted to kill me, to get custody of Courtney?" asked Claudia in disbelief. "Yes, your sickness was all down to him." Merde confirmed. "This man is actually more evil than Satan." Claudia said in astonishment.

This news overwhelmed Claudia, so she decided to change the subject and question Merde about the rats that he had mentioned in the reading.

"Merde, you said that the rat infestation in my home was a curse. How can that be possible?" Claudia asked curiously. "Well, the rats were not your normal everyday rodents. They were spirits." Merde explained.

"Excuse me." Claudia said in a shocked tone. "Well, a spirit can turn into any creature except a bee." explained

Merde. "Why?" Claudia asked. "Well bees are clean and they make honey." confirmed Merde.

"So, let me just make sure I understand what you are actually saying to me. These rats were actually spirits." Claudia repeated.

"Claudia, that's why you couldn't eradicate the rats from your home and all the poison in the world wouldn't have solved the problem. You were destroying the rats but not the spirit, because spirits live on forever. The spirit can multiply into dozens of rats, so when the rats died, the spirit just turned into more rats." Merde confirmed.

"Oh my God, I am shocked that these things are actually possible." Claudia said. "What you should have done to get rid of the rat problem, was to protect your home from spirits." Merde revealed.

"Things like a horseshoe, a tape measure and ammonia are good for protection." explained Merde. "I've heard about the horseshoe. But how does a tape measure or ammonia help?" Claudia asked.

"The reason why spirits are afraid of the tape measure, is because it brings back memories of when they passed away, when the tape was used to measure their coffin and spirits hate the ammonia, because it's like acid to the spirit. If you sprinkle ammonia in your home, the spirit will quickly leave, because the ammonia can burn them in a spiritual way." explained Merde.

"How interesting. People need to be educated about these things. I wondered why my life was so bad. I thought I was just an unlucky person. People need to look at their lives and if they are not fulfilled in certain areas of their lives, it could be caused by an evil force."

Claudia continued, "many people would say that to believe this is foolish. However, I believe God sent you to me to teach me about this way of life. If the non-believers affected by curses want to continue to be a slave to their enemies, then those jealous ones will continue to laugh in the misery they have caused. People have laughed at me for many years, but they can't anymore. I have been blessed with a miracle." Claudia said with passion and relief.

Merde smiled. "I like the way you talk. Could I invite you to give a speech at my next Psychic event?" Merde stated. Claudia was flattered. "Well, I don't normally do public speaking, but I will for you." Claudia said. Merde thanked her and said goodbye.

Steve dropped Claudia home just after midnight. Claudia was worried because she remembered that Merde said there was an evil spirit around her.

She went to collect Courtney from her neighbour's house and they both ran home. She was so scared and she wondered whether she should get a taxi to her parent's house or just stay at home and be brave. Claudia reluctantly opted for the latter.

As she slowly walked into her house, Claudia tiptoed and looked all around, half expecting to see the spirit. Ironically, Claudia was unaware that the spirit was right next to her the whole time.

Claudia put Courtney to bed, opened the bible and placed it at the top of the bed. Hoping this holy book would have the power to scare the spirit away. Claudia then rang her mother and began to tell her mother all that was revealed to her today. She finally went to bed at 3am.

Merde spoke to Claudia the next day and reminded her that she must get her treatment, as death was all around her. "I will get the materials to cleanse you and then I will provide you with a guard that you need to wear at all times, to protect you from any curses that people may try to put on you in the future." Merde explained.

All of this was still very surreal for Claudia, but she was glad that she had finally met someone who could help her.

The next day Claudia's mother came around, then shortly afterwards Merde arrived with Penny. Merde got to work and gave Claudia her treatment. At that point, she became cleansed of all curses, old and new. He also gave her a good luck charm to protect her from future spiritual attacks. Claudia felt uplifted, with peace in her heart.

Her depression magically disappeared, the obsessive love she had for Ricardo had gone, proving what she had believed all along, that her love for Ricardo was not real. A new person emerged within Claudia and she felt even better than before her depression, because she had curses on her before Ricardo made her ill.

Claudia had never felt so good in all of her entire adult life. Her nonchalant attitude and overwhelming happiness, gave her a sense of peace. As she lay down to rest, she entered into a euphoric transcendent state that was so strong, it made her weak.

She slept for a few hours and when she woke up, she felt like a new woman. She found her mother, Merde and Penny in the dining room, laughing and joking and feeling happy that Claudia was well again. "Did you have a good rest?" her mother asked with a wide smile. "Yes, it was lovely, I slept without a care in the world." replied Claudia.

"Look how your natural skin tone has come back." her mother said. Claudia turned towards Merde and asked, "Why did my sickness affect my colour?"

Penny immediately jumped in and explained, "Claudia, do you remember when I asked you why your skin had got so dark?" Claudia nodded. "Well that was because I was worried about you. It's a sign that you had a spirit on you, which was why I wanted you to get help as soon as possible." Penny declared. "Really?" Claudia said in a state of shock.

"Claudia, I realised that you were in a dangerous situation, because I saw what happened to my friend when she had a spirit on her. Her skin colour got darker, she became sick and eventually died of a stroke. Well, that's what the doctors claimed, but I know that the spirit killed her. I knew you needed to get help quickly." Penny explained.

"Well now I am the happiest person alive." Claudia said as tears filled her eyes. "I just want to let you know that I am feeling 100% better. That depression has now lifted. I am looking forward to the future now and I am excited about what God has in store for me. Thank you for getting me the help I needed and for your love and support." Claudia said with gratitude.

"When I was suffering, I had a great desire to talk and let my feelings out and you all listened to me, even though I kept repeating myself. You had patience with me and the talking slowly helped me through each day. Anyway Claudia is back, but in better form." Claudia announced.

"Many people didn't understand what I was going through, so they distanced themselves. But you two came closer to me and I am grateful for that." Claudia said passionately.

Penny and Claudia's mother were moved by her words. "You deserve to be happy. My support was from the heart, because I care about you. Now you can enjoy your life." Penny explained.

"It's your time now Claudia. The depression was not you. Just believe that good people still do exist. Know what you want, ask God for what you want, but make sure you are ready to receive the goodness he has for you, because it's going to be wonderful." Penny said softly.

Merde explained how this healing process would affect

her. "Claudia, now that you have had your treatment. Over the next week or so, you will feel very sleepy and at times you may need to rest during the day. Also you will quickly gain the weight that you lost, so take it easy over the next few days." Merde advised.

Merde then thought about catching the spirit. "Can you remove that evil thing from my house today?" Claudia asked anxiously. "No, I have to set a trap first. I need to throw white rice into every room of the house and it must be left for a few days before I can catch the spirit." explained Merde. Claudia was disappointed and fretful, because she knew she would be scared until the spirit leaves her house.

Over the next few days, Claudia was unable to sleep. She couldn't wait for the day when Merde was able to catch the spirit. She thought about the concept of what Merde was about to do and found it all unreal.

Merde is going to catch a spirit into a bottle and remove it from my house. How crazy is that? Claudia thought, but she felt relieved and didn't care what Merde had to do, to make her feel better.

Merde warned Claudia that as the days go by, she will notice that the rice will start to split. "When you see this, it means that the spirit is eating the rice." Merde explained. "Spirits eat?" Claudia asked in a disbelieving tone. "Yes." Merde said.

Because this was very normal for Merde, he responded as if to say, how could you ask such a silly question? "Merde, has the curse on my finances disappeared as well?" Claudia asked, "Yes, you will see a difference on your next pay day." Merde confirmed. Claudia reflected on the times when she didn't have enough money for food and how hard things were for her.

Merde was due to have his annual Psychic event the next

day and because Claudia had suffered the worst case of danger Merde had seen in a long time, he wanted Claudia to talk about her experiences. Claudia agreed and although she was nervous, she made a great speech.

Chapter 18

THE TRUTH ABOUT
THE LIES

MEANWHILE, THE 22ND February came and went, as Ricky and Annette anxiously awaited their blessings. "I went to see Louise today, but nobody was at home. I spoke to Claudia and she seemed to be okay. I thought Claudia would have been sick in the hospital by now. I mean the pastor did say that she was supposed to be dead already." Ricky said angrily.

"Whatever." Annette snapped. Annette was very jealous of Ricky's former girlfriend and she couldn't bear to hear that Claudia was still alive, because that meant she wouldn't have the opportunity of being a full time mother to Louise.

"I'll visit again over the next few days. I don't want Louise to be alone when it happens." Ricky explained.

In the proceeding days, Ricky visited Claudia to see if everything was okay with her. Although he had expected her to be sick, Claudia was as fit as a fiddle and she definitely didn't seem as if she was on her deathbed, as Ricardo had hoped.

"I went to Claudia's house again today and there's nothing wrong with her." Ricky admitted to Annette. "I couldn't believe she was so strong. She was standing there, sweeping the front yard. I just stood there, in shock." Ricky explained. "Oh stop talking about her all the time. I'm getting fed up of it." Annette said angrily. Oh dear, it seemed like Annette's insecurities had surfaced again.

The next day, Annette decided to call Pastor John. "Pastor, you said that we should receive our blessing on Friday, but it didn't happen." Annette declared to the Pastor. "I don't know what happened, my rituals usually work. I'll tell you what I will do, I will carry out another strong prayer and in 9 days time you will receive your wish." reassured the Pastor.

"Can you write down the details again, so that I can confirm I have spelt the names correctly? If I've made a mistake with the names, it weakens the work. Just text me over the information." The Pastor instructed.

Annette sent the text over to the Pastor and then she phoned Ricky. "Ricky, where are you?" she asked "I've just parked up outside. I'll talk to you when I get upstairs." Ricky replied.

Annette sat in the kitchen anxiously tapping her fingers on the table, waiting for Ricky to come in. "What did he say then?" Ricky asked, as he walked through the door. "There may have been a spelling mistake. The work is not so powerful when that happens. He asked me to text him the details again and then he will carry out the ritual again, which is expected to work in 9 days time." explained Annette.

"I hope this man isn't messing us around. This better work, otherwise he'll have me to deal with. We've paid him too much money for this to fail." Ricky fumed. "Babes, calm down. We must have faith. Just believe it will work." reassured Annette.

The phone rang, it was the Pastor. "Annette, I received your text and I noticed that I was missing the letter A in the name. The name that Ricky gave me was misspelt. That's the reason why the work was weak." explained the Pastor.

"Okay, because the mistake was our fault, I will give you £750 to buy all the things you need to get. Do whatever you want to Claudia, just make sure it's as powerful as it can be." Annette said deviously.

"Ok, I will buy the materials and make it stronger than before. Don't worry, I will set it up over my alter tonight and this time it will definitely work in nine days time, I promise you. Anyway take care of yourself." reassured the Pastor.

In the middle of the night, Annette and Ricky tossed and turned. Neither could sleep. "The Pastor said that you definitely spelt Claudia's name wrong, because he checked the paper that you gave him at the time." Annette revealed. "Damm" Ricardo said in frustration, as he sat up in bed.

"This has delayed the work. But never mind it will work next time, because Pastor now has all the correct information, plus I've agreed to pay him more money." Annette revealed. "Thanks babes, you're the best." Ricardo said as he leant over to kiss her. They spent the early hours talking about how happy they will be when the work is completed.

The next day, Annette met with the Pastor and gave him the £750, as promised. The Pastor went to purchase the necessary items. When he returned home, he went upstairs and laid out all the materials on to his alter.

He copied the information written in Annette's text, onto some thick cream paper and then he mixed his lotions and potions and prayed a strong prayer. Commanding the work to manifest in 9 days time.

Annette and Ricky waited in anticipation for their dreams to come true in nine days time. But unfortunately, they were to be disappointed for the second time. The Pastor called Annette the day after he set up the spell in a panic.

"Hello Pastor." said Annette. She put the phone on loudspeaker, so that Ricky could listen in on the conversation. "Look, this ritual is not going to work. I don't know what has happened, but when I went into my bedroom, I noticed that my alter has been damaged and all the material has been thrown on the floor. It seems like someone has cancelled my prayer and destroyed the work. This has never happened to me before, I'm so sorry." explained Pastor John.

Ricky shouted, "I want a refund, I want every penny back. We gave you so much money for you to do the work properly, but you failed us." Ricky said furiously. "Look I'll advise you to forget everything and move on with your lives." defended Pastor John. "Just accept that maybe it's not going to happen." he advised.

"You hypocrite, you stand there in church on a Sunday and encourage the congregation to believe that their lives will change for the better and then you tell us to forget our dreams." Ricky shouted. "I knew I should have asked Mr Yardley to do the work, instead of you. My mother has known him for years and he has never once disappointed her. You're useless." Ricky said insultingly. Pastor John didn't want to discuss the matter any further, so he immediately ended the call.

"How dare he put the phone down on me? Right I'm going over to that church to deal with him right now." Ricky said, as he picked up his coat.

Annette placed her hand on his shoulder. "Look Ricky, you can't mess with a powerful man like him. You don't know what he could do and I don't want anything bad to happen to you. Maybe it's just not meant to be." explained Annette.

Ricky punched the wall in anger and shouted, "Did you say it's not meant to be? Oh you're wrong, it's definitely meant to be and if Mr Yardley can't do the work, then I'll find someone else and I won't stop searching and I'll never give up, until I find someone that can give me what I want." Ricky said desperately.

Annette had a confused look on her face. "What about me? Why didn't you say that you won't give up until we, get what we want?" screamed Annette, emphasising the word we. "We, there's no we you stupid woman." replied Ricky. Annette burst into tears "But, I'm your wife, don't you love me?" sobbed Annette.

"Love you, I've never loved you. I don't even know why I married you. You failed me. There's no point in me being with you, now that I didn't get my daughter." Ricky said, hurting Annette even more.

"You used me. You took my money, I paid your bills, I bought your car. I didn't even see the £5000 you got for winning the DJ competition. I thought we really had something special, we were good together." cried Annette.

Annette followed Ricky into the bedroom, where he grabbed a bag and began to throw his clothes into it. "Well you're a fool. Listen, a word of advice for when you move on into another relationship. If your man doesn't introduce you to his family, he doesn't love you and if you have to buy a man's love, then it's not real. The divorce papers will be in the post. Have a nice life, see ya." Ricky said coldly, as he grabbed his car keys and slammed the front door behind him.

Annette ran after him and begged Ricky not to leave her. "I'm nothing without you." she said desperately.

Ricky raced down the stairs, without a second glance. Leaving Annette devastated and crumpled on the floor, crying like a baby. Ricky never really loved Annette and when their devilish, cunning plan failed, he left Annette in a heartbeat.

So there you have it. Ricky, better known as DJ Ricky is actually Ricardo. He had two children from two different women, Wayne from Elaine and Courtney from Claudia. He called his daughter Louise, by her middle name, because he didn't like the name Courtney.

Ricardo found it hard to move on from Claudia, after she finished the relationship and he spent the next few years wrestling with his emotions.

He had a stronger connection towards Claudia than he had with Elaine, because Claudia was his true love and he had stong feelings of having to protect his daughter.

Ricardo would regularly visit Pastor John with Annette, asking Pastor John to make up evil spells, that he would send to Claudia, to make her ill.

Ricardo set out to trick Claudia into loving him, so that she would allow him into her home. Once inside, he had the opportunity to place a potion of destruction in her attic, which strengthened the work.

Claudia gave Ricardo her money, not realising that he put a curse on her finances. During Claudia's illness, he got closer to her, to see with his own eyes that the curse he placed on her, was working and then he would laugh at her behind her back.

He convinced Annette that Claudia was evil and that she should help him destroy Claudia to get Courtney and because Annette was childless, she agreed. Placing curses on people was Annette's passion. After all, she was inadequate and had little confidence.

Moreover, towards the end, Ricardo stayed away from Claudia for 6 weeks and then subsequently visited her on the day of her death. Even telephoning Courtney's school, hoping they would give him the good news that Claudia had passed away.

Realising she was still alive, he visited the following two days, hoping that he would see Claudia breathe her last breath and then leave with Courtney in his arms.

Ricky was a broken man. For someone to go to great lengths to get what they wanted and fail, naturally will mess up a persons mind. The days leading up to Claudia's death, were filled with anxiety and excitement for Ricky and Annette. Because that was the day they expected to receive their blessings and Annette looked forward to the day of finally being a mother to Claudia's daughter.

As you can see, there is nothing to be gained for doing evil. You may win a few battles, but never the war. Imagine the shame they feel now that they have been found out. They will never be able to hold there heads up in Claudia's presence again.

Chapter 19

GENIE IN A BOTTLE

MERDE AND STEVE arrived at Claudia's house at 6am to catch the spirit. Merde got to work straight away and proceeded to communicate in a language that the spirit understood, in order to connect with it.

Claudia watched in astonishment, as Merde appeared to transcend to a higher realm and chant, and the way you would entice a dog with a bone, Merde tricked the spirit by pouring rice into a bottle.

After a short while, the spirit entered the wine bottle. Suddenly the bottle turned cloudy. Claudia stood back in amazement, she was very shocked at what she had just witnessed, but relieved to know that she could now begin to bury her horrible past and look forward to a brighter future.

As Merde was about to secure the bottle, he unexpectedly fell on the floor and began to groan in pain. Steve reacted quickly and immediately ran towards the bottle. Claudia was worried. "Steve, what's wrong with Merde?" she said worryingly.

Steve began to explain, "Well, when Merde covered the bottle, the spirit got angry and hit his finger with such force, that he fell on the floor. It was a good thing I was able to place the cap on the bottle, before the spirit had a chance to escape." explained Steve.

Claudia ran to Merde's aid and helped him back on to his feet. "Should I call an ambulance? I don't know what to do, Merde, will you be okay?" Claudia said hysterically.

Merde slowly sat down on the chair. "Pass me a beer." he instructed, still groaning in pain.

He quickly drank the beer and allowed himself time to recover and gain his strength back. "Not anybody can do this job and if you're not experienced, the spirit can kill you." warned Merde.

Merde and Steve quickly taped up the bottle to keep the spirit safely inside and Claudia was relieved that the deed was done. Merde was now ready to throw the bottle into a flowing river.

As Merde was about to reach over and pick up the bottle it started to shake violently. The bottle immediately turned opaque and then it became transparent, to reveal a series of unusual shapes, until a fuzzy image of a persons face formed.

"How dare you come in here and interrupt my job?" A voice bellowed from the bottle. Within no time at all, Claudia picked up her feet and ran out of the room, screaming in such fear that she had made herself sick. "Look you evil spirit, it's all over. You will never be able to harm Claudia or anyone else ever again." Merde snapped.

As Claudia cleaned herself up and bravely returned to the kitchen, the spirit immediately turned 180 degrees to face her. It had an angry look on its face, as it prepared to confess all to Claudia.

"Claudia, Pastor John woke me up after 120 years, 2 months and 12 days of resting. My job was to destroy you. I went everywhere with you and I would have continued to do so, until I killed you." the spirit revealed.

This is unbelievable, spirits speak, Claudia thought, stunned by what she was seeing. The spirit continued, "The first time I was supposed to kill you, it didn't work, so I returned to my master who strengthened my power, to make sure that it would work the second time around. If I had killed you, I would have been released from this job. Now I'm stuck in this bottle for eternity." explained the spirit.

"Good, you're a wicked spirit." Merde shouted. The spirit then turned to face Merde. "Who are you? Where did you come from? I was living here quite happily, until you came to mess everything up." replied the spirit.

It then looked at Claudia again. "You was supposed to die, so that your daughter would go to live with her father. This was the job that I was paid to do and I was to obey this order until the work was completed." said the spirit

"Look," replied Merde. "You had better stop talking, otherwise I will wrap this tape measure right around this bottle. Do you want to be reminded of when you were measured for your coffin? Don't mess with me you demon." Merde said angrily.

Claudia glanced over at Merde and shook her head in disbelief. She attempted to understand the concept of Merde having a conversation with a dead person, right here in her kitchen.

"I know you really need to confess and get stuff off your chest, but we've heard enough." Merde shouted, as he peered into the bottle. The spirit began to pace up and down. "Look, other than keeping me here, just release me and I promise I will never bother Claudia again." begged the spirit. "You're insulting me if you think I am that foolish to believe you." replied Merde.

"This hasn't been easy for me, either. I lost my freedom for all those months, following Claudia everywhere she went. I'm begging you to set me free." pleaded the spirit. "Listen, you will remain in that bottle forever. Your time is up" explained Merde.

In its anger, the spirit began changing into different shapes and images again. Then it remained silent for a while. "I'm sorry," the spirit said to Claudia. "Yes, I'm really sorry, that I didn't get to kill you." and as the spirit got angry, the bottle began to shake again.

"Quick hold it." Merde shouted to Steve. "I want Ricardo back and if I don't get him back, I'm gonna kill myself, how sad." the spirit said, mimicking the things that Claudia used to say when she was sick.

The spirit continued with the harassment until Claudia reacted. "Get it out of here, get that thing out of my house right now." Claudia ordered and then she broke down crying.

Merde quickly grabbed the bottle and left the house with Steve, to dispose of it. While in the car, the bottle became hot. "Steve, drive quicker this spirit is getting angrier." said Merde. "Alright" Steve said as he put his foot down on the accelerator.

As they arrived, Merde quickly got out of the car and ran to the riverbank, where he threw the bottle into the water. As the bottle dropped in, the birds flew out. Merde and Steve watched the bottle float for a while until it slowly disappeared.

The tiny bubbles that remained on the surface, indicated the spot where the bottle had sunk. Merde sighed with relief.

Claudia thought about the phrase, "A Genie in a bottle." She always believed that the things see saw on television could never happen in real life, but as they say, the truth can be stranger than fiction.

All that Merde revealed to Claudia was going round and round in her head. She had many questions that she needed Merde to answer. But one thing he had told her in her reading, played on her mind.

She picked up her mobile phone and called Merde. "Hello, Claudia." Merde said. "Hi Merde. I need to ask you something. When you read me, you said that the girl who introduced me to Ricardo was no good." Claudia clarified. "Yes, that's true. Cheryl is the worst friend you could ever have." Claudia stayed quiet. She remembered that she never told Merde Cheryl's name but Merde being a great psychic, was able to say her name with such ease, it was as if he knew her.

"What did she do, that was so bad? I mean I could tell she was jealous of me, but jealousy is not a crime." Claudia said, waiting in anticipation for Merde to reply.

"Yes, jealousy is a crime because if people are jealous of you, that means they don't want the sun to shine over your head. Listen, I didn't really want to tell you this, because I know it's going to hurt you. But if you insist." explained Merde.

"Claudia, Cheryl was sleeping with Ricardo before she passed him onto you. She knew his history and purposely set you up with a no good man. Hello, hello . . ." said Merde.

Claudia wasn't able to respond, she dropped her phone and collapsed on the chair. What Merde had told her, was going around and around in her head. This unexpected news had shattered her.

The fact of the matter was, Cheryl was sleeping with Ricardo and then she contrived to get the two of them together. At the time, Cheryl had her man and her kids, that meant she had been cheating on her husband. What a nasty worthless bitch, Claudia thought.

All these years, Cheryl had been laughing at Claudia, thinking that she was better than her, because she had the husband, the 5 bedroom house, the prestigious cars in the driveway and the 2.4 children. Claudia has none of these.

Claudia was in a daze when she called to tell her mother. "Mum, you will never believe this." Claudia said in disbelief. "What's happened?" her mother asked anxiously. "Merde told me that Cheryl slept with Ricardo." cried Claudia.

Her mum paused and said, "Oh my God, cousin Misty always used to say to me, are you sure Cheryl never had him first? But I told her no. This is why she asked you so many times to meet this man. I wondered why she was so interested in getting you to meet up with him. Now we know."

Her mother continued, "It all makes sense now. Claudia, do you remember Cheryl's wedding day? Ricardo arrived just before it finished and he was looking all shady? Well, this is the reason for his strange behaviour." explained her mother.

"Yes, I remember Ricardo was behaving funny that day." Claudia recalled. "They were hiding this dirty secret for all these years. My gosh, Merde can see so much. This man is definitely no fake. Cheryl knew that Ricardo was no good and by getting you involved with Ricardo, she knew that you would have a terrible life with this man." explained her mother.

"It is so sad to know that we were so good to these people and they turned around and did evil acts towards us. Even Miss Gloria, she couldn't destroy my life, so she tried to destroy yours. That spirit you saw when you were younger. I told her about it, because I thought I could trust her." thought Claudia's mother.

"Yes it makes sense now. I saw the spirit around the same

time that I got that premonition. When she realised I could see spirits, she made sure to hide it away from me, so that I would never see it again." Claudia concluded. "She wanted to make you live a life like her, unmarried and lonely, but she will never get her wish." reassured her mother.

After Claudia came off the phone, she knelt down beside her bed and broke down in a stream of tears. She then had a hot bath to calm her feelings. Claudia felt exhausted, after the day she had. But at least she knew who her enemies were and now she was free from evil and free from pain.

It was a rainy Tuesday afternoon. After leaving the drug store, Merde went to see his cousin, Jeffery to drop off another guard for him. "Hey Jeffery, it's been a long time." Merde said, as Jeffery opened the door. "Hey Merde, I'm glad to see you. Since I lost my guard, there has been pure destruction happening in my life." explained Jeffery. "Don't worry, everything will be alright now." Merde assured.

As Merde walked into the dining room, he saw a friend that he had not seen for a while. "Hey Carlos, what's been happening?" Merde asked with a massive grin on his face. "Merde, I haven't seen you around lately. Where have you been hiding?" Carlos asked.

"Well, I've been travelling up and down the country and I also spent time abroad. Whenever people are in trouble and they are desperate for help, they will even buy your plane ticket, which is what has helped me to see so many different countries around the world." Merde replied.

"Jeffery put this on please. It's a recording of my last psychic fair." Merde said, as he gave Jeffery the dvd. As it played, Merde began to name the people who appeared on the show.

"You see this lady?" Merde said, as he pointed to the

television. "Her name is Claudia. I healed her just recently. I am telling you, her problem was the worst that I have ever seen in this country. She only had a matter of days to live. I'm grateful that she was brave enough to talk about her experience." explained Merde. Jeffery smiled. "Umm, she looks nice. Merde you need to set me up with this girl. What's her number?" Jeffery asked keenly.

Merde patted him on the back. "Easy brother, she's not interested in any man at the moment. She's starting to find her way in life. Things that people take for granted, Claudia's beginning to appreciate it and enjoy it." explained Merde.

The conversation continued between the two of them, however, Carlos was not participating. He seemed uncomfortable. He began to get hot and sweat profusely. For some reason, Carlos was shocked to see this woman talking on TV about what she had gone through.

But why was Carlos so surprised? Why did he care? Did he know Claudia and if so how?

Chapter 20

MORE REVELATIONS

AFTER A WHILE, Jeffery turned to Carlos. "Hey Carlos, you're quiet. What's up? And why are you sweating so much? Do you want me to open the window?" Jeffery asked. Carlos was in a daze. He began to tremble, as he prepared to reveal the things he had been doing and who he had been doing them with.

"Merde, there's something I need to tell you." Carlos admitted nervously. "I recognise the girl on the dvd." Carlos dropped his head in shame. "Who? Claudia?" Merde asked. "Yes Claudia, I know her and the reason why I know her, is because I was the one that made her ill in the first place." Carlos admitted. Merde's face dropped, he knew what Carlos was about to reveal, but he asked him to tell all anyway.

"Well it started two years ago. I was approached by DJ Ricky." Merde interrupted Carlos. "Who's DJ Ricky?" Merde snapped. "Well, DJ Ricky is Claudia's child's father." Carlos explained.

"DJ Ricky came to see me and told me that his ex-girlfriend was evil and that she won't allow him to see his daughter. He claimed that she has poisoned the little girl's mind against him, to the point that the child had stopped calling him dad. Anyway DJ Ricky wanted Claudia dead, so he asked me to raise a spirit and send it to her, which was to eventually kill her." Carlos revealed.

Jeffery and Merde stayed quiet. They were shocked and surprised at what they were hearing. Carlos carried on. "I know where Claudia lives. I've been there a couple of times with DJ Ricky, to set up spells at her house. I made up spells in plastic bags, which I would throw into her garden, so when she picks up the bags it will make her more ill and strengthen the work. I have her picture, her name, date of birth the lot. DJ Ricky wanted Claudia out of the way, because he wanted his daughter to live with him." Carlos explained.

"Carry on, I want to know everything." Merde said abruptly, clearly upset with Carlos. Carlos continued, "His wife, Annette was in on it too, because she used to come and see me as well." Carlos revealed.

"Hold on, his wife?" Merde asked in confusion. "Yes, he's married." Carlos confirmed. "Claudia doesn't know they're married, when did they marry?" asked Merde. "I can't remember the date, but they got married on Ricky's birthday. Anyway, Annette used to pay me money to destroy Claudia. She couldn't conceive, that's why she was so desperate to raise DJ Ricky's child as her own."

Everyone paused, while Carlos carried on without interruption. "Annette was so besotted with DJ Ricky, that she didn't even realise he was cheating on her with a girl called Cheryl." revealed Carlos. "Hey, is he still seeing Cheryl?" Merde asked. "He was, but not anymore. He used to meet

Cheryl in hotels. He was even seeing Cheryl while he was with Claudia." Carlos explained.

"What am I hearing?" Merde said with shock. "Yes, DJ Ricky, admitted to me that, when Claudia was pregnant with his daughter, he slept with Cheryl and picked up a disease. He said that he had to attend the hospital to get an injection and during that time he kept away from Claudia" Carlos revealed. Merde shook his head in disbelief. "I even gave DJ Ricky a plastic bag with a seal inside. I told him to plant this in Claudia's house. All of this science work was to make it strong from all directions." Carlos revealed.

"Merde, Claudia was not supposed to have any money. I set the money curse on her, so that the pounds would disappear within days. I used to tell Ricky to bring me Claudia's money, so I can put a curse on her finances. The spirit was instructed to go to the cash point with her and force her to spend the money quickly. Merde, I can't believe that I did all these things to this girl and look at her now. She's so strong and healthy." Carlos said in shame.

"Carlos, I didn't know you were into these things. If it was not for Merde, you would have killed her and her daughter would be without her mother. I can't believe that you would do this, just for money. It's true, the love of money is the root of all evil." Jeffery said disappointingly.

Merde kept quiet, as he prepared to blast Carlos. "How can you fight against my client? How could you take up that job? That is evil work." Merde said, trying to contain his emotions.

Merde has healed many people that were in danger, but it's not everyday that he meets the person that caused his clients sickness and then to know that this same person, is also his friend.

"Carlos, I healed you. I gave you a guard to protect you

and you were so fascinated by the power that I have, you wanted me to teach you. But I never healed you, so that you can turn around and kill people." said Merde furiously.

Jeffery also started on Carlos. "Man you are selfish. You made sure that you guarded yourself, so if any evil turned around on you all, you would be the only one protected and your customers would be left to fend for themselves. Even though, you were the one that led them into temptation in the first place." Jeffery said angrily.

"Well Jeffery, it's every man for themselves in this life. You need to look after number one. I'm ashamed of what I've done, so Merde, I want to tell you that DJ Ricky is getting another person to help him. Although he was upset with me, we still talk sometimes. DJ Ricky told me that he has asked a man who doesn't live too far from here, to help him." Carlos admitted.

"DJ Ricky went to see this man last week and gave him pictures of Claudia and his daughter, because he wants the man to repeat the work that I did for him. He still wants his daughter you know." Carlos explained.

"This man is really crazy. He's still trying to do wicked things, but, he will never win over Claudia, now that she is protected. Do you know where he lives? Because I want to get the pictures back." Merde asked.

"Well his name is Mr Yardley." said Carlos, as he pulled out a pen from his coat pocket to write down the details. "This is his address." Carlos said as he gave Merde the piece of paper. Merde folded it and put it in his brief case.

Carlos was fearful and he made it clear to Merde where he stands with DJ Ricky. "Merde, I don't want anything to do with DJ Ricky. I won't be doing anymore work for him, but I'll still keep in contact with him, to find out what he's up to. I can tell you whenever he is planning something." Carlos explained.

"I can't believe you did the devil's work. Carlos, I'm disappointed in you, I thought you were a better man than that." Merde said emotionally.

"I'm going to head home guys. I'm sorry for everything, see you later." Carlos said, he quickly left feeling ashamed of himself.

"Merde, can you believe it? Carlos preaches in church as well. What a hypocrite." Jeffery said shaking his head in disbelief.

The next day, Merde got up early because he was determined to go to Mr Yardley's house to get Claudia and Courtney's pictures back. He wrote down the directions and made his way to the bus stop. The bus came within minutes.

Merde was anxious to get to Mr Yardley's house, but the traffic was delaying him. After 10 minutes, the traffic started moving again. Merde got off the bus and made the short walk to the house.

The house was a small, stone-pladded, two up two down detached house, on a quite street. Merde opened the gate, walked up the garden path and pressed the bell.

A tall slim man, in his late fifties opened the door. He was bald with a white beard. "Hello, can I help you?" Mr Yardley said in a deep voice. "I've come for a reading." Merde said, lying his way into the house. "Oh, I wasn't expecting any clients today. But okay, come inside and go into the room on your left." Mr Yardley said. Merde stepped into the house and Mr Yardley followed.

"So, how did you hear about me?" Mr Yardley asked. "Oh, through a friend of a friend." Merde said vaguely. As Merde took a seat at the table, he noticed a picture of Claudia and Courtney on the alter.

Mr Yardley gave Merde a pack of cards and asked him to shuffle them. Merde did as instructed and returned the cards to Mr Yardley. Mr Yardley then placed the pack on the table. Merde picked the top card and handed it to him. There was a long silence while Mr Yardley studied the card. He turned it back to front and upside down. Mr Yardley had a puzzled look on his face.

"Is there something wrong?" Merde asked sarcastically. Something happened to Mr Yardley that had never happened before. "Well, I can't read you." stated Mr Yardley. "Why?" Merde asked, pretending not to understand, even though Merde knew that Mr Yardley would not be able to read him, because he is more powerful than Mr Yardley is.

"I don't know, but I can't pick up any messages about you from the cards. It has never happened before." Mr Yardley declared.

There was a long silence, while Mr Yardley tried to find a reason for this occurrence. "You're a psychic aren't you?" Mr Yardley predicted. "Yes, my name is Merde." he revealed. "Oh yes, I've heard about you." Mr Yardley said, almost bending over to bow down to him.

Merde then pointed towards the alter. "I know the people in these pictures." Merde revealed. Mr Yardley was surprised, he sat up straight and repeated. "You know these people?" he said nervously. "Yes I do and I want the pictures, right now." Merde instructed.

Mr Yardley felt ashamed. "Ok, I'll give them to you. However, you know that I can't just remove them from the alter as easy as that. I have to carry out a ritual first." said Mr Yardley. "No problem, but you will have to do your ritual today, because I'm not leaving without those pictures." explained Merde.

Merde began to question Mr Yardley. "So how do you

know the man who gave you the pictures?" Merde asked curiously. "I've been working for the family for a long time, now. His mother first came to me over 30 years ago. I saw Ricardo last week. He was quite distressed and he kept saying that he wanted the child. He asked me to help him get custody of his daughter. I was about to light the candles to start the work, but instead I'm going to cancel this job. Look I'll destroy the candles to prove it." Mr Yardley stated.

Merde followed Mr Yardley into the back garden, where he smashed two glass-cased candles on to the concrete paving and then he melted the candle wax. "And I'm not giving them back their money either." declared Mr Yardley.

As they walked back into the front room, Merde asked, "So tell me more about the work you've done for the family?" Mr Yardley began to confess all to Merde. "Well the mother asked me to separate this girl, Claudia from Ricardo. She wanted their relationship destroyed, because she didn't think Claudia was good enough for her son. I asked her to bring an item of Claudia's clothing in order to carry out the work." Mr Yardley explained.

"She didn't approve of Philips relationship, or Jackson's or Trevor's, so she asked me to part them all from their girlfriends. The only son that was spared was Mitchell, because he ended up marrying her friends daughter, who she liked very much." revealed Mr Yardley.

Mr Yardley spoke for hours and as he talked, he performed his ritual and released the photographs, which he put into a black plastic bag and passed to Merde. "I won't be doing anymore work for that family. You can take my word for it." Mr Yardley declared.

It was time for Merde to leave. As he left, Merde sprinkled something outside the house. This was to weaken Mr Yardley's power and prevent him carrying out evil work in the future.

It was a bright sunny morning. Claudia saw Merde's name flashing on her phone and she picked it up. "Hi Merde, how are you?" Claudia said happily. "I hope you're not going out today, I need to come round straight away." Merde said anxiously. "Well yes, I was going to pop out for a couple of hours. What's the urgency?" Claudia asked curiously.

"You'll never believe what I found out." Merde said, as he began to explain all what Carlos had revealed. "So you see Claudia, it's important that we find that plastic bag in your house." Half an hour later, Merde arrived at Claudia's house. "Hi Merde, where shall we look first? Maybe it's behind the fridge." said Claudia.

"Wait, I've got something else to tell you. Do you know that his partner is called Annette and she's his wife, not his girlfriend?" Merde revealed.

"What?" Claudia said in disbelief. "I thought her name was Lucinda. When did they get married?" Claudia asked. "They married on his birthday." Claudia gasped. "Oh yes, I remember when he asked me if he could have Courtney for his birthday, he claimed that he wanted to take Courtney out to dinner with his mother. He even put his woman on the phone, but she was rude and we ended up arguing. That's why he was so desperate to have her on that day, he was probably going to make Courtney a bridesmaid." Claudia continued, "What a devious person, he was full of lies and deceit."

After she calmed down, they began to search for the bag. They moved the fridge, but it wasn't there. They then checked underneath the washing machine, but it wasn't there either.

Then Merde stopped. He closed his eyes and remained still for a while. "I'm getting messages, let's go upstairs and look inside the attic." explained Merde.

Claudia got the ladder out of the cupboard and Merde

climbed up and opened the lid. As soon as he lifted it up, he noticed a see-through plastic bag positioned on the edge.

Merde prayed before he picked it up and then he threw it on the floor. "Well, well, is this what you were talking about?" Claudia asked, as she attempted to pick it up. "No, no don't touch it." Merde shouted. "The contents are very dangerous, only experienced people like myself should handle it. I will destroy it." Merde explained. "I'm glad we found it. Thank you so much." Claudia said in appreciation.

Merde continued to search in the attic. He then found a bottle with red liquid inside. "Claudia, if I pour this liquid into water and it turns cloudy, then I'll know what it is." explained Merde.

Merde placed the bottle onto the floor and climbed back up the ladder. "There's a few old clothes up here as well, are they yours?" Merde asked. "No, I've never looked in the attic since I moved in here." replied Claudia.

"Old dusty clothes hanging around in your house are not good, they can bring bad energy." Merde said, as he threw the bag of clothes on the floor.

He then sprinkled house-clearing liquid into the attic and prayed again. This was to get rid of the negative energy. Merde then replaced the lid and came down. Then, they both went into the kitchen, where Merde used the crystal ball to inspect the seal.

The paper was very thick and yellow in colour and what they saw on the paper was very shocking. There was a drawing of a coffin and inside, there was something written down.

When Merde rolled the crystal ball over the paper, it had the word February. It also had Claudia's name written along the bottom of it, but it was misspelt.

"Oh my God, that was the month that I was supposed to die." Claudia said nervously. "Yes and because this was in the attic, right above your head, it would have made your sickness worse." explained Merde.

"And they spelt my name wrong, because they missed out the A at the end." Claudia noticed. "Actually, I'm not surprised he made a mistake, he never had any intelligence anyway." Claudia giggled.

"Well you should thank God, because that mistake, along with being born feet first, saved you and gave you more time to meet me. Right pass me some water." Merde instructed.

Claudia got a disposable plastic cup and half filled it with water. "Remember, I said if this red liquid turns white, then I'll know what it is?" Merde stated. Claudia nodded.

Merde than opened the glass bottle and poured some of the solution into the cup. The red liquid immediately turned white. "Yes, just what I thought. This liquid is to make a person go mad." explained Merde.

"No, way." Claudia responded. "Claudia, you were doomed. You were definitely supposed to die, but through the mercy of God, you were saved." said Merde.

Claudia breathed a deep sigh. It was clear to see how lucky she was. "So what are you going to do with these items?" Claudia asked. "I will pour this liquid away. Give me another cup of water?" instructed Merde. Claudia did as she was asked and Merde put the piece of paper, in the cup of water. "Leave this soaking in the water, until all the ink disappears." Merde advised. "Okay" replied Claudia.

Claudia then remembered the times Courtney would come home feeling ill, after being with her father. "Merde, can I ask you something? Courtney used to come home sick, after spending time with her father and I realised that when I stopped him taking her out, she no longer suffered the tummy pains or the headaches." Claudia explained.

"Yes, well he used to put powder in her food, to turn her

mind against you." revealed Merde. Claudia did not expect Merde to say something as horrific as this. "No way did he do this to his own child." Claudia felt hurt. "Yes he did, this stuff affected her and made her sick. It's unnatural for the body to consume these substances." Merde confirmed. Claudia shook her head in disbelief.

"But you suspected something, because you accused him of poisoning Courtney and then you stopped him being out on his own with her." Merde relayed.

"Yes, Courtney told me that when Ricardo would take her out to eat, she was never allowed to order the meal with him. Ricardo always made sure that she sat at the table. This would have given him the opportunity to administer the dose into her food." Claudia revealed.

"It breaks my heart to know that Courtney's own father would risk her life, for his own selfish gain. He could have killed her. I'm glad I followed my motherly instinct to protect my child. What a wicked, evil creature he is." Claudia expressed.

"So why did they try to take Courtney and not Wayne?" asked Claudia. "Whose Wayne?" asked Merde. "Courtney's half brother, he's about fifteen now." replied Claudia. "Oh, they wouldn't want him because he's too old. They wanted the younger one, so that they could get the opportunity to mould her. His wife would have felt more like a mother if she had raised the small one." Merde explained.

"They wanted to kill Courtney's real mother and replace her with a stepmother. Those two are beyond evil." said Claudia angrily.

Merde didn't want to give Claudia too much information straightaway. So, Merde waited until later on in the evening to tell Claudia about Mr Yardley. Claudia was astonished. "So the things that Mr Nelson told me back in the day was true. He told me that Ricardo's mother was trying to split us up, but I didn't believe him. I knew she was evil though. She was definitely trying to separate us, because she would say things to cause us to argue. But at the time, I really didn't believe that curses and spells actually worked." explained Claudia.

"Ricardo always used to complain that he had never seen inside the spare room, his mother had turned into an office, because she always locked it. Mr Nelson used to tell me that she was doing evil things in that room. It's sad that she would even destroy the happiness of her own children. She doesn't care about her sons at all, it seems like she enjoys making people suffer, even if it means hurting her own family."

Claudia continued, "She saw how sad and depressed Ricardo was after the break up and she had the chance to reverse the spell, that she had created. She has caused a lot of people unnecessary heartache. People will have happier lives, if others do not interfere." Claudia said holding back the tears.

"One person shouldn't have the power to wreck the lives of others. Why does this work?" asked Claudia. "Well this couldn't work without spirits and the magical science out there. That's why people worship the dead more than the living." explained Merde.

"You are protected now so don't worry, the power of evil will never be present in your life again." reassured Merde. "You see, people think they can do their wickedness behind people's back, but what is hidden in the dark comes out into the light." said Claudia.

"But remember, Ricardo is still trying to take Courtney away from you. He gave Mr Yardley your picture, you know the one you took at the shopping centre." explained Merde. "What? Oh yes, I remember he took a picture of me on his phone, without my permission. I wasn't happy about it and I tried to get the picture deleted. So that's why he wanted it."

Before Merde left, he told Claudia what Ricardo was

doing with Cheryl while she was pregnant with Courtney. This news really hurt Claudia and she began to get emotional.

Gradually things were becoming clearer for Claudia. After Merde left, she thought about all the things she had discovered and could not believe the endless shocking hidden truths about her past that were haunting her today.

Chapter 21

STATE OF CONSCIOUSNESS

CLAUDIA FOUND ALL that Merde had revealed plausible, but surreal. These disclosures were constantly going around in her head. Claudia had come to realise that the hidden sciences that were placed on her, had succeeded to destroy her, to the point where she could have lost everything, including her life.

Clearly there is something out there on a higher realm, a life that we do not feel apart of, but yet can be affected by it through the devilish actions of another.

Claudia recalled on her childhood experience when she saw the shadow of a spirit. Back then, Claudia knew there were higher beings out there, but she put it to the back of her mind, because of fear.

It made her wonder why we restrict our level of consciousness, to be satisfied with the basic information given to us. Only believing what is seen, but failing to explore the unseen. Claudia questioned why we don't carryout our own research, to find out whether the other life is real.

In Claudia's opinion, the people who were disbelieving would believe if they suffered as badly as she did. However, none of those who judged Claudia through her sickness, had actually walked in her shoes and if they had, maybe they would not have survived and fought against the spirit, the way that Claudia had. After all she was born feet first, giving her that extra protection.

Claudia doesn't have to take Merde's word for it, she can draw upon her own experiences. Merde mentioned that spirits talk. Well Claudia realised this, when she was in the apartment in New York and a loud deep voice bellowed her name. Even though nobody was there.

Claudia even discussed her sleep disorder with Merde, seeking an answer as to why she would, for a short while during her sleep, be in this paralysis like state and in her attempt to wake up, she'd struggle to speak or open her eyes. She would feel heaviness in her body and fight with herself, until she was able to rise. Claudia asked Merde about this, as she believed there was a spiritual reason behind it.

Merde explained that the spirit roams and if the spirit doesn't return before you are ready to wake, the body will be unable to move, until the spirit re-connects with the body. Merde's explanation made sense to Claudia.

Claudia concluded that the body is useless without the spirit and that the spirit controls the body. The spirit is a greater force than the flesh, because when a person dies, the physical is no more but the spirit continues its life as an eternal being.

Claudia wondered why God saved her life at that crucial point, knowing that people die everyday. Claudia's experiences and beliefs of the explanations given, had empowered her and some how she felt that she should be doing something with all this information.

She decided that she should be working alongside Merde, to educate people and heal the world, believing that this was the reason why she was saved.

Claudia did not think it was right to receive her blessing, without telling the people she cared about. She remembered the conversation she had with her mother about her cousin Shereen, who was still single and childless.

Claudia and Courtney put there coats on and Claudia drove to see her mother. "Mum, I feel that I need to tell Shereen about what I have been through. I want her to get help as well." explained Claudia. "Yes, that would be good. Her mother told me that Shereen has been feeling sad for a long time now, wondering when she will meet someone special." Claudia's mother explained.

"See mum, how can I receive my healing, without helping Shereen? I'm not a selfish person, I want good things for everyone. We grew up together and I don't want to see her grow old and lonely. I couldn't have that on my conscience." declared Claudia.

"Actually I want to tell the world about this life. It would end a lot of unnecessary pain and suffering." Claudia said passionately. Claudia contacted Shereen and invited her to her house on Saturday. Claudia couldn't wait for the day to come.

Claudia woke up early on Saturday morning to make her house perfectly clean, before Shereen arrived. "Courtney, tidy up your toys and put your books under your desk." instructed Claudia.

A little while later, the doorbell rang. "I'll get that mummy." Courtney said as she ran to open the door. Claudia was in the kitchen preparing lunch, when this tall, slim, beautiful woman with model like features walked in.

"Gosh, is this my little cousin Shereen?" Claudia said excitedly. "Yes Claudia, it's me." said Shereen, as they hugged each other for a while. It had been many years since they last saw each other.

"Let's sit down in the front room." Claudia said, as she grabbed two glasses and a bottle of her favourite wine. "Courtney, you have grown. The last time I saw you, you were a tiny baby in my arms. It's terrible that I've taken so long to come and visit you." said Shereen regrettably. "Don't worry, we all get caught up with work and living life in the fast lane." reassured Claudia.

"So, what's been happening with you over the years?" asked Claudia. "Well, I still haven't met my husband yet." Shereen chuckled and then she became serious. "I always used to go to church, praying for God to send a good man to me. But after years of doing that, I got fed up, because nothing changed in my life. I'm still single." explained Shereen.

"Good things have been happening to my friends, though. Last year, three of my girlfriends got married and two of them had babies. I don't know why these things are not happening in my life." Shereen said sadly.

"Courtney sweetie, go upstairs and watch a dvd. I just need to talk to Shereen." Claudia said, as she ushered Courtney out of the room. Shereen's eyes followed Courtney, until she disappeared up the stairs. "Your daughter is adorable." Shereen said enviously. "Thank you." replied Claudia.

"Shereen, look how beautiful you are. It must be shocking to most people, that you're not with someone. But I'm not surprised about that." stated Claudia. Shereen appeared startled. She didn't understand why Claudia would say such a thing, but she waited for Claudia to explain herself.

"Well, you are not going to believe this." Claudia paused for a while, trying to figure out the best way of telling Shereen about this ridiculous way of life. "I can't go through life without revealing something to you and what I am about to tell you, is really strange but definitely true." Claudia said cautiously.

Shereen was intrigued, but remained silent. "Do you remember Miss Gloria?" asked Claudia. "Yes, mum still sees her, she shops in the market down our way." said Shereen.

"Well, it used to take me a long time to form new relationships as well. I used to feel invisible, guys never noticed me and when I would go out to parties, I was never asked to dance. I always wondered what was wrong with me." Claudia explained. "I feel that way too." Shereen said in agreement. "Well, you know what? I believe in curses. Didn't they used to talk about curses in your church?" asked Claudia. "Yes they did." replied Shereen.

"Well, I believed that I had a curse on me and I worked out that it was Miss Gloria who placed it on me." Claudia declared. Shereen continued to remain silent. "Look, Miss Gloria never settled down with a man. Do you remember she used to change men as often as the weather? She told my mother that she believed that someone put a curse on her, to cause her to be unlucky in love." explained Claudia.

"Anyway, I met a Psychic. A really powerful Psychic, who confirmed this. Without telling him anything about my life, he told me that Miss Gloria had put a curse on me, by sending a spirit to follow me everywhere. Causing men to dislike me." revealed Claudia.

"Many other things were going on with me. I suffered a spiritual attack from Courtney's father, which made me depressed and suicidal. Shereen, this Psychic healed me and made me well again. Maybe he could heal you too. His name is Merde. He'll be able to explain to, you why your life is the way it is. I bet you, he'll tell you that Miss Gloria put the same curse on you too." Claudia said with excitement.

Shereen looked serious. Then she suddenly stood up

and her mood changed. "That's rubbish. The church used to brainwash us into believing that curses were real, that's the reason why I left that church. Those things don't happen in real life. You're watching too many movies. This Psychic is not God." Shereen said angrily.

"Keep your voice down, before Courtney hears you. I didn't say that he is God. However, God is the one that has given him the gift to see more than others and grant him the powers to heal. How can that be bad? Listen, I'm telling you about this out of the goodness of my heart, because I want the best for you. I want you to know what it's like to be blessed with a child." Claudia defended, she was shocked at Shereen's unexpected reaction.

Then Shereen calmed down. "I need to go." she said. "At least have lunch with Courtney and I." persuaded Claudia. "Sorry I can't." and Shereen, with her disbelieving attitude, quickly grabbed her bag and left.

Claudia looked on and watched Shereen drive off, down the road. Then she set the table for lunch and called Courtney down to eat. "Where's auntie Shereen?" asked Courtney. "She had to go home." explained Claudia. "Oh, I thought she was going to eat with us and stay for the day. It's not even dark yet." Courtney said sadly. "Yeah, she had something important to deal with. Never mind, hopefully we'll see her again soon." reassured Claudia.

After their meal, Claudia telephoned her mother. "Hello, so how did it go? Has she agreed to see Merde?" asked her mother eagerly.

"Mum, she doesn't believe in curses." interrupted Claudia. "What?" her mother was surprised. "She said that those things can't happen, he's not God and accused me of watching too many movies." explained Claudia.

"Mum, her outburst was unnecessary. I mean, if she

didn't believe in it, she could have calmly told me so. I would have respected her views. But I definitely don't respect how she behaved today." said Claudia.

"So, you probably wish that you never told her now." assumed her mother. "No I don't, there's always a risk that people could turn against you, but I will never regret trying to help another person. If Shereen never gets married or never bears a child, it's her loss. The main thing is that I am healed." explained Claudia.

"Mum, it seems that for Shereen, the truth hurts, but for me, the truth has set me free. Look, Shereen is not the first person to disagree with it and she won't be the last." Claudia continued, "However, for me, what was the alternative? Depression, mental hospitals and then death or accepting the help and getting well, as I am now. For those people who saw how I was suffering, now they can see with their own eyes that I am better again." explained Claudia.

"They should be happy for me and if they're not, then I can honestly say that those people probably rejoiced when I was sick and they themselves must have wanted me to either go mad or watch me pass away. Anyway mum enjoy your evening, bye."

As the weeks went by, she hoped that Shereen would call her. What she was not expecting, was for Janet to get in touch with her and tell her about Claudia's business. "Hi Claudia, It's been a long time, how are you"? Janet asked. "I'm good Janet, how are you?" replied Claudia. "I'm well, listen, Shereen told me about the conversation you had with her. I warned her that I was going to tell you about it. She's not happy, but a least she can't say that I'm talking about her behind her back." explained Janet.

"What, I don't believe it. I told her, so that she could get the help. I don't remember telling her to spread the news and tell the world about it. Shereen has told me private things about herself, but I would never dream of telling anybody else. I am surprised at her. She betrayed my trust." replied Claudia furiously.

"Never mind Shereen, I believe in the spiritual world and I really want to see this Psychic. Anyway, when was you going to tell me about this amazing man." Janet said excitedly. When Claudia heard Janet's enthusiasm, her anger lifted and she felt happy that Janet wanted to be healed.

Chapter 22

BORN AGAIN

CLAUDIA WAS GETTING better and better everyday and she now felt strong enough to know the date, of when she was supposed to die. She was ready, because whatever that day was, it would be a date that would never come around again.

She decided to phone Merde. "Hi Merde." Claudia said. "Who's this?" Merde asked. Merde had healed so many people, that sometimes it was difficult for him to remember everybody's name. "Have you forgotten me already?" Claudia laughed.

"Ahh yes, Claudia." Merde recalled. "Anyway, Merde. I am ready to know my death date." Claudia said nervously. "Are you sure you want me to tell you?" confirmed Merde. "Yes, time moves forward, not backwards, so that date can never be repeated." explained Claudia. "Yes that is true." Merde agreed. "Well, the date that was set for you, was the 22nd February." Merde confirmed.

Claudia paused and gazed up towards the ceiling, as she

tried to remember what she would have been doing on that day. "The 22nd February? That was a couple of weeks before you healed me. I can't remember what happened on that day." Claudia was puzzled.

"Claudia, your death time had come. You don't realise the amount of evil that was around you. However, because the spirit failed to do the job on 22nd, it was getting fed up and angry. Ricardo then put a 9 day spell on you, so on the 9th day, the spirit would have definitely killed you." Merde confirmed.

"Claudia you were lucky when I healed you, I had to work on your case quickly, because there wasn't much time. I healed you only one day before your second death date." Merde stated. "It's shocking that someone is told the date they were supposed to die." Claudia said emotionally. "Merde, I'm going to tell my mother. She has a photographic memory, so I'm sure that she can remember what happened on that day."

Claudia rushed off the phone and quickly called her mother. The phone rang a number of times, then it switched to voicemail. Claudia re-dialled, desperate to get through to her mother. "Pick up, pick up" Claudia said anxiously.

"Hello." her mother answered. Claudia was relieved. "Great Mum, you're there. Listen, Merde told me the date of when I was supposed to pass away." Claudia revealed. "Really, when was it to be?" her mother asked with a nervous disposition. "February the 22nd, You've got a good memory, do you remember what happened on that day?"

Her mother paused. "I'm trying to recall." her mother said, desperately trying to evoke the events of that day. "Yes, that's it, do you remember when you went to collect Courtney after our shopping trip? The teacher told you that Ricardo phoned the school, because he claimed he was worried about you? Well that was on the 22nd February." her mother established.

Claudia became nervous. "Oh yes, that day Ricardo came to my house and then he came back again the next day and then again the day after that." Claudia remembered. "Merde is so right. I found it strange that I had not seen Ricardo for weeks and then he came to visit us over three consecutive days. Yeah and I remember he kept asking me about my health all the time, which I found weird." Claudia said with surprise.

"Mum do you remember, I told you that the third time he came to my house, he got out of his car and stood there looking at me with his mouth wide open. Obviously he was in a state of shock, because he couldn't believe that I was still alive." Claudia said, as she tried to comprehend all of these revelations.

"I told you he was up to something." her mother said angrily. "How could Ricardo do all of this to my child? We treated him so good, better than his own mother had. I never knew that he would turn out to be such a wicked person." her mother said angrily. "Never mind mum, He didn't succeed."

Claudia's mother quickly came down to Claudia's house, to continue their conversation.

Then Courtney came into the front room and placed Claudia's arm around her shoulder. "Mum, don't get angry, but when I used to visit my dad, his girlfriend used to tell me to call her mum." Courtney admitted.

Courtney then sunk her head into Claudia's lap, waiting for her mother's reaction. Claudia took a deep breath and looked over at her mother. Claudia could see that her mother was angry and before her mother could start, Claudia signalled for her to say nothing.

"Tell me more, Courtney." Claudia said gently. "Well I didn't want to, but she used to bully me into calling her mum, saying it wasn't respectful. Also my dad would be in the bedroom with her, whispering and when I used to go into the room they would stop. Dad would send me back into the front room." explained Courtney. "Don't worry, this is all over now."

Claudia put Courtney to bed and came back downstairs to talk to her mother. "So, they were having private conversations, planning for the day that Courtney would come to live with them." Claudia fumed. "So evil." replied her mother. After her mother left to go home, Claudia went into Courtney's bedroom and hugged her while she slept.

When the morning came, Claudia phoned Merde to ask him to come around, because she wanted to speak to him about something. Merde was in the area and a short while later, he knocked on the door. "Hi Merde, come in." Claudia said. Merde followed Claudia into the kitchen.

"When I was younger, I saw a shadow, it moved across the wall, and then it turned up the radio in my parent's bedroom. I know that was a spirit." confirmed Claudia. "Yes, spirits can show up in all different forms. They can appear as themselves, or they can present themselves in the form of any animal or creature, except bees, remember?" Merde explained.

"When I saw the ghost, my mum got Mr Nelson to come and pray it out of the house." explained Claudia. "That wouldn't have solved the problem, because it could have easily come back in, through an open door or window." explained Merde.

"I should have used ammonia, I remember you said that ammonia burns the spirit?" Claudia laughed, fascinated by what she had learnt over the weeks. "Yes in its own spiritual way." replied Merde. "I am really glad that I'm being educated by you, my spiritual teacher." Claudia said gratefully.

It was a Saturday afternoon. Claudia decided to spend

a lazy day at home, while Courtney played outside the front with her friends. Deena phoned Claudia to tell her that she was going to drop by, before she does her grocery shopping. She arrived shortly afterwards.

"Hey girl, how are you?" greeted Claudia. "I need to let off some steam. This guy is really getting on my nerves." Deena said angrily as she came in and followed Claudia into the dining room. "What's happened?" Claudia asked with concern. "The children's father was supposed to take them out today and at the last minute he cancelled, without good reason. They were all dressed and ready, waiting for him to turn up and then he lets them down, again." Deena fumed.

"Well it's not good that he breaks his promises. Come and sit down, it seems like you need a drink." Claudia said sympathetically. "Well I would if I wasn't driving. Anyway, how are you doing? It looks like you've got over your feelings for Ricardo." said Deena.

Obviously, Claudia had told Deena at the time about her depression and her love for Ricardo. But because the spiritual life is something of a sensitive nature, Claudia had carefully selected the people she decided to tell about it. Everyone but Shereen believed in it.

Therefore, because of this, she thought it best not to tell Deena the details of how she got better. "I was being stupid. I think I was lonely. I'm just looking forward to the future when Mr Right comes along." Claudia said with a smile.

"Is there such thing? I mean the amount of guys I've dated, I should have met the right one a long time ago." Deena said sadly. "Anyway, I've just realised that I've never even seen Courtney's father before. What does he look like?" Deena asked curiously.

Claudia looked puzzled. "Are you sure you haven't seen him before?" asked Claudia. "No, we got back in touch after you ended the relationship with him." Deena confirmed. "Okay, I'll just pop upstairs, to see if I can find the last remaining photo that I have of him. But it may take me a while." Claudia said, as she left the room.

Deena decided to check on the kids playing outside. Claudia soon returned with a picture of Ricardo, he was sitting on the sofa at her parent's house with Courtney in his arms.

"Is this Ricardo?" Deena asked. "That's him." Claudia replied. "I don't believe it, this is the guy who was in that DJ competition I invited you to, remember? And he actually won." revealed Deena.

"He won? He didn't tell me that he won a competition, what did he win?" Claudia asked out of curiosity. "A trip to New York and I think it was £5000." confirmed Deena. "What?" Claudia gasped. "Are you telling me that he won £5000 and didn't give Courtney a penny of it? I can't believe it. You couldn't get any lower than that. When I asked him for maintenance, all he would give Courtney was pennies. I can't believe the selfishness of the man." Claudia fumed.

"He seemed like a nice guy, how could he not share his prize money with his own child? I have to admit, I did fancy him when I saw him. But Clarissa was the one that was really crazy over him." Deena admitted. "Girl, as you can see, looks doesn't mean a thing. Ricardo needs to come with a warning sign saying, this man will seriously damage your health." The pair chuckled.

"Did I tell you that Ricardo slept with Courtney's Godmother, Cheryl. She's the one who arranged for me to meet Ricardo on a blind date." revealed Claudia. "No way, who's Cheryl? Was she the one that I saw at your house, when you celebrated Courtney's first birthday?" asked Deena. "Yes, that's her." replied Claudia.

"Yuk, how grotesque. How could he lower himself to sleep with that? If I were you, I would have punched the bitch in her face." Deena said angrily.

Deena was a no-nonsense woman and a fighter. If she was in Claudia's shoes, there was no way she would have let Cheryl get away with it. "Don't worry the, universe will punish her for what she's done." Claudia declared. "Anyway, I must go, I haven't even cooked dinner yet." Deena said, as she got up to leave.

Claudia said goodbye to Deena and her kids. Then she checked to make sure that Courtney was safely playing outside with her friends, before returning to the living room to relax. She began to flick through the channels with the remote control, but could only find a wildlife documentary on the television.

Suddenly there was a knock at the door. Claudia would normally ask who the caller was before opening the door, but on this occasion, she didn't. When she opened the door there was nobody there, but she did notice a sweet scent outside her house.

She assumed that the children in the neighbourhood, were playing knock down ginger. This is where children would knock on someone's door and then run away. This was the game that she herself used to play, when she was a little girl.

Claudia shrugged and returned to the living room, looking through the TV guide, determined to find a program of interest.

By now, it was 5pm and Claudia went to bring Courtney inside. As Claudia opened the door and stood on the doorstep, Courtney came running around the corner. "Mum," Courtney said, quite concerned. "Look." and she pointed to her bracelet. Claudia examined the bracelet and realised it was broken. It had split down the middle and the red stone on the front of the bracelet, was missing. "Don't worry Courtney. I'll ask Merde to get another one for you." explained Claudia.

When they got back into the house, Claudia telephoned Merde. "Hi Merde, its Claudia." "Hi Claudia, how are things?" Merde asked. "We're good. Listen, the bracelet you gave to Courtney is broken." explained Claudia.

"How did it break?" Merde asked. "I'm not sure, but it happened when she was playing outside." Claudia explained. "Alright then, I've just finished reading someone who lives not far from you. I'll be at your house in about half an hour." Merde said.

Claudia waited for Merde to arrive. A short while later, the door knocked and because Claudia was expecting Merde, she opened the door, without confirming whom the caller was. When she opened the door, again nobody was there. But she smelt that same sweet scent, as she had done before.

Claudia was puzzled by this, but then she thought nothing of it. A short while later, the door knocked again. Claudia made sure that this time, she confirmed who the caller was. "Who is it?" she asked. "It's me, Merde." he replied. "Hi Merde." Claudia said, as she greeted him with a smile.

Merde followed Claudia into the kitchen. I need to read you and look into my crystal ball to find out what happened, but firstly I want to see the bracelet." Merde explained. "Okay. Courtney, come and bring your bracelet." shouted Claudia. Courtney came down and found them in the kitchen. "So how are you Courtney?" asked Merde. "I'm fine, thank you." replied Courtney.

Merde took the bracelet and inspected it. "It's been damaged. But don't worry, it's on consignment, so I'll get another one for her." Merde confirmed. "Okay, thanks for that." Claudia said with gratitude. "Oh sweetie, you can go back to watching your dvd in your room." Claudia said.

"It seems like a spirit may have damaged the bracelet." Merde revealed. "Please don't tell me, this wicked man is still trying." Claudia said with disgust.

"Let me read you." Merde said and he placed the crystal ball on to a piece of cloth, to keep it still and then he put the pack of cards on the table. After he prayed, Claudia gave Merde the cards one by one.

Card no 1

"Ricardo went to see a woman two weeks ago, to put another curse on you."

Card no 2

"Ricardo is still trying to get your daughter"

Card no 3

"He knows he can get wealth off your daughters head. Like a house and money from the government"

Card no 4

"Did you hear the door knock and realise nobody was there?"

Claudia jumped, "Yes, twice before you arrived. I heard the door knock and nobody was there. I thought it was just children playing games. Both times I smelt something sweet." Claudia said. "Well that was the spirit that knocked the door. It came for Courtney, to make her turn against you and ask to be with her father." Merde explained.

Claudia shook her head in disbelief.

Card no 5

"The spirit destroyed the bracelet out of frustration,

because it couldn't get to carry out the work. Luckily, Courtney is protected."

Card no 6

"Ricardo wants to take you to court. That's why he has sent this spirit to Courtney, to force her to tell the Judge that she wants to be with him."

Merde continued through the reading, with Claudia giving Merde the cards one by one. After the reading, Claudia began to look over all the things Merde had told her. "Merde, nothing that this man does, should surprise me anymore, but it still does." Claudia said.

"Well, even though this bracelet is damaged, it is still powerful. But the other guard that Courtney is wearing, protects her more. Just thank the day when God sent me to help you and your daughter." Merde smiled.

"It's a shame you answered the door to the spirit, you should have known better. It probably circulated outside, because it couldn't get into your house. It seems like it tried a few times, but failed. But it's definitely gone, because I never saw it when I arrived. Remember I can see spirits." explained Merde.

"Okay this man is getting ridiculous now. I have never heard anything like this in my life. When a relationship doesn't work out, most people usually move on with their lives and form new relationships. But no, this crazy, mentally disturbed, evil man thinks that I should die, as my punishment for getting rid of him." Claudia declared.

"I ended the relationship years ago and he still want's revenge. This is precisely the reason why Cheryl kept telling me to meet him. When I said I was not interested, she continued to bring up the same thing for weeks and she wouldn't have given up until I agreed to meet up with this guy." explained Claudia.

"At the time, I thought she was a nice person and valued our friendship. I thought she cared about me, but years after I finished with Ricardo, I wondered why she was so keen for me to meet this man. I still can't believe that she slept with him."

Claudia continued, "Ricardo probably treated Cheryl in the same way he treated me, with the jealousy and the anger problems. She's poison. Not only will Ricardo suffer, but so will Cheryl, because they will pay back for all the wickedness they have done in their lives." Claudia said passionately.

"Claudia, I saw something else in the cards." admitted Merde. Claudia became a bit nervous, but wanted to hear it. "The spirit that was sent to you years ago, clouded your eyes and brought on your migraines." explained Merde.

Claudia reacted, "What?" As Merde began to repeat what he had said, Claudia interrupted him. "I heard what you said to me. I just can't believe it. Before I started university, my eyesight was good, but two months into my law degree, I noticed that I couldn't see the board clearly. Then I had to start wearing glasses." explained Claudia.

"So, who did this to me?" Claudia asked, waiting in anticipation. Merde paused for a while. "It was Miss Gloria." Merde revealed. "Her again. I just can't understand it. This woman is old enough to be my mother. I was an innocent child. How could she do this to me? Why was I such a threat to her?" Claudia said angrily.

"Even though you was a young girl, she was jealous of you. She didn't want you to get married or have a successful career. These people rejoice when you fail to make something of your life, don't you understand?" Merde explained. "So she caused my migraines. I remember there were so many times that I would suffer such severe migraines, that sometimes it was impossible to study."

Claudia continued, "I always wondered why I was the only one in the family to wear glasses. My parents still have good vision and Clint's eyesight is alright. I thought it was because of all the studying." Claudia said and then she went quiet.

She began to reflect on how many people hated her and the great lengths they went to harm her. She suffered unnecessarily at the hands of others.

A feeling of sadness came over her, as she felt like she was the most hated person on the planet. But then she was soon over it. "They have failed. I have my family, my career and I have my life back. I am a survivor." Claudia said as she raised her hands in the air.

"Will my eye sight improve then?" Claudia said optimistically. "Well remember, this curse has been soaked into your eyes for a long time. It will improve, but I can't guarantee that you will never need to wear glasses in the future. There is an improvement, because your eyes used to be red, but I can see that they are getting clearer now." confirmed Merde.

"That's true. Mum used to think that I had been crying, because my eyes were so red. Nowadays I have noticed that for a short moment, I can read the smallest text from a distance. But then the sharpness fades and my vision becomes blurry again." explained Claudia. "It will get better. Just continue to pray. Don't worry, you're alright now." reassured Merde, as Claudia hugged him in appreciation.

"Anyway, I've got to go. I have somebody else to read."

Claudia walked Merde to the door and said goodbye. After she closed the door, Claudia leaned back against the door and she looked up and thanked God for everything.

Chapter 23

WHAT GOES AROUND COMES BACK AROUND

CLAUDIA'S MOTHER WOULD often say, "If you sow good seeds, you will reap good fruit and equally if you sow bad seeds you will reap rotten fruit." which means the same as, "What goes around comes back around." However, Claudia wondered if whatever you give out really does turn back on you?

Well, months after Claudia was healed. The events that unfolded around her, proved that this saying was true. Evil is like a boomerang, you throw it out and it comes straight back to you.

Cheryl was Claudia's university friend and she forced Claudia to get together with Ricardo. Cheryl failed to tell Claudia that she had an affair with Ricardo, prior to passing him on to her and she had expected that her lies and deceit would remain a secret forever.

Eventually, Cheryl's husband found out that she cheated on him. He also learned that 9 years ago, she created a hate spell to cause him and his family to argue and split apart, because she was jealous of the relationship her husband had with his family. Sadly the spell did work.

Eventually her husband divorced her and reunited with his family. Since then Cheryl has been homeless, jobless and continues to have lots of boyfriends.

Claudia remembered how she never really liked Cheryl in the first place. She was loud, bossy and embarrassing and if Cheryl never forced their friendship, Claudia would have happily left Cheryl at the university gates.

Cheryl forced Claudia to do things she didn't want to do and she continuously failed to respect Claudia's views, which made Claudia realise that Cheryl was never a real friend.

Claudia allowed Cheryl to control her life. There was no way Claudia would have met Ricardo, if Cheryl hadn't pestered her into meeting him. Claudia initially did not want to meet Ricardo, telling Cheryl several times that she wasn't interested.

The Angels were definitely talking to Claudia at that time, but she ignored the messages. Cheryl had an agenda and she pushed Claudia into the path of an evil man. This ultimately could have led to her death.

Anyway, someone must have told Cheryl that Claudia knew about her dirty secret, because Cheryl suddenly stopped calling Claudia, only weeks after she was healed and for the first time, she missed Courtney's birthday. The guilt and the shame she felt, caused her to stay away and Claudia never heard from Cheryl again.

Miss Gloria was the person who put a curse on Claudia, at the age of thirteen, to prevent her from getting married.

She also tried to blind her to prevent her from getting a good education.

Claudia recently saw Miss Gloria at a wedding, that her mother had invited her to. When Claudia and her mother arrived at the church, they sat at the back.

Some familiar guests arrived and they greeted Claudia and her mother upon their arrival. Although Claudia's mother and Miss Gloria stopped talking many years ago, her mother used to tell Clint and Claudia that when they see Miss Gloria, they should still speak to her, because the disagreement was hers and not theirs.

When Miss Gloria arrived at the church, she smiled at Claudia, expecting her to say hello, as Claudia used to. However, Claudia responded by ignoring Miss Gloria and turning her face away from her. This was the first time that Claudia came face to face with Miss Gloria, since she found out about all the evil things she had done to her.

"Mum, this woman has the cheek to smile at me, after all that she has done." Claudia said angrily. "You should give her a dirty look and stick your two fingers up at her. But we are in the house of God after all, so that wouldn't be appropriate, maybe next time." replied her mother. Claudia laughed.

Throughout the ceremony Miss Gloria, looked puzzled, wondering why Claudia declined to speak to her. She then began to appear agitated and couldn't relax in her seat.

Whenever Miss Gloria's eyes met with Claudia's, Claudia would give her a blank stare. After the service had ended, the bride and groom walked down the aisle to leave the church and the guests followed.

As Claudia and her mother walked towards the car, they happened to bump into one of Miss Gloria's daughter's. "Hi Claudia, how are you? I haven't seen you in ages." said Francis. "Yes, it's been a while." replied Claudia, forcing a smile.

"Look, my mum's there." Francis said to Claudia. As Claudia turned around, she saw Miss Gloria standing behind her. Claudia paused and stared deeply into Miss Gloria's evil eyes. Then Claudia gave her a dirty look, as her mother suggested and then walked off.

Francis was left shocked, that Claudia had not spoken to her mother and Miss Gloria felt embarrassed.

It's ironic, because after Claudia saw Miss Gloria at the wedding, Claudia had a dream that she was getting on a bus and Francis was the bus driver.

As she walked onto the bus and down the aisle, she saw Miss Gloria in her dream. When Miss Gloria saw Claudia, she ran to the back of the bus, trying to hide behind the seats hoping that Claudia would not see her.

When Claudia told her mother about this dream, her mother said that Miss Gloria was trying to hide, because in real life she is ashamed, now that Claudia knows about her evil actions.

Lately, Miss Gloria spends her days alone, with no family around her. She is ill and bedridden.

Where Ricardo was concerned, Claudia got the satisfaction of seeing his downfall right in front of her eyes. One day, Claudia's mother invited her to a healing service at her church. "I'm healed already, there's not a shred of evil in my life," Claudia said proudly. "but anyway. I'll go along with you."

The Pastor greeted Claudia and her mother when they arrived at church, "Claudia, I haven't seen you for along time, it's nice seeing you again." said the Pastor cheerfully. "Thank you." replied Claudia. "Your mother told me the reason why you were sick. She told me that you suffered a spiritual attack, but God has made you well again." the Pastor said. "Amen." Claudia said in agreement.

Claudia was impressed with the recent renovations in the hall, but returning to this church brought back horrible memories for her. The last time she was here, she was very sick.

Claudia took Courtney to the Kids Zone and then returned to the main hall and sat down next to her mother. The organist played beautifully in the background, while the parishioners arrived. As Claudia looked behind her, she recognised someone that she really didn't want to see, walking down the aisle on the extreme left.

Claudia was stunned. She hastily began tapping her mothers shoulder. When she got her mothers attention, she discreetly pointed over to where the person was standing. "Oh Lord, is that Ricardo?" her mother asked. "Yes, what is he doing here when he lives so far away? I wonder if he's stalking me." Claudia said angrily.

They watched Ricardo position himself right at the front of the church. Towards the end of the service, the Pastor said, "If anybody is suffering greatly in their lives and they want God to touch them. please come forward."

Ricardo didn't waste any time, he was the first in line to receive a prayer. "I don't believe it, Ricardo has gone up to the front. Does he expect God to bless him after all the wicked things he's done in his life?" Claudia whispered to her mother. "He has no shame." replied her mother.

Ricardo stepped forward and the Pastor placed his hand on the top of Ricardo's head. Then he began to pray, "Oh God I ask you, to heal this man as he is not well. Give him wealth, as he has problems in his finances. God, give him happiness because he is sad." then the Pastor suddenly stopped and quickly removed his hands from Ricardo's head.

He continued to pause for a short while, then he spoke. "I am getting messages, you are not a well man and the reason for that is because you have been trying to make others sick and now it has fallen on you." revealed the Pastor.

Ricardo was surprised and other than attempting to leave, he remained motionless. Claudia and her mother were even more surprised.

"You should go to the front and say something" whispered her mother. "What? Tell the whole congregation that he's the father of my child, no thanks. I'd be too embarrassed to admit that. No, I've cut all ties with him now and I don't want to be linked to him in anyway, shape or form." replied Claudia, unimpressed with her mother's suggestion.

"Stop carrying out evil acts." the Pastor shouted to Ricardo. At that point, Ricardo's knees wobbled and he fell to the ground. A woman immediately got up and came forward to help Ricardo. "Please, Pastor." The woman said. "He's suffering."

The Pastor dismissed her statement and carried on talking to Ricardo. "You continue to send spirits to your enemies, to destroy them and the people you are trying to harm are God's children. Don't you know that God protects his worshippers?" The Pastor asked.

Then he continued, "What you are doing will turnaround on you, the devil will make sure of that. If you're on the devil's side, you will be the loser. You need to cleanse your heart and give your life to God. You can't serve both. I am unable to heal you today." the Pastor revealed.

"You need to go away and think about your life. If you are for God, God will be for you but if you are for the devil, the devil will disappoint you. When you decide to serve God, only then can we accept you and pray for you, now leave." The Pastor ordered, as he raised his arm and pointed to the exit doors.

Ricardo was speechless and shaken. The ushers guided

him down the aisle and out of the church. As he was led away, he shouted. "I want the child. I want my daughter and I'm not going to give up until I get her."

Those were chilling words for Claudia. His determination to over power her, almost caused her to lose her life and clearly he wasn't about to give up. "Well I'm not going to give up on protecting myself and my child either." Claudia said, quietly as if to respond to Ricardo's statement.

After Ricardo left, the Pastor did a final prayer, before the service ended. "I'm going to talk to the Pastor." Claudia said to her mother and she made her way to the front to speak to him. "Come Claudia." the Pastor beckoned. "Pastor, that man you spoke to just now, he is my daughter's father. He's the one who made me sick." admitted Claudia.

"Really? Well as you can see, I picked up a lot of things about him. But I still didn't reveal everything in front of the congregation. I am shocked to know that this is the same person, who was trying to destroy you. We must have a forgiving heart, but he will not receive blessings if he doesn't put his wicked ways behind him." explained the Pastor. "Thank you Pastor. I'll come back and visit soon." Claudia said cheerfully "Make sure you do." the Pastor replied.

"Mum, thank God Courtney was not around to witness this." a relieved Claudia said. "That's very true." replied her mother. Claudia went to collect Courtney and then they left.

Ricardo on the other hand was in a desperate state. As he got into his car, he decided to call Pastor John. "Pastor, its Ricardo." he said. "Oh hello Ricardo, I haven't heard from you in a long time. How have things been?" he replied. "Not good." Ricardo admitted. "Why haven't things been good with you?" asked Pastor John.

"Because I don't have anyone to help me. Everything I have tried has failed. The spirits I sent to Claudia's house have come back. They can't get to do the work. She must have a powerful person around her, protecting her. I just need to get a stronger person to back me, so that I can succeed. I will not be the loser." Ricardo said angrily.

"The last time I spoke to you, you said that you were getting Mr Yardley to work for you. What happened?" Pastor John asked, knowing that Merde got Mr Yardley to cancel the work.

"I don't know what happened. I went to see him. I gave him the photos of Claudia and Courtney and I paid him. But I haven't heard from him since. I keep calling him but he won't answer his phone." Ricardo complained. "He took my money and didn't do the work. That man ripped me off. Anyway, do you remember you told me that a man healed you, years ago? What was his name again? Oh, it was Merde, wasn't it?" Ricardo asked.

"Yes." Pastor John admitted reluctantly. "You told me that he was good. Where can I find him?" Ricardo said impatiently. "Are you still trying to get your daughter back?" Pastor John asked, surprised that Ricardo still had not let go of this absurd obsession. "Of course, I'm never giving up." Ricardo said in a frank way. "So, where can I find this guy?" Ricardo said persistently.

Pastor John paused and then he smiled a devious smile. "Well, he doesn't live in this country any more, he's gone back to his homeland." said Pastor John. "Really? Okay, I'll see if my brother can pay for my plane ticket, because I need to find him." Ricardo said with enthusiasm.

Based on what Pastor John had told Ricardo, Merde was a very powerful man, probably the most powerful person anybody will ever meet. Ricardo had some hope in his life again.

"Wait a minute. Why do you have to get your brother

to buy your ticket? Why don't you buy it yourself?" Pastor John asked. "Well I'm not working at the moment." Ricardo replied sheepishly.

"Ricardo, you're a big man. You need to sort your life out and earn a living. How are you going to look after your daughter, when you can't even look after yourself?" Pastor John said sarcastically. Ricardo began to get uptight. "Listen, I don't care if I am sleeping on a park bench, with the help of Merde, the judge must give me my daughter."

After the conversation, Ricardo started to make arrangements to get the money together, so that he could track Merde down. Little did Ricardo know, he was about to be sent on a wild goose chase to find him, when in fact Merde was actually right here in this town.

Carlos told Merde about Ricardo wanting to find him and Merde told Claudia. She was in hysterics. "Claudia, if I happen to meet Ricardo, I'll embarrass him and tell him about all the evil things he has done in his life. He's your enemy, I never help those who have fought against my client's, so he's wasting his time." said Merde.

"Yeah and he'll be wasting his money too, trying to find you. I hope he does go abroad and then gets stranded over there." said Claudia. "Better still, he needs to know that the person he so desperately wants to meet, is the same person who made me well." Claudia chuckled.

"Well if he finds out that I'm the one who helped you, someone would have to call the ambulance for him, because he will definitely collapse in shock." As they carried on in laughter, Claudia remembered that her mother used to say that one day she would get the last laugh and now she definitely has.

Ricardo did eventually travel to Merde's homeland.

He began asking people in the neighbourhood of Merde's whereabouts. Some people told him that Merde was living in England. Others told him he was in America. He didn't know what to believe. Ricardo realised that he had a wasted visit, his mission had failed and he had no choice but to return home.

Ricardo resorted to begging friends for money, as he wanted to save up in the hope that he will meet Merde, one day. He continued to make applications to court for child contact, but the cases were always dismissed, due to his bad character.

Annette remained childless. This was her punishment for destroying the lives of so many people and trying to kill Claudia to get her child.

They never expected that Claudia would be healed by one of the most powerful men on earth, who saved her only one day before she was due to pass away. They never thought that someone would bring Claudia back on her feet and make her stronger than they are today.

Ricardo claimed he had loved his daughter, but a man that wanted to murder his daughter's mother and risk poisoning their own child does not love that child. This is the actions of a selfish man who wanted personal gain, but failed.

It was later revealed that Annette caused the death of her friends, Lydia and Julianne. She was jealous of Lydia's stunning looks and hated the fact that her man lusted after Julianne, so she decided to get them out of the way. She had no problem in eradicating those people she found to be a threat, including Claudia.

Eventually, Ricardo and Annette's marriage ended, after a string of violent arguments and they remained penniless and homeless. Their friends and family turned against them and Ricardo's children never wanted to have anything to do with him again.

Annette now lives with her mother, whereas Ricardo continues to prey on gullible women, who take him under their wing until they eventually see sense.

Ricardo could not accept that his evil plan didn't work and like a fool, he still tells people that he will not stop until he kills Claudia. However, Claudia believes in the power of her protection and is not at all concerned about Ricardo's death threats.

She has now moved on with her life and Ricardo would do well to do the same. It is time he forgot about Claudia, instead of living this obsessive, pointless, existence.

Ricardo and Annette had craved for everything and in fact, they were left with nothing. All their evil actions had turned back around on them, ten times stronger, causing them to spend the rest of their lives in misery.

Even after all they had done, it was not the end for Claudia. It was just the beginning. They had dug a pit for Claudia, but they fell into it themselves.

All those people who hurt Claudia and attacked her behind her back, like vultures, had lost and in the end Ricardo, Cheryl, Annette and Miss Gloria, really did lose their powers and their evil reign was over forever.

Chapter 24

HEAL THE WORLD

CLAUDIA CONTACTED MERDE to arrange for Janet to see him. Janet was happy with her reading and even happier with her treatment. She felt like a weight had been lifted off her shoulders.

Claudia and Janet told selected friends and family about Merde and his amazing powers. They all believed and one by one, Merde cleared away the obstacles out of their lives. Even Felecia and Clint couldn't believe how so many things were holding them back in their life.

Claudia still believed that she should work with Merde, because her desire to help others was still strong. Not only did she want to help the people she knew, she wanted to reach out to those she didn't know.

Therefore, Claudia decided to tell Merde. She was nervous because she thought Merde might think the idea was silly. But despite this, she had to at least ask him, even if nothing materialises from it.

"Hi Merde." Claudia said down the phone line. "Hello, Claudia, how is everything?" Merde asked. "I'm good. Merde, I would like to propose an idea to you. I think more people need to know about you. I was thinking that we should hold events, where you can explain about the spiritual world to people." suggested Claudia.

"You can carryout readings, offer healing, they can ask you questions. What do you think about that?" Claudia spoke passionately. But, there was a long pause, which made Claudia feel uncomfortable.

"Claudia, do you know how long I have been waiting for someone to be willing to work with me? I wanted to hold regular spiritual events along time ago, but it's easier to work alongside someone else. Yes I want to do this." Merde said happily. Claudia was excited.

In the coming weeks, Claudia started to plan the first event. She found the premises, booked the date, printed the flyers and hired the camera operator. The DJ's announced the event on the radio stations and before you knew it, this spiritual event was the talk of the town.

The event was now three weeks away and Claudia, her mother and Courtney went to collect the tickets from the printers. As they left the shop, Courtney saw a familiar face coming up towards her. "Hi Louise" a lady said, as she approached them. "Hi" Courtney said feebly. "How are you? I haven't seen you in a long time." replied the lady. "Anyway it's nice to see you again. Take Care Louise, bye." said the woman, as she kissed Courtney before she left.

During the conversation, Claudia had a puzzled look on her face and she wanted to ask the woman who she was and why she was calling her daughter Louise. But she didn't want to be rude, so she patiently waited until the woman left, before she questioned Courtney. But Claudia's mother got in there first.

"Who was that?" Claudia's mother asked. "That's Annette." Courtney replied. "Who?" said Claudia, mystified. "That was Annette, dad's girlfriend." Courtney said nervously. "I'm confused, I thought her name was Lucinda." Claudia said, pretending to be uninterested, but all the time she discreetly fixed her eyes on Annette's movements. By now, Annette had crossed the street and was yards down the road.

"When I first met her, they called her Lucinda, but after that dad always called her Annette." explained Courtney.

"Just wait one minute, I need to pick up some medication from the drug store. Mum, take Courtney to the car please. I'll be back soon." Claudia said. She began to act shady. "Okay" said her mother seemingly concerned.

As the pair made their way back to the car, Claudia quickly dodged traffic to catch up with Annette. She followed Annette into the shopping centre and challenged her. "Hi Annette." Claudia said as she walked alongside her.

Annette turned to look at Claudia. "Yes, I'm Annette, do I know you?" Annette responded. "Annette, don't tell me that you don't recognise me. You've seen me so many times before, in the photographs that you and you man have of me. Remember?" Claudia said sternly and as Annette turned away from Claudia, Claudia clenched her fist and punched Annette in her face. Annette let out a loud squeal, as she fell backwards to the ground.

"Who are you?" Annette screamed. "Who am I? Today I'm your worst nightmare." shouted Claudia. "That's for bullying my child into calling you mum and for putting poison in my daughter's food. I can't believe you paid money to kill me. Would you like it if I did the same to you?" Claudia said angrily.

Claudia continued, "You're a witch and a devil worshipper and you have the audacity to go to church. Well, you won't find the devil in the church." Then Claudia went up close to Annette and bent down, Annette flinched and guarded her face with her hand, as she prepared for another blow.

"And how dare you, disrespect me on the phone? You don't know me, but you thought you had the right to tell me about my life, saying that I was depressed and in darkness. Well Annette, Lucinda or whatever the hell your name is. I'm happy, now that God has saved me from evil people like you and actually you look like you're the one whose depressed and in darkness." Claudia boasted. "Who's laughing now, Annette? Me. Your task failed. What you wanted for me, you will get it back and I hope you and your man rot in the pit of hell. Oh yeah, I forgot, you don't have a man anymore because your precious Ricardo left you."

When Annette realised that Claudia knew this, she began to sob. "Bitch, I told you that you were second best. You must feel really bad that you did so much to please Ricardo and you still couldn't hold on to him. You're lucky that I didn't give you a real beating after what you did to us, but you're not worth it." Claudia screamed.

Claudia was so enraged, that she began to pant heavily. However, she felt satisfied that she gave Annette what she deserved. Claudia turned around, leaving Annette crying in the middle of the shopping centre, cradling her bruised eye.

Claudia quickly fixed her hair and composed herself, before returning to the car. Courtney noticed her mother across the street and wound down the window. "Mum, why did you take so long?" Courtney asked. "Oh, sweetie, I just couldn't find the medication that I wanted, never mind, let's go home now." Claudia explained.

Claudia's mother looked over at her with raised eyebrows

and Claudia looked back, winking her eye. Her mother smiled, as she knew what Claudia had just done.

Finally, it was the day of the event. Tickets sold like hot cakes. Courtney stirred early from her sleep. "Mummy she said, wake up, it's your show today. Now, what are you going to wear? You need to look smart mum, because you're gonna be on TV. You're gonna be famous?" Courtney said excitedly.

Claudia smiled. "Well, sweetie. If I've got to be famous in order to help people out there, then I think I can cope with that." Claudia replied, as she squeezed Courtney's cheeks.

The hours passed and Claudia prepared to get ready for the show. She looked in her wardrobe and pulled out a number of dresses. "Not that one, no, not that one" she said as she continued to look.

Then she took out one of her favourite outfits. A nice blue Versace style dress, she matched the dress with a pair of suede black high heeled shoes and added a large beaded necklace with matching earrings. With her hair newly cut into a bob and her subtle makeup shades, she was ready to go.

"Mummy, you look lovely." Courtney said with approval. "So do you, gorgeous." Claudia said proudly. "Hi five" said Courtney, as they smacked there hands with one another. The cabman impatiently beeped his horn. "Hello, sorry to keep you waiting." said Claudia, as they quickly sat in the car. "There's one pick up before we go to the hall, here's the details." Claudia leaned forward and gave the taxi driver a piece of paper with the relevant addresses written on it.

They soon arrived outside Merde's house. As Merde opened the front door, he emerged with a crisp white suit, with even whiter shoes. His hair was neat and he wore lots of gold around his neck.

"Hey Mr Slick" Claudia hollered through the rolled down window. "You're looking good." Claudia complimented.

"So are you." Merde responded as he sat down in the front passenger seat.

Everyone was in high spirits, as they looked forward to the event. Claudia was slightly nervous, because she offered to be the presenter. She didn't like public speaking, however, because she was doing Gods work, she felt that she had to do it.

Claudia read over her notes, reciting the introduction and familiarising herself with the order of the day. The roads were clear, so they arrived at the venue quickly. A security guard was on the door to collect the tickets, the camera operators had set up their equipment and now they were ready to start.

Claudia gave Merde and the camera operators a copy of the agenda. Then they carried out last minute preparations, rearranging the seating area and adjusting the mike stand. Gospel music was playing in the background, while they waited for the guests to arrive.

For the next hour, there was a steady stream of people and almost every chair was taken in the 200 seated auditorium. Claudia stepped up onto the stage and opened the evening with her introduction.

"Welcome to a night of spiritual awareness. The shocking truths and hidden sciences will be brought to you tonight. I am privileged to introduce to you a powerful psychic, who has an amazing gift from God. He can reveal to you your past, present and future. With his abilities, he can identify your sickness and provide treatment to heal you. Please welcome Merde." There was a round of applause, as Claudia gave Merde the mike.

"Good day lord, good evening lord and good night lord. Welcome to all people present. Coming here today may be the best decision you have ever made, because this could change your life." Merde said, as he addressed the audience.

"Most people know one way of life and that stems from what they see, what they hear and what they read. They know what's going on above, but they don't know what's going on underground. I'm talking about the spiritual world."

Merde continued, "Many people don't believe that spirits are real. However, I see spirits all the time, because of the gift that God has given to me. All those people that believe in God or a higher being, should also believe in spirits, because God is a spirit." Merde revealed. "If God is so great, that he can breathe life into us and make us into a physical form, why is it so hard to believe that we cannot transcend into a spiritual existence, when we die?" Merde declared.

"You can't see God or hear God, but he is there. Likewise, you can't see dead people and you can't hear them, but they are definitely there. In the spiritual world, there is no such thing as death, because the spirit lives on forever." Merde explained.

"Now, let me tell you how the dead can affect the living. In an ideal world, spirits would live in a world separated from us. That way, most people would live happy lives. However, what happens in reality is that sometimes spirits are raised and brought into our lives, by people who want to do wicked things."

Merde continued, "Before I explain how spirits can harm you. Remember, the believers of the spiritual life have a great advantage over the non-believers. Why? Because you can't see spirits, you don't see what is harming you." Merde revealed. "If you become ill, it's easy to be misdiagnosed by the doctor, because sometimes your symptoms may be similar to that of a real medical illness. There is a chance that you could end up taking medication for an illness, that you do not really have, which can be dangerous." Merde explained.

"These evil doers will win and successfully destroy your life if you don't try to get spiritual help. For example, people will raise spirits and talk to them. They will give the spirit your name and date of birth, so that the spirit can find you and then they will be instructed to harm you. The spirits can get into your mind and your body and make you suffer a terrible illness. Sometimes the sufferer may hear voices or become suicidal. Whatever happens, you have to be smarter than the spirit and use things that the spirit does not like. This will prevent them from destroying you." Merde stated.

"If you come into your house backwards and face the spirit, strangely the spirit will become too scared to follow you into your house. This is because the spirit feels that you have discovered what they are doing to you." Merde explained, as he handed out leaflets, explaining the simple things people can do to protect themselves.

"Believe it or not, the things that people do in life they continue to do in death. A singer will continue to perform in the spiritual world and if you go into the cemetery at night, it resembles a busy town. I see many spirits at night, just walking up and down as if it's rush hour. You need to realise that death is not the end, it's just the start of your spiritual existence. Believe in all that I am telling you and you will be alright in life." Merde then ended his speech with a prayer.

After a short break, the gospel singers entertained the crowd, while Merde carried out the spiritual readings. Claudia ushered each person into a room, to have their private reading. An hour into the readings, Claudia called the next person on the list. "Please can Shereen come in for her reading. Is Shereen here?" hollered Claudia.

Suddenly, a woman came from behind the door and nervously walked up to Claudia. She had a sorry look on her face, as she leaned forward and rested her head on Claudia's shoulder. Shereen looked up into Claudia's eyes and made an attempt to say sorry, but her emotions prevented the words from coming out of her mouth.

Claudia smiled and wrapped her arms around Shereen, as she wiped the tears from her eyes. At that point Shereen knew that Claudia had forgiven her. Claudia signalled for the next person to go in, while she spent a little time with her cousin.

"Months after I saw you, my life was still the same and I had no hope of it changing. However, I was ashamed to contact you, knowing that I told everyone how crazy you were to believe in such nonsense." Shereen admitted. "Now, I realise that it's not nonsense and either I remain single and unhappy for the rest of my life, or I swallow my pride and come to see you. Because you are my ticket to happiness." explained Shereen.

"Well through Merde, God is your ticket to happiness." Claudia said as she ran her hands through Shereen's tall hair. "I'm surprised to see you." Claudia declared. "Well, I noticed the event flyer in my local hairdressers. When I saw Merde's name on it, I realised he was the same psychic that had healed you. It was easier for me to face you here, than call you on the telephone." explained Shereen.

It was now Shereen's turn to see Merde. "Can you come with me? I'm a bit scared." Shereen said, deep breathing to calm herself down.

The pair walked into the room and saw Merde sitting behind the table. Claudia went up to Merde and explained that Shereen was her cousin and she will be staying for the reading to support Shereen.

"Shereen, Merde is not going to give you a full reading this time. He's just going to give you a hint, because you're nervous." explained Claudia. "Okay." replied Shereen.

Merde carried out his usual ritual and shuffled the cards.

"Who is Marvin?" asked Merde, after Shereen gave him the first card.

Shereen gasped and covered her mouth. "Oh my God, he's a guy that I liked years ago." confirmed Shereen. "Well, he wasn't a good person. He got close to you, so that he could use you." Merde stated. "Yes that's right, I used to buy him gifts and pay for all the restaurant meals, but I didn't get nothing back in return. He stopped calling me, when I stopped spending my money on him." Shereen confirmed.

"Who is Uncle Max?" asked Merde. "That's my dad's brother." replied Shereen.

Shereen and Claudia waited for what he was about to reveal, hoping it would be good things. "Uncle max is a nice person, with a caring heart. He used to bring you sweets when you were small." The girls nodded in agreement and smiled.

Merde spent a short time revealing factual things about Shereen's life, until the brief reading came to an end. "Thank you, so much." said Shereen. Claudia was puzzled, she had expected Merde to tell Shereen that Miss Gloria was to blame for her singleness, as she believed that her suspicions were right.

When Shereen and Claudia got up to leave the room, Merde shouted. "Oh, and who's Miss Gloria?" As soon as he said that, Shereen collapsed on the floor, in tears. "Well she's the one responsible for destroying your love life." said Merde. "I knew it." Claudia shouted. "I just knew it was her."

Shereen cried because of all the unnecessary pain she had endured, being single for all those years and because of the joy she was certain to have in the future. Knowing that after her healing, she will have a normal life.

Shereen couldn't wait to have her treatment and two days after being healed, Shereen was a new woman. She felt light as a feather and as free as a bird. Shereen wanted to thank

Claudia for telling her about Merde, so she gave Claudia a card and a nice gold chain in appreciation.

"Oh you didn't have to do that." Claudia said, as Shereen fixed the chain around Claudia's neck. "Let's go out tonight." Shereen suggested. "Okay, sure, why not." replied Claudia. "I'll invite Felecia and Janet. It's been a long time since we all had a night out together." Shereen said excitedly.

After Shereen left, Claudia took Courtney to her parents house, then she returned home to get herself ready. She pinned up her hair, put on her little black dress and her high heels.

Shortly afterwards, Shereen arrived in her posh car with Felecia and Janet. Claudia got in and they made their way to the club. As they parked up, Shereen asked Claudia to look after her car keys, as her bag was more spacious.

This was the first time they were all out together, since all the bad stuff dropped off them and now they were able to put Merde's powers to the test. To see if the men really will notice them tonight. Felecia and Janet never have any problems getting the guys so as usual, the men in the club surrounded them.

The girls really enjoyed their evening and as the end of the night approached, the DJ typically played the slow tunes.

But old habits die hard, so Claudia, feeling uncomfortable, decided to find a seat at the back of the club, to avoid the embarrassment of being left without a partner to dance with. "Where are you going?" said Shereen. "I'm gonna get a drink, does anybody want one?" asked Claudia. "No, thanks." the girls replied.

As Claudia walked off, she changed her mind and decided to go and sit in Shereen's car, instead. Claudia was so used to hiding herself away at parties, as she had done for so many years, that she naturally did it again tonight.

After an hour, Claudia returned to the party. She noticed

that Shereen was having fun, dancing with a very attractive man. Shereen was holding him tight, as she serenaded him. Claudia smiled. She was happy for Shereen.

As the guests prepared to leave the club, Claudia decided to wait for her cousins outside. "Claudia, where did you go? We were looking for you." Janet asked, as the girls walked towards her.

"Well you guys were getting down to some serious dirty dancing, so I left you to it." Claudia teased. "Claudia, I've got his number, I can't believe that I've got the number of a gorgeous, attractive, good looking, sexy, hunk of a guy." Shereen said excitedly, fluttering her eye lids, as she thought of her man.

"This is such a new experience for me. I mean, I've been chatted up by granddads and the not so attractive guys, but never anyone that I've been interested in. I feel like one of those 16 year olds whose old enough to date. I definitely have a lot of catching up to do." explained Shereen.

Shereen was too tipsy to drive, so Felecia drove them home. Evidently, Shereen was no longer affected by the man curse, but for Claudia, she still had to prove that she was free from it. Claudia looked over at Shereen and she saw that Shereen was on a high, still mesmerised by this guy that she met only a few hours before. Claudia had never seen Shereen this happy and it was priceless.

As the months went by, Merde's good name became infectious. Knowledge of this powerful man began to spread like wild fire and soon everybody was talking about him.

Claudia continued to work alongside Merde and people far a wide came to see him. They worked tirelessly to educate and heal the nation. The popularity and demand for this psychic grew so much, that they began travelling to neighbouring towns, to cities and then all around the world.

Many people's lives had changed for the better and those held back by curses, began to achieve with happiness, being brought into their lives.

It was the start of Autumn, and Merde and Claudia were in America, preparing for a very special day. Because in a couple of hours time, they were going to be holding their biggest ever televised event. They were full of excitement, as they made there way to the arena.

Claudia started by introducing Merde to the guests and the crowd applauded as Merde began to pray and then he proceeded to talk about the spiritual world. The audience were fascinated. They asked many questions, as they were keen to know more about life after death. There was gospel singing and readings and when the night ended, Claudia gave a closing speech in front of 10,000 guests.

"Good night and thank you for attending a positive evening of spiritual awareness. I hope you all now have an understanding of how powerful the hidden sciences can be. I myself have been a victim of many spiritual attacks in my lifetime." Claudia revealed.

"It all began when I was thirteen years old and I heard a voice in my head, telling me that it will be difficult for me to meet a partner in the future. I actually now believe that this warning, was the angels talking to me." explained Claudia.

"If you are in tune with your spirituality and you listen very carefully, you will hear those angels talking to you too. Through my challenges, I called upon the lord to solve my problems. It was too big for me to deal with, but nothing is too great for God."

Claudia continued, "I can only describe my pain and suffering as if I was hanging from a cliff top. Could you imagine the pain you would be feeling by holding on to that cliff? Knowing it would have been easier to let go. However,

I was patient and I held on, until God sent his messenger to heal me and he did heal me, at the right time, following his own timetable." Claudia explained.

"Yes, I took anti depressants and attended counselling sessions, but it did nothing for me. I never knew I could feel as good as I did when I was healed, it was instant." Claudia spoke passionately.

She continued by saying, "Whether you believe in the power of science or not, it will affect you if those people around you are jealous. I have realised that the power of jealousy, could lead to hatred and even death. You need to be protected to survive in a world controlled by science. We need to know both sides of the coin."

Claudia continued, "I can't make you believe in the spiritual life, but I feel that I must try to educate people. If things are not right in your life, bad luck may not be the reason. It could be an evil force. Evil fails if you eliminate it from your life."

"Listen, if you are going to war, you need to know what your enemies are doing, so that you have the best strategy, the best armour and the best equipment to defeat them. This principal also applies in your personal lives. You have to provide a good defence against your enemies, so that you can win your own personal war." Claudia explained.

"God may have given you your blessings, but there could be a hand that has prevented it from reaching you. When you remove the negativity and the bad energy, happiness will seep into your life. However, if you don't, then your life may not be the way you want it to be. You will be forever seeking happiness and never finding it. Don't let evil take away your dreams."

Claudia continued with complete emotion. "I thank God for clearing the obstacles out of my path and for knocking down those mammoth walls that surrounded me. I used to worry about my life wondering why it was like this."

"Was I such a horrible person that I should never find happiness? I would ask myself. People go to their graves, never knowing the truth, never knowing that their life could have been better, but for the evil people who had laid down curses on them. Preventing them from achieving inner peace and happiness." Claudia said passionately.

"I have a message to the people that placed such curses on me. I am no longer tied down by your chains of hell. I have come from being in the deepest valley and now I have risen to the top of the highest mountain." Claudia spoke eloquently.

"You have lost your power and control over me, for now and for evermore. Your physical existence, is fuelled by evil thoughts, uncontrollable jealousy and deep hatred. Now my darkness has turned to light and my night has turned to day."

"How ashamed are you now. Knowing that what you quietly did behind my back, has now come out into the open. What didn't kill me has made me stronger. As the saying goes, don't trouble, trouble until trouble, troubles you, otherwise it will end up costing you, So think about that, whenever you are tempted to do wrong to others. Evil doers never win. They are the ones that ultimately pay the price, because what goes around will definitely come back around, no matter how long it takes."

"I don't think the shadows of my experience will ever go away, but this is the happiest I have been in all my adult life. Now, I am living a life without struggles and I'm free, because the truth has set me free." Claudia said emotionally.

"I have a dream, that one day we will live in the way God wants us to live. That we shall all have authority over our own lives. I want all of mankind to have the choice of getting married, starting a family, buying a house and having wealth."

"So that we all shall live and not just exist. So that another human being will never have the power to control our lives and change our destiny. So that you will no longer be frozen and stuck in a time warp, where you do not progress when everyone around you is." Claudia said passionately.

Claudia ended her speech by saying. "I fell down, but the important thing was that I got back up. I wish to express my deepest thanks to Merde, the man who God sent to heal me. Merde, I salute you. I have received God's blessings and it is wonderful." Claudia said, as she turned towards Merde.

"To the audience and everyone around the world, remember this is your life, you have one life. Live it the way you choose to and never ever let anyone stop you from fulfilling your dreams. Stay protected, stay healthy and stay blessed. Thank you and Goodnight."

The crowd expressed how much Claudia inspired them, by honouring her with a standing ovation and a deafening round of applause.

As she left the arena and walked towards the exit, someone tapped her on her shoulder. When Claudia turned around, she recognised a familiar face. "Jaz" she screamed with excitement. Jaz wrapped his big arms around her and rubbed his smooth skin against her face, as he kissed her cheek.

"I can't believe you're here." Claudia said with total elation. "Well when I heard you were in town, I thought I should support you the way you supported me, when I launched my book. Anyway, I really believe in your campaign. My granny used to tell me about the spiritual life, all the time when I was a boy. That was an amazing speech and a great event." Jaz said and while he admired what was before him, Claudia noticed that Jaz looked at her, in a way that he hadn't done before.

"Claudia, you look absolutely amazing." he said, unable

to disguise his attraction for Claudia. "Well you don't look so bad yourself." Claudia replied with flushed cheeks.

Jaz remembered that the last time he saw Claudia, she was a thin, troubled, desperate woman with the world on her shoulders. Now she is a new woman, sexy, voluptuous and feisty. Jaz couldn't take his eyes from her.

"Clint told me that you got married. How is your wife?" asked Claudia out of politeness.

"Well, Clint forgot to tell you that I got divorced. She wasn't right for me you know, totally unambitious. She was only interested in the money, but didn't support the work that I had to do to make the money. Anyway, enough about me, have you eaten? Because we could grab something. I know how much you like your Italian food." Jaz said hoping that Claudia would accept.

"Sorry Jaz I wish I could, but I have a taxi waiting outside to take me to the airport." explained Claudia. "You're leaving town tonight?" asked Jaz. "I'm afraid so." replied Claudia.

Jaz's smile turned into a look of disappointment. "Well that's a shame, don't worry. Clint gave me your number, so I'll give you a call very soon. I'm still writing you know, maybe you could refine my next manuscript." said Jaz. Claudia chuckled.

"Actually, do you remember the last time you were here? You said that a writer needs to have something interesting to say. Well you have no excuses now, everything you spoke about today should be written in a book. It could help sufferers around the world. But, if nothing else, it would be an interesting read. So you better get started." Jaz said persuasively.

Claudia smiled, "Well if I find the time to write a book, I'll definitely call you for advice." she replied.

As he walked her to the taxi, Jaz couldn't resist giving

Claudia one last hug before she left in the car. On her way to the airport, Claudia reflected on the success of the event and smiled, feeling satisfied that she was helping to do great work on earth, knowing that this is truly the purpose of her life.

Claudia's final thought of the day was about God. She reflected on how he made her strong from birth to fight the bullets of evil and when she had no strength to fight any longer, he performed a miracle in her life and saved her from her enemies.

As Claudia boarded her flight and flew from White Plains, New York to Miami International Airport, Claudia felt blessed that she was finally in a good place in her life.

She no longer had to fight against those fierce waves anymore, everything just flowed, life was easier now. And as for Jaz, well his positive reaction towards her proved that after many years, she is finally noticed and appreciated by men.

By the way, Claudia now lives in America. Merde did mention that one day she would settle in the States.

To ✍B from Mother

Printed in Great Britain
by Amazon